DEATH ON THE POINT

No. 2 - The Blackwell Series

DUANE WURST

ISBN-10: 0-9883947-2-3
ISBN-13: 978-0-9883947-2-8

Text and cover design by Duane Wurst, Berne Studio
Cover images © Duane Wurst

Printed in the United States of America

Acknowledgments

Writing is a solitary adventure. Because I have a loving family, I have never felt alone. My wife let me have my space while encouraging me to continue. I wish to thank Sharon for reading and proofing my work. She kept prodding me to finish the next chapter, because she wanted to read what happened. Sharon, I love you.

I also thank two women who helped edit my book. My stepdaughter Cyndi Krzysik has a technical writing background and did a great edit of my book. M. Teresa Calkins, a member of my writing group in Pigeon, also edited my book. Their comments helped me catch grammar errors, and they found those obvious errors that only an outsider would see. Thank you both for helping to make this book a success.

The Huron Area Writers Group and The Thumb Words Work Group listened, read, and advised me. They have been there when I needed a shoulder to cry on or an incentive to keep going.

Comments

"Loved the entire book. I loved how fast moving it was. Just when you thought Colton's life was going to settle down a little, something else would happen that kept me on my toes. The sense of humor that was placed throughout had me chuckling out loud. I especially LOVED the end! That was pretty funny!!" Cyndi Krzysik

Chapter 1

Meeting Colton Blackwell

Colton had to clean the barn crammed with hundreds of milking cows in their stalls. The automatic waste system could not handle the job; so the supervisor instructed Colton to clean the floors using a small Bobcat loader. An overpowering smell made him gag. The heat, high humidity, and lack of any breeze allowed the gases to concentrate several feet above the ground, at the level of Colton's nostrils. He could ask for a face mask to filter the air, but the supervisor would just laugh and tell him to get back to work. The dairy farm was large, but not big on following safety rules. In another two hours, he would have the concrete cleared of waste and his night shift would end. Instead of causing any trouble, he decided to just get the job done.

Colton heard a voice from behind him. He turned and saw the supervisor standing with a young Mexican boy.

The supervisor yelled, "Colton, turn the loader off and come here."

It was unusual for Tom to be here this late at night, so Colton stopped and jumped off the loader.

"What's up, Tom?" Colton asked. "Who is your new friend?"

Tom suggested they step outside the barn into the fresh air. Colton took several deep, cleansing breaths while he studied both Tom and the youngster.

Tom was at least twenty-four years old, but he had the build of a middle-aged heavy beer drinker. Close to three hundred pounds with a scraggly beard that hid the pockmarks on his face. The boy couldn't be over thirteen. He looked as if he had missed too many meals, and his eyes were bloodshot. Colton concluded that the youngster was too young to be working for the dairy legally.

"I've got a job for you," said the burly supervisor. He put his hand on the boy's head and continued. "This is Tony Lopez. He will work here, and I want you to show him the ropes. Give him a locker and show him what you do every night."

"Good to meet you Tony, my name is Colton."

"I hope you speak Spanish, Colton, because Tony doesn't know much English. You know Spanish, don't you?" asked Tom.

"It's been over three years since I had my Spanish class in school."

Colton turned to the teen and said in Spanish, "Hello, Tony, my name is Colton. I will show you what to do here."

"Are you the owner of this place?" Tony asked in Spanish.

"No. I am definitely not the owner," Colton said.

"What did he want to know?" asked Tom.

"He asked if I was the owner," Colton said, laughing.

"Well, boss, show him the ropes and then get to school. I know you're working overtime, but I can't afford to have you getting into trouble for being late to school again."

Colton spent the rest of his shift helping Tony get organized. The two talked about their work, and Tony opened up about himself. It surprised Colton to learn that Tony was not an American citizen or even in the United States legally. Some men smuggled him and his father and sister into the country a few months ago. They all worked at different businesses and lived in a group home outside of Bad Axe. Over fifteen people lived in the old three-bedroom farmhouse.

Looking at his watch, Colton realized that he only had half an hour to get ready for school. He worked a full ten-hour shift, and would rather be at home sleeping instead of going to school for another seven hours. A good education was his only hope for the future, and he did not want to work at dirty jobs the rest of his life. "An education," as his dad always told him, "is the key to a good job." Two things his father never had.

Colton rushed into the employee bathroom, took a quick cold shower and threw on the clothes he wore to work. There was no time to stop at home for new clothes, so he splashed on some aftershave and jumped into his Jeep. Even after showering, the smell of the farm would linger on him all day.

It'll be close, but Colton must get to school on time. Mr. Dinger, the first hour teacher, warned him yesterday that being tardy one more time would make him ineligible for football, and Colton considered football the most important thing in his life, next to his family. If possible, he would love to attend college on a football scholarship. At seventeen, he was looking forward to a great future. He has the grades and plays football well enough to attract a college scout's attention.

Colton's yellow Jeep flew down the dusty road and came within inches of rolling into the ditch as he made the last turn before the school drive. The buses were gone, and only two students still walked toward the high school. There is less than one minute to go and at least one hundred yards to go. The doors of the school flew open, and he ran down the hall past his locker toward the open door of Mr. Dinger's history class.

"Cathy Adams?" The teacher read the class roster in his usual monotone voice.

"Here."

"Carol Bailey?"

"Yes."

"Colton Blackwell?" Mr. Dinger looked up from his list. He knew Colton was not at his desk.

"I'm here, Mr. Dinger." Colton gasped as he hurried to his place in the back of the classroom.

"You're late, Colton. You missed the last bell by over a minute."

"Sorry, but I was here before you counted me absent or tardy, wasn't I?" he asked, with a pleading expression running across his face.

"Yes, you're safe for another day, Colton."

"Dave Brown?" the teacher continued.

"Where were you, Colton?" whispered Connie Jackson, as Colton slid into his seat.

"I got off work late, and then I almost killed myself getting here."

"That Jeep of yours has four-wheel-drive, why not go cross-country?"

"You're hilarious, Connie. I wish I could have slept before I got here. Sometimes I can go home and sleep for a few hours after work. Today, I had to show a new worker the ropes. I can't believe the kid doesn't know English and isn't even a legal worker. It's crazy, you know? He is only thirteen, an illegal immigrant with no education." Colton looked up and realized the teacher intended to tell him to be quiet. He smiled and opened his book.

"Today, we will cover the early pioneers. Open your book to page 98, and let's read together," Mr. Dinger instructed. The class let out a sigh of pain and opened their books. Several students asked if they could get their books from their lockers, and Mr. Dinger spent several more minutes asking, "Why would anyone come to class without a textbook?"

The hour dragged on forever. Colton tried to listen and follow along with the lesson, but his eyes kept closing. Whenever he felt like he was about to nod off, Connie poked his arm with her pencil. At the end of the hour, Colton had a small bruise on his upper arm.

"Sorry about that," laughed Connie as they walked out of the classroom. "I have art class. What class do you have this hour?"

Colton thought for a moment and then said, "Trigonometry with

Mr. Sellerman. If I'm lucky, I can get a little rest. I would love to hide in my locker and sleep for a few hours, but that will never happen."

"Well, good luck. You know, Colton, you should just stop working so many hours. If you keep this up, you will get in trouble at school and lose the job anyway." Connie liked Colton, but she could see he was overextending himself.

"Thanks for the advice." Colton had no intention of following it.

He had been working at the dairy since the first of summer. The owner liked his work and asked him to keep on working full time. Knowing he could not legally work over 15 hours a week while attending school, Colton did not inform the school he was working full time. This omission could land him in deep trouble.

As Colton entered Mr. Sellerman's classroom, he saw a comfortable-looking seat in the back corner of the room. He worked his way to the seat, sat down, and put his head back. Thinking about work, the Mexican boy he was training, and the football game coming up on Friday night, Colton drifted off to sleep. He heard his name and let out a low, "Here, sir."

Chapter 2

The Algebra Dream

The roar of the crowd becomes a thrilling mind rush. The game, tied at seven to seven with two minutes remaining in the fourth quarter. And the Lake Huron Loons have the ball on the fifty yard line. In the huddle, quarterback Aden Carville repeats Coach Talbert's instructions for the next two plays. The first play will be a hand-off to the halfback and a run to the right, followed with a second play, a quick pass to Colton, the wide receiver. The second play will be a tremendous surprise, because there won't be a huddle, nor will there be any more timeouts. This is the last chance to win the championship. Losing is not an option.

The Loons are in an "I" formation. Down, get set, hut three. Everyone on the field hears the loud snap. The crowd roars as Aden hands off the ball and the play gains five yards for a second and five.

But wait, the team lines up at the scrimmage line again, and the Bad Axe Kings look around in wonderment. What's going on? The center snaps the ball, and Colton breaks through the dazed defense and brushes off the man guarding him. He runs to center field, looks back at the ball as it glides into his hands. Pulling the ball close to him, he is off. In unison, the cheerleaders jump with their pom-poms streaking green and white against the azure blue sky, and Colton's teammates create a safe zone leading down the center of the field. No one can catch the cheetah-like Colton now, and it's a touchdown! The fans in the stands are on their feet while the coach jumps up, laughing with joy, and the

Bad Axe coach protests the play to a referee. The touchdown is good! There are no flags on the play. The Lake Huron Loons have won the championship!

The team carries Colton on their shoulders and set him down in front of the admiring cheerleaders. Linda, the beautiful head cheer-leader, jumps into Colton's arms and gives him a huge and lingering full mouth kiss.

"Colton, Colton, Colton," the chant gets louder.

Mr. Sellerman... now standing over the sleeping Colton yells, "Colton! Colton, how do you simplify this equation?"

With no response, he picks up Colton's textbook and slams it on the table next to Colton's ear. The class is silent, astonished at the loud crack the book has made.

A shocked Colton jumps up, only to have his knees hit the bottom of his chair-desk combo. He flies forward, his face crashing into the back of Aden Carville's head. Sliding down Aden's back along the chair, Colton's bloodied face hit the floor.

"Oh my God," screams Mr. Sellerman.

"Why did you hit me, sir?" Colton cupped his hand to his nose and felt blood pouring out.

"Colton, you were asleep, and I tried to wake you. Go clean up in the restroom and then get yourself down to the office; I will be there in a few minutes. It looks like we have some explaining to do to the principal."

Colton pulled himself off the floor and put his chair upright. Someone handed him some tissues for his nose, and he limped toward the doorway. He turned and asked, "Which one of us is in trouble, Mr. Sellerman?"

"I would imagine we are both in for a lecture."

On his way to the office, Colton stopped at the restroom and ran cold water over his face. His nose was no longer bleeding, but his left eye swelled shut, and there was a small gash on his right cheek. It looked like he was in a cage fight instead of his trigonometry class.

As he combed his dark brown hair, a big grin ran across his face. The image of Linda Canberry, the head cheerleader, in his arms kissing him on the lips, came rushing back.

Wow, I have to get to know her; he thought.

Visit The Principal

As Colton walked into the main office, he heard the head secretary, Ms. Downer, talking on the phone.

"He's here now, Mr. Sellerman. I will have him stay here until the next hour. Yes, I will let Mr. Zeller know what happened." She turned to Colton and said. "Did you hear what he said?"

Colton nodded.

"Find a seat in the conference room and wait."

The large room was modern and quiet. Colton walked around looking at the pictures on the wall. There were drawings of all the school buildings that make up the Lake Huron Community School District. Compared to city schools, LHC was a small school district, with only eight hundred students. Colton's junior class had close to a hundred students. However, in Huron County, LHC was one of the largest. Students from many communities came to this school, making a diverse student population.

Serving a farming community, LHC schools offer many opportunities for both children of farmers and students like Colton, whose father was a foundry worker before they laid him off last year. Today, like many other men, Colton's dad takes any job he can find to help keep his family afloat.

Colton gives his family most of the money he earns. With five people in his family, his father's income is not enough to keep everyone fed and clothed; especially with the high cost of utilities and auto fuel. Without Colton's income, his family would not have a home.

It was apparent that the principal and Mr. Sellerman would not be coming in to talk to him until the end of the hour, so Colton pulled one of the overstuffed leather chairs out from the table and sat down. His body molded itself to the chair, and in a few minutes he fell asleep again.

Colton saw a foggy view of the kitchen, his mom crying, and his brothers and sisters sitting at the dinner table with nothing but straw on their plates.

"I'm sorry, kids," his mom said. "Colton lost his job, and now we cannot eat regular food. The cows enjoy straw, and if you chew the straw, it might help. Just be sure you don't swallow. You may get ill."

Everyone is now crying. The kids are losing weight right before Colton's eyes. He sees them dying because of his foolish behavior.

He ran out of the house and into the woods. On his knees, he asked God to end this suffering. "Please, God. Don't let my family die because of my sins." Tears ran down his cheeks, but in the distance he heard God calling.

"Colton. Colton. I am here to talk to you."

Mr. Sellerman put his hand on Colton's shoulder.

"This is how he was in class, Mr. Zeller."

Colton opened his eyes with a start. He looked up at the two men, rubbed his tear-filled eyes, and smiled sheepishly.

"Was I asleep again?" He asked.

"Yes, now we need to find out why?" Mr. Zeller pulled up a chair and sat next to Colton at the huge oak table. In his hands was a green and white folder with Colton's name and address printed on the tab. "Mr. Sellerman, why don't you sit down and see if we can figure out why Colton has this sleeping problem."

Colton smiled and said, "I can tell you. I didn't get enough sleep last night."

"That's a great start, Colton. Please tell us why you didn't get enough sleep?" As Mr. Zeller asked, he looked through the folder with Colton's name on it. Unsure of the information in the folder, Colton felt uneasy.

"Ah... perhaps it was because I worked at the Smithford Dairy last night for a few hours. You are aware I worked there full time during the summer, and they asked me to keep working, ah... part time?" The school approved a fifteen hour work permit for the job, but if they learned he worked more than that, they would force him to quit his job.

Mr. Zeller looked into Colton's sleepy eyes and said, "Colton, ever since the first of the year, your first hour teacher has been warning you about being late. You were tardy over five times, and you have not been doing as well on your grades as you could."

"That is not true, sir. I'm getting an A in American history. In fact, as far as I know, I never get a grade lower than *A* in any of my classes," Colton retorted. "The part about being tardy five times is correct, but I have good grades."

"Yes, but we are worried because you could be the valedictorian next year if you can keep your grades up, and if you continue being tardy and falling asleep in class, your grades will go down. Colton, you could lose your opportunity to win a scholarship to college."

Mr. Sellerman turned to the principal and said, "Perhaps Colton should quit working nights. That would solve the problem."

"Colton, could you stop working or work fewer hours?" Mr. Zeller asked.

Colton feared this was where they were heading; quitting was not an option because as long as his family needed his help, he would continue working.

"No! I will try to get more rest before school, but I will not give up my night job."

"Even if it means jeopardizing your future?" asked Mr. Zeller.

"It won't. I will go to college, and nothing, including my job, will keep me from reaching that goal," insisted Colton.

Mr. Zeller picked up the folder and stood. Turning to Colton, he said, "Just remember, Colton, we are working on your behalf. If I can do anything to help you, please ask."

"Yes," injected Mr. Sellerman, "and I apologize for my actions this morning. I didn't expect that you would react the way you did. I wanted to wake you, and now you look like I beat you up."

"Don't worry, sir. I realize it wasn't intentional, and I will try to stay awake in your class tomorrow."

Chapter 3

The Art of Explaining

Miss Carol Downer gave Colton a hall pass to get into his third hour chemistry class. Entering the classroom, the students turned to the front of the class and listened as Colton explained why he was late. The teacher, Mrs. Quick, gave Colton the test the class was taking. With only fifteen minutes left in the hour, Colton went to his seat and worked. A few of the students attempted to quiz him about his bruised face, but he shrugged them off, keeping his head down while concentrating on the test.

It only took Colton ten minutes to finish the test, a few minutes before most of his classmates. He sat thinking about the day's events: He almost killed himself trying to get to school, got a bruised arm in first hour because Connie Jackson poked him every time he tried to sleep, and then, he got beat up by the trigonometry teacher. What else could happen?

It would be difficult to keep his promise to the principal. Colton considered that there are only 24 hours in each day. If he works eight hours, goes to school seven hours, and attends football practice for two hours, he is left with seven hours. Sounds good; seven hours of sleep would be great. The problem is that in seven hours, he must drive to work, home, and school, eat dinner, and do chores at home. That only leaves him with four hours of sleep. Doing the math only made Colton more tired. As he walked out the classroom door, Lacie Wooddell ran up to Colton and grabbed his arm.

"So, I hear Mr. Sellerman beat you up in second hour? Tell me all about it in art class."

"It was an accident, Lacie. Mr. Sellerman tried to wake me up, and I sort of jumped out of my chair and into the back of Carville's head. It's no big deal, just a stupid accident."

"You were sleeping again?" Lacie asked. Being Colton's steady friend, she was familiar with his problem.

"Yes, again," Colton responded as the two came up to the art room door. With her back to the wall, Colton put his arms out to each side of her and looked into her beautiful blue eyes. "Can we sit together this hour? I need to talk to you about some crap that's happening. For now, I have to get things under control, but I'm afraid I will lose it. It's getting too complicated. Even my dreams tell me I have to get my crap together."

"That sounds serious. You know I'll do anything I can to help, Colton. Just ask."

The two walked into the classroom just as the bell rang. They convinced Jerry to move so the two of them could sit at a table together. Jerry wasn't happy, but he felt sorry for Colton, with his face looking like he was in a war.

"No problem, man. You know, Colton, you look... like... you know, terrible. Can you see out of that eye?"

"It's getting better. I can see well enough to know you still can't draw in perspective," Colton said, looking down at Jerry's drawing.

"Man, it's an abstract. It's not supposed to be in perspective. For someone who's a genius, you know, you don't know crap about art." Jerry picked up his drawing and moved down the table.

Jerry was right. Colton had a photographic memory, could pass any test without studying, but in art or music, he got A's only because he tried. Mr. Swansear, the art teacher, didn't grade on talent alone. If you tried hard, you got an A. This was one class where Colton had to try hard.

"Tell me all the bad stuff, Colton," insisted Lacie. She was sincere in her desire to help Colton. The two had a history based on mutual trust. Like best friends, they confided their dreams and fears to each other. Lacie wanted to be a registered nurse or physician's assistant, planned to attend a community college and get her degree from one of the local universities.

"Well, you know about my job. No one knows I have been working forty hours a week, and it's getting hard to balance all of my activities," Colton told Lacie, who had a shocked look on her face.

"Damn you, Colton. You promised you would only work part time after summer." Lacie was uncharacteristically upset. Colton had told her at the beginning of the school year that he would cut down on the hours he worked. They talked about all the activities they would have during *this*, their junior year in high school: sports, honor society, student government, and the prom.

"I tried to, but Dad needs help keeping the family above water. My paycheck has helped, and I am afraid that without my income, Dad might lose the house," Colton explained as he worked on his watercolor.

"Will it help your family if you end up dead? You need enough sleep to keep healthy. How can you drive, work, and play football if you are sleep deprived? God, Colton, you're smart enough to know you could kill yourself by overworking," Lacie scolded.

"Always the nurse, aren't you, Lacie? But I appreciate your looking out for me." Colton put his hand on hers to show his appreciation.

"It won't help to schmooze me. You need to find another job or cut back on the hours," she offered. "Remember, you are not responsible for your family. You can help, but it is not your job to be the adult."

"Damn, you're tough!" Colton smiled. "I have another problem you might help me solve. Last night I had to train a Latino boy. He doesn't speak English, is only thirteen years old, and he is an illegal. What would you suggest? Shoot him at dawn?"

"No, but you should explain the situation to someone. There have been several farmers caught using illegal immigrants in the past few months. They only pay a small fine and then turn around and hire more illegals."

"I wasn't aware of that. This is the first one I have met. There are several Latino workers on the farm, but I don't know if they are legal or not. At least they speak English. Tony doesn't know any English," Colton said as he continued painting.

"So, if I turn him in, that would solve all my problems? I would get fired and not be working too many hours."

"Sounds like a plan," Lacie said with a laugh. "But I am serious."

Artsie Smartsie

Mr. Swansear, the art teacher, pulled up a chair and sat next to Colton.

"I understand Mr. Sellerman did a number on your face in trigonometry today. What did you do, forget your homework?" Mr. Swansear laughed.

"Everyone blames Mr. Sellerman, but it was my fault. I fell asleep, and he tried to wake me."

"I know; it makes for a more interesting story." Mr. Swansear smiled, and then continued, "You know, if you need any help, I'm here. I know you have been working hard for the last while. In fact, I have seen you fall asleep in this class more than once this year. You're not the only student to do that. I offer a good place to get rest. Anyway, the offer stands."

Colton smiled and said, "Thanks, sir. I appreciate your offer. My night job is impeding my day job, and I have to decide how to handle the situation."

"Been there, done that," Mr. Swansear said as he got up from the chair. "I worked my way through college and spent many a day with toothpicks keeping my eyes open. The trick is, you can't do it too long, or you will make yourself sick."

"Got it, and thanks."

Lacie smiled and said, "I'll keep pestering him until he fixes the problem."

"You do that, Lacie. Oh, and you better get working on your mosaic project. It's due in a few days, and you need the grade."

"I'm close to done," she said as she worked on her picture. With half of the hour gone, the two refrained from talking and worked in silence. Other than the occasional sound of music coming from the headphones of students listening to their MP3 players and phones, the room was silent. Colton wished he had brought his headphones, but he only had a cell phone, and they are not supposed to be used in school. The administration thinks the students will text all day. Instead, the students use their Wi-Fi enabled iPod or iPad and play games, listen to music, and surf the web. *Got to love tech toys,* Colton thought.

A few minutes before the bell, everyone cleaned up their area, and then it was an enormous rush to be first in line at the door.

"Stay in your seats," Mr. Swansear yelled, to no avail.

Lacie and Colton were the last to leave. They walked out holding hands and headed down the hall. On the way to the cafeteria, everyone who had heard of Colton's morning adventure wanted to see his messed up face.

"I feel like a carnival freak on display!"

"Better you than me," Lacie shrugged as she continued down the hall. "You should be used to it, though. After every game, you walk the halls like a big hero and shake the hands of all your admirers."

"That's different. This time, I'm not proud of my actions."

Colton didn't mind being the center of attention, provided it was for a good deed. But, like most kids, he hated to have everyone looking at him when he did something wrong. There is no scorn like the scorn of one's peers.

"You want to sit with me at lunch?" asked Colton. The two used to sit together every day, but this year, Lacie had been spending more time with her girlfriends.

"No, I promised to help Kathy with her algebra and her boyfriend problems."

"Is she still with Gordy Lackwater?"

"Are you kidding? That was so last week. She's with Aden Carville now. You know your quarterback?" Lacie laughed as she teased.

Colton knew Kathy changed her boyfriends more than she changed her tight jeans.

"So she's the girl Aden keeps talking about. Dang, I didn't know she was that kind of girl. According to Aden, she's hot. I mean... volcano hot!"

"That's the problem. Aden tells everyone that Kathy does all kinds of things with him, and she has done nothing. She likes him a lot, but he will brag himself right out of having a great girlfriend."

"Well, maybe I can help. I'll be seeing him at football practice, and I can put in a few words to set him straight."

As the two parted, Lacie turned and said, "Thanks. Just don't tell him where you heard this."

"No problem. I'll tell him I read it on Facebook or something."

Chapter 4

Sports Talk

Colton spent fifth hour sleeping. It was study hour, and Miss Walker, the instructor, suggested that if he had his work done, he could rest. She knew about his "sleeping problem" and didn't feel it would be a problem if he spent the hour in the back of the class, sleeping. It was very unconventional, much like Miss Walker herself.

Colton breezed through English class, reading the entire hour. Mrs. Castle's substitute teacher allowed the class to do homework or read the book they were all doing as a class assignment.

Steinbeck was an easy read, and Colton could relate to the hard luck of the Joad family. Tears filled his eyes as he read. Compared to the migrants during the Great Depression, Colton's family was rich. He could see a little of himself in the main character, determined to help his family succeed.

The bell startled Colton, and he headed to last hour physical education class. Because Colton was on the football team, Coach Talbert had him working on the weight lifting equipment. He would get enough exercise after school, but it was important for him to keep up his strength, and the equipment was the chosen method.

With several other team members, Colton worked through the day's routine. The routine, as set by Coach, comprised leg extensions, squats, leg presses, leg curls, seated dumbbell presses, stiff leg dead lifts, incline sit-ups, and 20 to 25 minutes of cardio. It would take Colton the entire hour to work through today's routine, and when he finished, instead of showering, he would get suited for football practice.

As Colton finished putting his football pads on, Coach Talbert asked him to come into his office. The two sat at the large cluttered desk, and Coach said, "Colton, I know what happened today. I keep a tight rein on my first team, and I want to make sure there won't be any problems with your ability to play on Friday. This is our second game, and it looks like we could have a decent year. God knows it's about time we won the division title."

"Yes, I understand your concern, and there will be no problem with my game. I have a few issues to take care of with work, but I will be ready." Colton said. "And sir, we will win Friday, and we will be district champions come November. I feel we have a great chance."

"Attaboy, keep up the spirit and let's get on the field. Did you get through all of your reps today? It looks like you have been doing a great job building muscle. Now let's see if we can teach you how to catch a few more of Aden's tosses. After warm up, we'll toss a few balls, and assistant coach Jeff can give you a few tips on keeping the football after you catch it. Last Friday, you lost two balls because you didn't grip them right."

The two walked through the locker room; Colton grabbed his spikes and put them on at the door. It was a crisp fall day, just perfect for football.

With every practice, Colton could feel himself becoming a better player. All he needed now was to make sure he could get rest. Sleeping in school is a major problem in need of a solution.

Walking out to his car, Aden came up from behind and slapped Colton on the rear. "Hey Colt, it looks like I should pass to you more often, considering how you were catching them today."

"You do that, Aden, and we might win Friday. Oh, and I hear you might lose that nice girlfriend of yours."

"What? Who have you been talking to?"

"Kathy knows you have been telling lies about her. Look, Aden, you don't have to brag to make yourself the big man at school. As quarterback and captain of the football team, everyone knows you and looks up to you. Don't brag about what you are doing with your girlfriend because she won't stay around if you keep it up."

Aden looked like a deer caught in the headlights of a truck. "I.... I didn't lie. Well... not much."

"We all know what you do, and it looks foolish for you to keep telling everyone what a great lover you are. Learn to keep your mouth shut, and you might keep that nice girl longer than your other girlfriends." Colton pushed the key in the door of his yellow Jeep Wrangler and pulled the door open. He slid into the driver's seat and opened the window. Aden stood there, looking like he might cry.

"You might be right, Colton. I like Kathy a lot. She is funny, and she puts up with a lot of my crap. She is a nice girl, Colton, and she doesn't put out, like I told the guys. In fact, the most we've done is kiss."

"That's good. I'll let my sources know you won't shoot off your mouth, and maybe you can keep her."

"Thanks pal. And get something on that eye; it looks gross all puffed up like that. Sellerman sure did a number on you."

Colton groaned, "He didn't do this. It was my fault."

"Whatever you say."

Aden turned and walked to his beat up brown 1994 Camaro. When he turned the engine over, blue smoke rolled out of the tailpipe. Even though it had seen better days, it still sounded hot. Colton considered his old Jeep and smiled. He loved his yellow Jeep. Even if it wasn't hot.

Dad To The Rescue

Colton pulled up to the large farmhouse featuring white siding with blue shutters, two stories, four bedrooms, a detached garage, and a mortgage that was killing his parents. This is home to Colton, his parents; Cyndi and Adam; two younger brothers, Jason and Terrance, and a younger sister, Stephenie. His dad's car was in the garage, so Colton parked in the driveway. The doorway opened, and Colton's youngest brother ran out to greet him.

"Hey Terry, how was school today?" Colton yelled out to his favorite little brother.

"Awesome. We played football in gym class, and I got to be the quarterback. I was good, but I couldn't throw so well. Will you teach me tonight how to throw?" Terry begged.

"Sorry, kid, I have to get sleep. Got to be at work in a few hours, and I'm dead tired."

"Shoot. Oh well, I can throw at the tire by myself, I guess."

"You do that. Keep practicing and you'll be on the Pee Wee team in no time," Colton said as he opened the back door.

Colton's mom stood at the stove, stirring a large kettle of soup. She turned and gasped at the sight of Colton's swollen face.

"Oh my God, what happened to you? I take it football practice didn't go well?" she asked.

"Long story, but it was from second hour. I had an accident in trigonometry. Is Dad around, Mom?"

"Sure, he's in the dining room, working on bills."

"Bad time to talk to him?" Colton asked. Bill time meant a lot of pressure on Colton's dad.

"Tonight he has good news. Talk to him. I know he wanted to talk to you when you got home."

Colton walked into the dining room and saw his dad with a stack of bills in front of him. He looked up, and seeing Colton, he smiled. "Evening, Colton. I have good news."

"And I have bad news. Who should go first?" Colton knew he had to do something about his job, and he hoped his dad could suggest a solution.

"You can. It sounds serious, son."

"Well... I seem to have trouble staying awake in school. Today, I fell asleep in trigonometry, and this is the result," he pointed to his swollen eye.

"You're working too many hours on the dairy farm? I feared this would happen. I told you, you don't have to keep working like you have been, Colton."

"But you and Mom need the extra money," Colton insisted.

"We did, and it helped us get through a dry spell. But my news changes all of that. I got my job back at the foundry, and I start tomorrow, with an increase in wages, and guess what?"

"I don't know. What?" Colton asked.

"They want me to go to college, and they will even pay for it. Imagine, your old man will go to college, even though I only have a GED. I guess they realized that I have brains even if I don't have an excellent education. They want me to go into management, and I'll earn twice what I earned last year." Colton's dad grinned from ear to ear. It was the happiest he had been in months, and Colton was proud of him.

"I always felt you were better than the jobs you ended up with, Dad. You're smart, and I'm glad they realize it."

"I may be smart, but without a diploma it's hard for the boss to know that."

"Dad, I'm proud of you." Colton walked over to his dad and gave him a bear hug. The two hugged for several minutes with tears running down their faces.

Colton's dad, Adam, pulled away and looked at his son with a huge smile. He said, "Now for the better news, Colton. You can take over my delivery job. I talked to the managers of the newspaper, and they said, As long as I keep the route in my name, you can deliver the papers."

Colton thought for a few minutes and then asked, "How much will it pay, and how many hours will I have to work?"

"Put it like this, you will earn as much as you have been putting into the pot here, and you will only work 16 hours per week: Tuesday, Thursday and Friday mornings from two to five, and Sunday morning from one to eight. Your mom will collect the money from the stores every Wednesday afternoon. That will save you from having to take off from school."

"Dad, that sounds too good. What's the catch?"

"No catch. It's a good job if you can remember all the stops. There are over 200 deliveries to homes, and then there are ten stores you deliver to. On Sunday, deliver up to eight hundred newspapers. Trust me, it gets busy, and if you miss someone, they will complain to your boss."

Adam had taken the job after he got laid off from the foundry. It didn't cover the bills, but along with a few odd jobs it helped keep them afloat.

Colton thought about the idea and said, "When can you show me the route and when can I start?"

"Bravo! You will love this. You can quit your stinky farm job tonight. Wait until you finish your shift and then tell the supervisor you can't come back."

Adam pulled the papers from the table and handed them to Colton. "This is a detailed list of the deliveries, and these are the store deliveries. You can study them, and the map. I will drive the route with you after school tomorrow if you feel it's needed. With your photographic memory, you won't have any trouble remembering the stops."

Chapter 5

Goodbye Night Job

Colton felt good about the afternoon's events. After dinner, he excused himself and headed up the stairs to his bedroom. On his way, he checked his messages and noticed that Lacie Wooddell had texted him and asked that he call.

He lay across his bed and dialed Lacie's number, eager to tell her about his dad's advice.

"Got your message. I have major news to share tonight," he said.

"So do I." Lacie sounded as if she had been running. "Let me catch my breath. I took a few sprints after dinner, and now I'm walking. I wanted to tell you I talked to my uncle, Ned. He is a county patrolman."

"I hope you didn't tell him about the illegal kid at work." Colton became agitated. "It isn't up to you to report him. He did nothing wrong!"

"Hold on, Colton. I would never do that, so I asked him a hypothetical question. I told him I heard about a guy in Sandusky who was hiring illegal workers, and I asked what would happen," she said.

"OK, so what did he say?"

"Well, there have been a lot of problems with the farmers hiring these illegals. He said last week they raided a farm where there were over six Latino men working. They will process the illegals and return them to Mexico. The owners just get a slap on their wrists, pay a small fine and go back to doing it again."

Lacie stopped walking. "He says anyone who knows about illegal workers should report them."

"I imagine he would say that, but I won't be around the farm after tonight. That's my news. Dad got his job back, with higher pay. From now on I'm doing his paper route, so I'll work fewer hours. I'm telling my boss to take the dairy job and shove it!" Colton said.

"That's great. So you won't be sleeping through class?" she asked.

"That's my hope, Lacie. I enjoy working at the dairy, but not during school. My body can't take the punishment."

"Well, we can talk about your body another time. I have to do homework, which I don't think you have ever done," she said.

"Hey, I do homework, but I don't do it at home," Colton said. It was true; he always got his work done at school.

"OK, smarty pants. Good luck tonight, and remember, turn them in for hiring illegal workers," she advised.

Colton considered playing a game on his computer, but decided that sleep was more important. He got ready for bed and set his alarm clock for nine p.m. That would give him half an hour to get ready for work. Tonight Colton would sleep well, and tomorrow he would celebrate his new job.

Colton was dead to the world, and when the alarm rang he jumped up, thinking it was his phone. When he realized what time it was, his whole body slumped. He hated the thought of going to work tonight. Why not just call in and tell the boss he quit? Heck, why bother working at all tonight? He almost convinced himself it was a smart move not to go, but his conscience wouldn't let him. He had to tell the supervisor face to face why he was quitting. That's what a man would do, and even though he would rather be a little boy tonight and sleep, he will man up and get ready for work.

In the kitchen, Colton packed his breakfast and heated a mug of coffee. He didn't enjoy taking energy drinks because of all the additives, but strong coffee would keep his eyes open all night. Trouble was, he would crash and burn at school when he couldn't drink coffee.

What Else Could Go Wrong

Pulling into the parking lot, Colton could see that Tom, the supervisor, was there along with most of the regular night crew. As he parked his Jeep, a red Ford pickup drove up and young Tony, the Mexican illegal worker, got pushed out the open door. The driver swore at him and told him to get to work and stop crying like a baby. The truck then sped off, creating a cloud of dust as it drove down the road.

Tony picked himself up from the gravel parking lot and walked toward Colton. His face had bruises, and he had a broken lip and swelling around his black eye.

"Can you help me, Colton? I need to stop that man. He will rape my little sister, and I have to kill him," the boy said in Spanish.

"Hold on, kid. Slow down and tell me what happened," Colton said.

Tony took a deep breath and told Colton how the man who keeps the illegal workers in the farmhouse tried to rape his sister last night. His dad fought with the man, but the man was much bigger and beat his father. Tony tried to stop the man himself and attacked him with his fists. The man beat him and said that if they tried to stop him again, he would send them all back to Mexico.

"My dad fears him," said Tony. "But I will kill him if he touches my sister. I am not afraid of the stupid gringo. Will you help me? You have a car. Can you drive me back to stop him?"

"No, but I will call the police, and they can stop him."

"No! No! You cannot call them. They will take us away and send us back to Mexico. I have to do this. Please help me," Tony pleaded.

As they were talking, Tom came out of the barn and yelled at them to get to work. Colton told Tony that he would help later, but now they have to work so Tom, the supervisor, doesn't get mad.

Colton didn't know what he should do. Calling the police would stop the man from molesting Tony's sister, but it would hurt Tony and his family. Doing nothing would also hurt them.

"Tom, do you have a minute?" Colton yelled. He told Tom what Tony had told him. Colton did not feel equipped to handle this situation by himself. Perhaps Tom could come up with a plan.

"What do you need, Colton?"

"There is a problem with Tony. The guy who brought him here from Mexico is trying to molest his little sister. Tony says he wants to stop him, but he doesn't want the police called."

"Holy crap. Sounds bad, but it's not our problem. Keep this quiet, Colton. We don't need this kind of stuff spreading to the other workers. I know the guy. His name is Bill Smittwell, and he's just bluffing. There's nothing to worry about," Tom said.

Tom kept looking down at the driveway, kicking gravel with his feet. Colton believed Tom knew more than he was letting on, and he may have felt this could become a big problem for him.

"Tom, I should also tell you I'm quitting after tonight. I can't keep working these hours while going to school, so Dad got me a job with the newspaper. I start tomorrow."

"Damn you, Colton. We put a lot of training into you. You can't just quit like that. Man, you got to give us more notice."

"You're lucky I gave you any notice. I wanted to call yesterday afternoon, but Dad said I should do it face-to-face, like a real man." Colton said.

"Well, I don't want you doing anything stupid, like calling the cops. I will take care of Tony, so get your stuff out of your locker and head home. I don't want you here if you will not stay on the job."

Tom's decision surprised and relieved Colton.

"I still think you should call the police about Tony's sister. That Bill Smittwell guy can't get away with molesting her, even if it means that Tony and his family have to go back to Mexico."

"Damn, Colton; keep out of this mess, and don't do something stupid. Do you understand? You could get many people in trouble, including you and your family. Colton, do you understand what I mean?" Tom asked again. He looked straight into Colton's eyes now, and Colton knew Tom meant his statement as a threat.

"Got it. I won't do anything I shouldn't," Colton said. He wasn't lying because he knew he should contact the police. Sometimes you can't look the other way.

"OK, now get your stuff and scram." Tom took out his cell phone and started back to the milking parlor as Colton walked into the employee room. Tony had left for work, and two employees were sitting at the large table. Colton got his things from the locker as the two men looked on. He had seen them many times, but never talked to them. Both were in their thirties, well built, looking like motorcycle gang members. Not the type that Colton socialized with. The largest man's arms had many tattoos, and he was talking on his cell phone.

Colton carried his belongings out toward his Jeep in the employee parking lot. He turned back and saw two men following him. He hurried to his vehicle, but the men caught up with him, grabbed him by the shoulder and spun him around.

"Kid, we'll show you what happens when you screw with things you shouldn't," the largest and gruffest man said.

The second man grabbed Colton's arms from behind and held him tight. Colton tried to squirm out of his grip, but he couldn't move.

"You some kinda smart ass kid, ain't ya?" the man standing in front of him said. He then pulled his arm back and gave Colton a punch in his abdomen, and with his other fist, he hit him on his left jaw. Colton flew back in pain.

"I won't do anything wrong, so you don't have to beat me. I get the idea," Colton yelled out.

"Hit him again, Joey; he doesn't act like he gets the idea."

Two more punches to his stomach, and another swipe at his jaw. The pain was more than Colton had ever endured. It felt like his guts were on fire, and he felt like his jaw broke. He could taste blood in his mouth, and his eye swelled shut again. The last blow was a powerful kick to his groin. That is the last he remembered. He fell to the ground as the man holding him let go. The two men were laughing like maniacs as they kicked him several times in the ribs and legs and finally pulled him up and set him in the seat of his Jeep. Colton looked like he had just been in an accident, slumped over the steering wheel.

"When he wakes up, he'll know we mean business," Joey said. The two walked to the milking parlor, congratulating each other on their handiwork.

An hour passed before Colton regained consciousness. At first, he thought he had fallen asleep while watching television. Then he couldn't understand why he was in the Jeep and why, in God's name, he hurt badly. Suddenly he remembered what had happened and cringed in pain. He started the Jeep and eased out of the parking lot.

Straining to stay on the road, he drove just over ten miles per hour until he was a few miles away from the dairy. He pulled off the road and dialed 911.

"This is the Huron County Emergency Services. How can I help you?" came a woman's soothing voice over the phone.

"My employer beat me up... an illegal immigrant named Tony intends to kill Bill Smittwell because he's trying to rape his sister, and... uh... did I tell you I got beat up and don't feel so good?" Colton told the operator where he was, and then passed out.

Dreams may reflect the events of the day, our plans for the future, past lives that may or may not have existed, and perhaps our most inner and crazy thoughts. Tonight, Colton was not dreaming. Like someone who goes under for surgery, Colton drifted in and out of existence. He remembered being beaten, being tired, and calling 911. The conversation with his dad telling him to be a man and man up kept ringing in his mind. *Is this what being a man is all about? Getting your ass beaten by two thugs?* He asked himself. *I don't want to be a man. Why can't I be a little boy forever?*

Flashing lights were all around him. He thought he was at the county fair again. He had so much fun there last month. Bright lights, flashing lights, spinning lights, rides with lights…

"Sir, can you get out of the car? Are you the person who called 911?" the police officer asked.

She turned to her partner and said, "Get the breathalyzer; I believe this kid is drunk."

Colton turned toward the policewoman and whispered, "I don't drink. I got beaten up by two guys at the dairy down the road. I was the one who called you for help."

Moving her flashlight around, the officer yelled to her partner. "Bring the first aid kit, and call for an ambulance. He's been beaten, and it looks serious."

"I need to see your ID. Can you get your ID out of your pocket, or do you want me to get it?" she asked.

Colton worked his hand into his back pocket. He grimaced in pain as he pulled the billfold out. "Here, you get it," he said, as he handed the billfold to the officer.

The officer looked over the license and registration. "Colton, just relax. We have EMT people coming, and you'll be OK. Can you explain what happened?"

"I went to work at the dairy, and an illegal immigrant who works there told me he wanted to kill Bill Smittwell, the guy who keeps him and his family at a farm south of Bad Axe. They are all illegal immigrants. Anyway, the guy has been trying to molest his sister. That's Tony's sister, not the guy's. She is under thirteen, and... Damn my guts really hurt. You need to stop that Bill guy because kids shouldn't get molested by old men, and young boys shouldn't kill them. You know?" His words faded off.

Colton hurt all over. Even after getting hit on the football field, he had never felt this bad.

He opened his eyes and realized that now he was lying in the back of a strange van, with guys looking down at him, putting needles in his arm and taking his blood pressure. He flinched when a woman rubbed something on his face.

"It's OK. I'm just cleaning this cut. Someone did a number on your face," she said.

"Yes, but my guts hurt more than my face. I feel like I took a bullet to the stomach. He kicked me hard, and he didn't have soft shoes on. Steel-toed boots in the groin."

"Ouch. That could be why you have pain in your gut, and you have bruising on your abs. Clear imprints of several enormous fists."

Colton could feel the van moving and asked, "Where are we going? I need to tell my parents."

"We're going to the Pigeon General Hospital. Don't worry about your parents. The police already contacted them; they will be at the hospital when we get there," the EMT said as he checked Colton's blood pressure.

Chapter 6

Will He Live?

Colton did not remember the ambulance reaching the hospital. The paramedics pushed his stretcher into the emergency room, where saw his mom and dad waiting for him. Together they rushed to Colton's side.

"Mr. and Mrs. Blackwell, let us get him into an exam room before you join him," the emergency room nurse said.

"No, we are his parents, and we will stay with him," said Colton's dad. He held onto Colton's hand as they wheeled him into a small room.

Colton was now conscious of where he was. He could feel himself getting stronger, and the pain subsided.

"My name is Nancy. We gave him a mild pain reliever, and all of his vital signs are good," the nurse told Colton's parents. "The doctor will be with you in a moment, but your son is not in any danger. I don't think we need to keep him overnight. The EMT staff saw no signs of broken bones or concussion, just a lot of bruises and a few cuts on his face."

The tall, thin doctor walked in and conferred with the EMT personnel. He checked their paperwork and then turned to Colton. "Hi, I'm Doctor Brown, and I see you took quite the beating. Look at this light and follow it." He moved the light back and forth, watching Colton's eyes. Then he looked into Colton's eyes, ears, and mouth and felt his side. Colton grimaced with pain when the doctor touched his side...

"I take it that hurts?"

"Yes, I feel like someone dropped me from a ten story building," Colton said.

"Well, it's not that serious. We will take a few X-rays to make sure that nothing's broken, but it looks good. You don't have a concussion, just some bruising. In a few hours, you should be able to walk and then leave. I will give you a prescription for a mild pain reliever, which we can fill at the pharmacy before you leave."

Colton asked, "Can I go to school today? I have about five hours to rest before I have to be in class."

"It's your choice, but wouldn't you like a day at home?" asked Dr. Brown.

"No, I hate missing school. I have a perfect attendance record, and a beating shouldn't ruin it," Colton laughed and grabbed his side.

"If the x-rays are clear, you can go home and to school."

"Thanks, Doc." Colton turned to his mom and dad. "I did what you suggested, Dad. I told Tom that I quit, and I also tried to help an illegal immigrant save his sister from a molester. They beat me because they want to keep me quiet."

"You did what was right, even if it cost you this pain. I'm sure it makes you feel good inside, doesn't it?" his dad asked.

"I will tell you in a few days. Right now it hurts inside."

Colton's mom, Cyndi, took her son's hand and said. "Colton, get some rest. We will wake you when they're ready to release you. Uncle Stan brought your Jeep back home, so you won't have to worry about it. And the police said, "We will contact you later."

Colton missed the last part of his mom's message as he drifted off to sleep.

Duane Wurst
Good Night Colton

The two biker dudes walked out of the bar, and Colton knew they were out to get him. As he walked down the dark street, they stayed just a few paces behind him. He ran, and with every step; he heard four steps catching up to him. Colton reached the Jeep, opened the door, and grabbed his baseball bat. Turning with full force, he swung the bat into the face of the first man.

Crack, the man's head burst into a thousand fragments of light. The second man screamed and ran for cover.

Colton yelled, "That will teach you. Never, ever, threaten a Loons football player." He laughed and stepped into the Jeep. As he lifted his leg, a hand grabbed his ankle. He looked down as the headless man bit at his leg, pulling him down to the ground. The man turned into a mad dog, gnawing away at his leg, holding it in his mouth like a pit bull.

"Colton, wake up," his mother said as she pulled on his leg. "The doctor said, you are fine, and we can get back home."

"I thought you would chew my leg off," Colton said.

"What? Chew your leg off?"

"Oh ... Sorry, I was dreaming." Colton sat up, holding his side and grimacing with pain. As he slid down from the gurney, his mother held his hand to steady him.

"I'm OK. I can stand by myself, Mom," he said.

"OK, but if you need me, I'm here."

"I have to use the bathroom. Where is it?" he asked.

The nursed pointed out the men's room, down the hall, and Colton shuffled toward it. It took a while, but he reached the room and closed the door.

Looking in the mirror, Colton didn't expect to see the bandage over his left eye. There was also a small bandage on a cut under his right eye. Bruises covered most of his face, but his pain was from the kicks he received to his side and groin. He pulled up his shirt and gasped. There were huge black blotches along his left side. No blood, but he was black and blue. His stomach also had two black imprints of a fist.

When he got back to his mother, Colton asked where his dad was.

"He went back with the kids. He has to go to work in the morning and wanted to remind you about the delivery tonight. If you can't do it, let him know." She said.

"I will do it. I have the map, and I remember all the house numbers. What time is it, and did you hear if they got the guys who did this?" Colton asked.

"It's two in the morning. Uncle Stan took your Jeep back to our house, and I haven't heard from the police yet, but I have signed the papers to get out of here, so let's stop talking and get home."

Together they walked through the emergency room exit toward Cyndi's old Chevy S-10 pickup. Colton and his dad had worked many hours to keep the little truck from falling apart. They both laughed when they calculated that there was more Bondo on the body than there was metal. But it ran well and took her wherever she wanted. Colton loved working with his dad. They had many similar interests, and both seemed to have a gift for remembering every detail. They would test each other whenever they took on a project, to see who could remember the instructions best. Colton always won, but his dad was a close second.

Colton's bed felt wonderful, and the fall air felt cool but not cold. Colton's mom opened the window and gave him a comforter to keep warm. She said she would wake him in time for school, but if he wanted to sleep in, she would call the school. Before she left his room, he was sound asleep. The pain pills were working, and he felt better. He would have a good four hours of sleep; a long needed night of rest.

No Breakfast In Bed

"Colton, it's six o'clock. Do you want to go to school, or stay home? I can bring breakfast up to you," Colton's mom said from the hallway.

"I will shower and get dressed, so I'll be down in a few minutes," Colton said. "Mom, could you make me some French toast? That would be great, but I can eat downstairs."

"French toast it is. Did you hear, Terry, Steph and Jason? Breakfast is in fifteen minutes, and the school bus in forty-five. So let's get going," she said.

Colton's pain had subsided, and the cool water of the shower seemed to work wonders. He avoided getting water on the bandage covering his eye. Instead, he used a washcloth and worked around it. The first pair of jeans he tried was too tight, so he decided on the red stretch jeans that his sister had bought him for Christmas last year. They looked silly, and he only wore them when she asked him to. But now they felt comfortable even though they looked skin tight.

"I love those jeans, Colton," Steph said as he passed her in the hallway.

"They sure are. Thanks again," he said.

"That white bandage over your eye is gross, so you should use a black patch, like a pirate."

"I would, but I don't have one."

"I do," yelled Terry from the bathroom. "It's in my dresser drawer. I got it last year for Halloween and never used it."

"Bring it down for breakfast, Terry. I don't want to mess around in your drawers. I never know what will jump out."

"OK," Terry yelled back.

At breakfast, all of Colton's siblings were examining his wounds and asking about his beating.

"Why didn't you fight back?" asked Jason. "I thought you were a tough guy."

"It's hard to fight with a big guy holding your arms behind your back. I wanted to fight, but I couldn't."

"Did they knock you out, like they do on TV?" asked Terry.

"Yes, I saw stars, but enough of this... I'm heading to school and the bus will be here soon for you guys," Colton said.

"Mom, tell Dad I will need the keys for the storage locker so I can pick the papers up tonight for the route, and I also need the bags."

"I can get them ready for you," his mom said. "Your dad has a class at Delta College tonight, and he won't be home until ten."

"Thanks, Mom. Love you, and I'll see you after football practice."

"I don't want you playing football tonight, Colton," she insisted.

"Only if I feel better; if not, I will just watch. But I don't want to miss anything, because I will play on Friday, no matter what."

"Yes, and be sure to walk with a limp... and you should wear a hook on your hand... like a pirate," his mom said.

"I like it," said Steph. "You're a pirate in red tights... cool."

Chapter 7

A First - Colton Is Early To School

The school bell rings at seven forty-five each morning, but today Colton walked through the doors fifteen minutes early. He couldn't remember the last time he had been early to school. He didn't run through the halls; instead; he limped to his locker and then sat down on the floor. As students passed him, they asked if he was OK.

"Sure, just waiting for the bell to ring," he replied.

Lacie saw him and sat next to him. "OK, Colton. What happened? There has to be a reason you look like a dejected pirate."

"The pants don't make my stomach ache because they are elastic, and the patch hides a gross bandage covering my eye," he told her.

"Is this from yesterday's events, or did something new happen?" she questioned.

"New. I got the crap beaten out of me last night. Spent most of the evening in the emergency room," he said. He raised his tee-shirt so she could see his bruises.

"Holy Jesus, Colton. Who did that?"

"Some creeps at work. I quit my job and threatened to call the police and report the illegal immigrant worker. You know, the kid I told you about yesterday. Well, Tony's keeper, a Bill Smittwell from Bad Axe, tried to molest his twelve-year-old sister, and Tony wanted me to help him kill the man. I wanted to call the police, but my boss didn't like me messing with things that could get him into trouble, so he sent his boys to give me a warning." With some effort, Colton worked his way back into a standing position.

"That looks painful," Lacie said. "Did you call the police? Knowing you, you figured you could handle this all by your macho self!"

"I called the police, and I was not macho," he said. "I passed out and was a real mess. Not macho at all."

The first bell rang, and the two headed to their class. Mr. Dinger, the first hour teacher, didn't expect to see Colton in the class early. He became concerned when he realized Colton looked like a wounded pirate. He asked if he was OK, and Colton said, "Everything is fine. I don't understand why you think something is wrong, just because I'm walking with a limp; have a patch over my swollen eye, and have more bruises than you can count on two hands."

Mr. Dinger asked no more questions about Colton's condition.

Most of first hour, Colton spent explaining the situation to his classmates. Everyone wanted to know what had happened last night. A few had even heard something on the morning news about a teenager being beaten and a dairy farm raided by the police. For the second day in a row, Colton was the talk of the school.

Walking into Mr. Sellerman's class, Colton approached the teacher's desk and said, "I want you to know these wounds aren't from yesterday, Mr. Sellerman. I had a little bad luck last night, and I got beaten up."

"They talked about you on the news this morning. And I assume then that it was the farm you work for that got raided?" he asked.

"Yes, I am sure it will be all over the newspapers too. I saw nothing, and I don't know what the police did. Last night they said they would call me today."

"Well, take a seat, Colton. I promise I won't beat *you* again today. You know, more students think I did that to you yesterday. It's kind of nice. When I make a threat now, the students listen," Mr. Sellerman said with a wicked laugh.

It surprised Colton how much he enjoyed listening to Mr. Sellerman teach. This was the first time he had been wide awake during his trigonometry class. He never studied because when he was ten, he took an online college trigonometry class and now he can do any problem that Mr. Sellerman throws at him. He often wished that he could just skip ahead, but an easy "A" was nice. Colton also studied other online courses because they were free, and he enjoyed learning on the computer. He could skim over the lesson and, with his photographic memory; he soaked the knowledge up, like a sponge.

As he limped down the hall toward chemistry class, Seth Seamoore, Colton's longtime friend, came up behind him and snapped his stretch jeans. "Nice jeans, Colton. Is this your new look?" he joked.

Colton knew Seth's voice and didn't turn around. "No, smart ass. These were the only jeans I had that didn't crush my bruised abs," he said.

"I heard you got the crap beat out of you. What were you doing wrong this time?" he asked.

"Nothing. At work, I told my boss I would report an illegal immigrant worker to the authorities. My boss took offense and had his goons do a number on me."

"Cool. You attract exciting situations. I don't have fun like that," said Seth.

"Hey, spend more time with me and I'm sure I can get someone to beat the crap out of you, too," said Colton.

"What class do you have now?" asked Seth.

"Chemistry, but we can eat lunch together, and I'll tell you all the details."

"Sounds like fun. See you then, Colton."

Seth turned into Mrs. Castle's English room as Colton turned down the hall toward the chemistry lab.

As the day progressed, Colton felt much better. He always seemed quick to heal when he didn't have to dwell on his pain. Keeping busy was his best medicine.

Lacie caught up with Colton in the hallway after third hour. "Colton, walk with me to art class."

"Sure, Lacie, I would have called you last night after I got out of the hospital, but I fell asleep before I got a chance."

"No problem. I'm just glad you didn't get killed, or something worse."

"And what would be worse than getting killed?" he asked.

"I don't know. Perhaps being in a coma... in a vegetative state... unaware you will always be in a hospital bed with machines keeping you alive."

"That's gross, but at least in a coma you could wake up. Dead is dead. The end... all done... no second act," he said.

As they entered the art room, the telephone rang, and Mr. Swansear, the art teacher, called for Colton to come up to his desk.

"The office wants you to go down there. Someone is here to see you," Mr. Swansear said. "Hope everything is OK. You look rad in that outfit. We should have a picture done so someone can paint it."

"I'm not sure I would like that, but I am sure students have taken my picture already. I keep seeing flashes when I walk down the hall," Colton said.

Colton walked toward the office. He could see that two state troopers were standing next to the main desk, so he stopped into the restroom first. He knew it would take time to go over the events with the officers, and a pit stop now would save him later.

Trooper Laurie Was Nice

The Michigan State Troopers were standing in the main office talking to Ms. Downer, the school receptionist.

"Colton will be here in a minute. I saw him slip into the men's room a second ago. Oh, here he comes. You can use the conference room for your interrogation, or whatever you need to do," Ms. Downer said in a nervous voice.

The female state trooper, Laurie Claybern, replied, "That would be very nice. We only need to ask a few questions. Colton was a hero last night. He brought down a ring of illegal alien smugglers, and he may have put away a rapist."

"You don't say," said Ms. Downer. "I always liked Colton; he is an outstanding football player and a smart student. I think he is one of only a few all *A* students."

Colton opened the glass office door and walked over to the Troopers. "I'm Colton Blackwell. I assume you want to talk?"

The three walked back to the conference room and sat down. Ms. Downer made a cup of coffee for everyone and then left the room.

Sipping his coffee, Colton let out an enormous sigh. "It was quite the night. One I hope never gets repeated."

"Yes, Colton," Trooper Laurie said. "I talked to you last night and took a statement while we were waiting for the ambulance. I see you are doing better. You looked terrible when I first saw you."

"I feel better, but I still can't see with my left eye, and I have a ton of bruises."

"Laurie, let's get down to business," said the second officer. He was a muscular older trooper with a gruff demeanor. "Colton, we need to verify the accuracy of the statement you gave Trooper Laurie last night."

"Steve, this is my interview. I will ask the questions, not you. Is that understood?" Laurie asserted.

"Yes, but we don't have all day."

"Colton, I would like to use a recorder. Is that OK with you?"

"Sure, record away," Colton said.

Laurie pulled out a small recorder and turned it on. Colton could see by the red light that it was now recording.

"Re-interview with Colton Blackwell, age 17 at LHC High School.

Colton, would you tell us what happened last night? Use your own words, but don't embellish the facts."

"Well, it started the night before. I was at work, and the supervisor asked me to train a Mexican boy named Tony. The boy is thirteen years old and doesn't speak English. I spoke Spanish, so we talked and I showed him the job. In my conversations with Tony, I learned he was an illegal immigrant and that he, his father, and sister lived in a farmhouse south of Bad Axe. Tony said they had to live there with several Mexican families who were all illegal."

"Kid, get to last night," said Trooper Steve.

"Take your time, Colton. Steve is just a little impatient," Laurie said, giving Steve a look of disapproval.

"Well, I talked to my friends, and they suggested telling the authorities about Tony. I didn't want to get the boy in trouble, and I felt relieved when Dad gave me his job delivering newspapers. I could quit my job at the dairy, and I wouldn't have to deal with the problem."

"That's nice, but not relevant," inserted Steve.

"Steve, do you want to leave the room? I will not remind you again. This is my interview, please keep your thoughts to yourself," Laurie warned.

Colton could see that the two troopers did not have a good working relationship. Perhaps, he thought, it was because Laurie was a woman and Steve was an old trooper. Bad blood, he concluded.

Colton continued, "When I went to work last night, I saw Tony being thrown out of a red pickup, driven by a man who I learned was Bill Smittwell. Tony and I were the only ones in the parking lot, and he wanted me to help him. He had been severely beaten and said that he and his father got in a fight with Smittwell because the man had attempted to molest his twelve-year-old sister. I told Tony I would call the police, but he said if I did they would send his family back to Mexico. I calmed Tony down by promising I would help him stop

Mr. Smittwell."

Colton stopped to take a drink of coffee. Trooper Steve spoke, but Laurie stopped him before he could.

"Continue, Colton," she said.

"The supervisor, Tom, came out and told us to get to work. Tony went in, but I stayed back to talk to Tom. I explained Tony's situation and suggested that I should call the police. He threatened me and told me to mind my business. I then informed Tom that this would be my last night working, and he got mad and wanted me to leave. He insisted I was not to call the police."

Colton thought for a moment, and then said, "I went into the break room, used the bathroom, and went back to get my belongings. I saw two guys whom I didn't know but had seen on the dairy before. I think they work in the field, or something. Anyway, they were sitting at the table, watching me. When I left to go to my Jeep, I noticed they were following me. They stopped me. One guy held my hands behind my back, and the other guy beat me. I think I must have passed out, because when I woke up, I was in my Jeep, slumped over the steering wheel. I drove off and called 911."

"That matched your statement from last night," said Trooper Laurie. "I want to inform you, Mr. Smittwell is being charged for bringing illegals into the country. Tony, his dad, and sister have pressed charges against him for molesting the young girl. They will receive immunity, and Mr. Smittwell will spend many years in jail. The two guys who beat you pled guilty to assault, so you will not have to testify against them. They may spend several years in jail as they both have several other warrants out for their arrest. And the dairy is being charged for hiring illegals. The owner says he did not know what his supervisor was doing, but they will pay a small fine and will probably continue to hire illegals. Do you have questions, Colton?"

"Wow! All that, and I don't even have to talk to the district attorney?" Colton asked.

"That won't be necessary. Sometimes it works out that way. We needed your interview for the record. If something changes, you may be called to testify, but I don't expect that to happen."

"Thanks, officer. I appreciate the way you handled this, especially last night. I was out of it, and your calmness helped."

"That's my job, Colton. To help," Laurie said. "OK, Steve, now we can go." Walking out of the office, Laurie turned to Colton.

"Colton, consider a profession in law enforcement. You had a good grasp of details and handled yourself well under pressure. Trust me, not all state troopers are like Steve over there. Most troopers are caring, understanding people, like you." She said goodbye and shook hands with Colton.

By the time the interview ended, it was past lunch. Ms. Downer suggested Colton go to the kitchen to get something to eat. She gave him a pass, and he headed down the hall. In the kitchen, the cooks were delighted to see him. They made him a sandwich, gave him pizza, and offered him a super-sized salad.

"This is better than any school lunch," Colton said, and then suggested doing this every day, but the cooks rejected the idea.

A Visit With Coach

Colton spent the last hour in the weight room talking to his buddies. He didn't do his routine because he was still sore. After school, he walked into Coach Talbert's office to tell him he couldn't suit up for practice.

"Colton, I hear you talked with the police. Care to tell me about it?" he said.

"I'm not in any trouble, if that's what you were thinking," Colton said.

"Well, dressed like a pirate in red tights, I didn't know what to think. I heard about your adventure last night, and your dad called to let me know what happened. I'm glad you're done with that damn job, because I need you concentrating on football."

"Coach, I'm the one happy about the job, but I will still work nights. I'm doing a newspaper route that takes three hours a night, three days a week, and six hours of work on Sunday morning. I will be home in time to get rest before school, and I shouldn't have any more problems being tired or late," Colton said.

"Great, and when will you be back for practice?" asked Coach Talbert.

"The way I'm healing, I think I can suit up tomorrow. I can watch practice tonight, but I don't think I'm ready to get hit anymore today."

"No, go home and sleep. I want you to heal, but if you like, you can use the whirlpool before you leave. That should help those bruises, and after you use the whirlpool, get an ice pack from the freezer and use it on any swollen areas."

"That sounds great, Coach. I'll see you tomorrow, then."

A half hour in the whirlpool allowed Colton to relax, but when he put ice on his swollen abdomen, the pain was shocking. After experimenting, he got to where he could tolerate the ice for a few minutes. He walked to his Jeep as the team came back from practice. The day was exhausting, but Colton felt comfortable. The worry he had for his family was easing, and now he didn't feel pressured to help because his dad had a new job, he had a new job, and everything felt better.

Colton got that strange feeling you get just before the roof collapses. It can't last; something always happens when things feel good. Call it a premonition, or whatever. Colton knew this bliss would not last forever; he wasn't that lucky.

Chapter 8

Paper Boy

Pulling his Jeep into the driveway, Colton could see his younger brother Terry throwing the football at a large tire hanging on the garage wall.

"You're doing well, Terry," Colton said.

"I still miss too many times. To become a quarterback, I have to always hit my mark. That's what Coach says," Terry explained.

"Well, not all quarterbacks always hit the mark. Even Aden Carville misses some. And I don't always catch his throws. We can only do our best."

"I want to be the best, Colton. I want to be on the varsity team just like you when I grow up," Terry said.

Colton walked over to him and gave him a big hug. "You will be because you have the drive and determination to succeed. I used to spend all my time catching Dad's throws. I guess I always wanted to be on the varsity team, just like you," he said.

"Do you work tonight on the farm?" Terry asked.

The two brothers talked for quite some time. As brothers, they were close. Terry idolized Colton, who saw himself in his younger brother. They both loved sports and were very intelligent. Colton tried to spend as much time as possible with his brother. It was important to him to be a part of his life. His other brother, Jason, appeared to be jealous of Colton and often criticized him. When Colton tried to spend time with him, they ended up in an argument about something.

Their sister, Stephenie, was a sassy, outspoken girl. Colton loved her attitude but did not feel he had much in common with her.

"Want to play a computer game tonight, Colton?" asked Terry.

"Sorry, little guy, but I have to do my paper route. I start deliveries tonight, and I have to get to bed early so I can get up at one in the morning."

"Can I go with you? Sometimes Dad would let me drive with him. I fell asleep before we got done, but I was a big help to him," Terry insisted.

"I'm sure you were, but tonight I have to learn where all the stops are, and that takes concentration."

Colton went into the big farmhouse while Terry continued playing football.

"Mom, I need the bags for tonight and any instructions Dad left for me."

Cyndi, Colton's mother, was in the kitchen making dinner. She yelled back to Colton. "Look next to the back door, in the box. All the bags are there, a list of the stops, and a flashlight for finding the house numbers. The key is to the storage shed where you have to pick the papers up. There is also a key for the newspaper racks you have to put papers in. One key fits all the racks."

"Well, that covers everything. What's for dinner?"

She poked her head through the archway and smiled. "You look like you're feeling better than you did this morning, and we're having meatloaf and boiled potatoes. Dinner will be ready in thirty minutes. Tell your brothers and sister."

At the table, Colton told about his visit with the police, and he went into detail for his siblings about the night's adventure, answering a dozen questions. Terry told about his football activities, Jason said little, and Steph talked about her new best friend at school and how they would spend the weekend at her place.

"Only after I approve," her mother insisted. "I have to call Madison's mother before I let you spend the night, Steph."

"Awe, Mom, I'll be fine. They only live a few miles from here, in Elkton."

"We'll see, dear."

After dinner, Colton put his delivery supplies in the Jeep and checked the oil and tires. Once satisfied that there were no problems, he went up to his room to surf the web, check his Facebook page, and talk with Lacie.

Lacie had become his best friend. He wasn't sure if he wanted a boyfriend / girlfriend relationship, but he loved confiding in her, and she was the ultimate sounding board. She told him what she thought, even if it wasn't what he wanted to hear. Tonight was no different. She reminded him he wasn't the hero that everyone says he was because he didn't want to call the police until he had to.

"You need to be more decisive, Colton. You're like most men; you go along with the flow, trying not to make waves. Sometimes you have to take a stand. Like when I told you to call the police the other day after you told me about the illegal immigrants. You didn't want to get anyone in trouble. If you had called the police then, you wouldn't have gotten beaten up."

"Yes, Lacie, you were right, and I'll try to be more decisive. I have a new job, and I will adjust my attitude."

"Good. You know I love you, Colton."

"Love you too, and I'll see you in art class."

"You can tell me all about delivering newspapers," she laughed. Lacie had told Colton that she thought he could find a more adult job than being a newspaper boy. This didn't bother Colton. He knew his dad enjoyed the job, and even his brother, Terry, was impressed.

So Many Stops

Every time Colton came close to falling asleep, he became uncomfortable and had to turn over. His ribs would hurt. He then turned over, and his abs hurt. The pain soon became uniform, and his entire torso ached, so he got up to use the bathroom and take one of the pain pills the doctor had given him.

The alarm rang at 1:00 a.m., and Colton was groggy from the medication, but he didn't want to mess up his first day on the route. His dad depended on him.

To wake up, he jumped in the cold shower, shivered into his jeans, the only pair that still felt good, and checked his eye. Still swollen, but better than yesterday. Colton removed the bandage the doctors had applied and realized that he needed the pirate patch because it kept him from seeing double. Before leaving the house, Colton filled a large insulated mug with coffee, and grabbed a large cola.

At the storage unit, there were two cars parked next to the building. Colton remembered his dad telling him two other drivers shared the unit. He drove up and parked behind an old 1989 Plymouth Voyager van. Colton got out of his Jeep and walked to the storage unit.

"Hey, Rob, look at the pirate! Sorry fella, we have nothing for you to pilfer, or plunder, or whatever a pirate does," said the large red-headed man. He smiled with a broad grin and gave a hearty laugh, followed by a few minutes of coughing.

"Hey, Joe, why don't you have another cigarette?" teased Rob.

"I'm Colton Blackwell. My dad is Adam Blackwell. I'm sure you all know him," Colton said.

"Sure do," said Rob, a young and handsome man in his twenties. "Your dad is the greatest. Couldn't ask for a nicer guy."

"I know," said Colton. "He got a new job and I'm taking over his route. I assume the papers aren't here yet?"

"Like usual, they're late. Oh, speak of the devil, here comes the truck now. Stand back and let him park here. The driver will show us our pile of papers, and we can unload them into our vehicles. Count your papers, Colton; you don't want them to be short," said Rob.

Colton loaded ten bundles of twenty-five newspapers into the back seat of the Jeep. The driver gave him some loose papers and a list of changes for the route. He saw that there was a new subscriber on Elm Street in Caseville and one subscriber who requested that he put the paper on the porch because she had knee surgery last week.

By 2:00 a.m. Colton finished his first stop a few miles south of Bay Port. He completed the rural roads of southern Bay Port and dropped papers off at the Bay Port Store and at a gas station. He marked down how many papers each business received because they would have to pay for the ones they sold. After an hour of driving, Colton became tired, but he had over two more hours and another hundred and fifty papers to deliver. By three-thirty, Colton was at The Point.

The Point, a large residential peninsula jutting into Lake Huron's Saginaw Bay, stretched out into the lake over two miles and had hundreds of resort cottages and homes on both the north and south side. The north side was on Lake Huron, and the homes were huge and expensive. On the south side, there were many roads with canals running between them. The homes were smaller, but still impressive. There were also homes on the south that faced Saginaw Bay. These homes had a beautiful view of the lake and woods that ran along the lake on the other side.

Colton knew these roads because he had driven before with his dad, and yesterday, he had studied them on Google Earth.

Colton noticed the houses were close together, and the mailboxes were on both sides of the road. As he looked for the house numbers, he realized some homes had one address, but the mailbox was on another road. Trying to match the house with the correct box took longer than he expected. Also, hundreds of deer walked around in the dark. Colton enjoyed hunting deer and knew you can't hunt in a residential area, but he still wondered why someone didn't catch some of these deer and eat them for dinner.

To Colton's amazement, it took over an hour to do The Point. He still had Caseville and many rural roads north of Pigeon and Elkton to deliver. With eyes that were growing tired, and time running out, he continued his route. Colton's dad told him that the first couple of days would take longer, because he had to learn where the stops were. It would appear that Dad was correct.

After delivering all the papers on The Point, Colton headed down the main road to Caseville. He delivered papers as he went, often having to use a flashlight to check house numbers. Some homes had special tubes for the newspapers, others were commercial mailboxes with newspaper slots, and several homeowners wanted the paper tossed in their driveway next to the side door. Colton remembered the new instruction for the woman on The Point who needed the paper delivered to her deck. He asked himself, *Should I go back? It's already late, and I don't want to be late again for school?* After deliberating, he headed back to The Point. Requests to deliver to the door were not unusual. There were several homes on The Point where Colton had to deliver to the back door because the owner was elderly and could not walk out to the road. These were an inconvenience to Colton, but his dad said they would tip him extra every month.

Upon returning to Caseville, Colton delivered over fifty papers to the businesses. He then spent half an hour looking for a road he didn't know. He used his cell phone to get on the internet, something he hated to do because of the cost; and he found a map. The road had two names, one on the sign, and one for the legal addresses.

It was now five-thirty in the morning, and Colton had another seventy-five newspapers to deliver. He did the math and realized that he would not get anymore sleep tonight. He would be home by 6:30 and would have to be in school an hour later. Resigned to these additional facts, Colton trudged on with his deliveries.

He delivered his last paper at 6:45 and had seven miles to drive to reach home, was tired, and he had to stop somewhere to relieve himself. He stopped along the deserted county road and checked to make sure no cars were coming. Before he finished, a police light flashed behind him. He zipped his fly and tried to look like he needed to check his tires. The police officer walked up and asked what his problem was.

"I finished delivering my newspaper route, and it sounded like my back tire might be low on air, so I stopped to look," Colton said.

"OK, and why are you dressed like a pirate?" the officer asked. He shone his light into Colton's face and laughed. "Aren't you Colton Blackwell, the kid who broke the illegal immigrant smuggling case last night?"

"I was there, but I broke nothing. In fact, I was the only thing that got broken."

"I understand you got quite a beating," the officer said. "So what are you doing this morning, dressed like a pirate?"

"I deliver the *Metro Press* newspaper. My dad used to have the route, but I will do it from now on." explained Colton.

"OK, kid. Just make sure when you use the outdoor facilities, you don't have someone watching. It is illegal to expose yourself in public," the officer warned.

Colton smiled and said, "Yes, well... I don't have a flat tire, sir."

Chapter 9

Sounds Like A Repeat

It's seven-thirty in the morning, and Colton could go home; get changed into some clean clothes, have breakfast and be an hour late to school, or he could rush to school, and still be late. He thought about the advice Lacie gave him last night. She suggested he must be decisive, so he jumped in the Jeep, and raced off to school.

"I will not be late. I will not be late," he kept repeating, hoping it would help. The last turn was another two-wheeler, and he slid to a stop in the parking lot. There were no buses and no other students. Colton ran through the school doors, past his locker and into Mr. Dinger's history class, just as the teacher called his name.

"I'm here, Mr. Dinger," Colton said as he walked to his desk.

"Well, I see the pirate has returned. Colton, I thought you said you wouldn't be late again."

"Sorry, Mr. Dinger. My new job took longer than I expected," Colton said.

"Dressed like that, you must be a server at a pirate-themed restaurant?"

The class laughed at Mr. Dinger's comment, and Colton felt belittled.

"No, sir. I'm a paperboy," Colton said.

The class laughed even louder at Colton's comment.

"That's enough of this. Let's get down to history. Colton, take your seat, and will someone pass him a book from the shelf?" Mr.

58

Dinger said.

Colton grew tired as the day dragged on, but he didn't fall asleep in any of his classes. He spent most of art class talking to Lacie about the week's events. Colton tried to convince her that delivering newspapers was a valid job, given the amount of money he would earn. His new income impressed her, and she agreed it was better than his job at the dairy, as far as the hours and smell.

"You know, Colton, those tight jeans are rad. Like, they look like something that Andy Warhol would have worn," Jerry Cultrain said.

"You would look good in them, Jerry. You're skinny enough for the look. I think they make me look fat. I bulge out of them too much."

"No, you don't. They show your muscles off, and you have a nice butt," Lacie said.

"For sure, man, I would have said that too, but it sounds weird coming from another guy, you know?" Jerry said.

"Yes, I know, Jerry."

Jerry is a throwback to the 1980s. He loves pop art and punk music, dresses in garage sale specials, and keeps his hair long and curly. Last year, he wore dreadlocks because he loved Black pop culture. This year, he is the ultimate hippie.

The rest of Colton's day went smoothly. No surprises and only a few people teased him about the way he dressed.

During the last hour of gym class, he looked at his eye and decided that the patch could go. He could see even though he had a nice shiner. Lifting weights was not a problem, and he realized he was almost healed from his misadventure.

After he suited up for practice, Coach Talbert called him into the office.

"Colton, do you feel well enough to practice?" he asked.

"Sure do. I told you I wouldn't miss tomorrow's game with the Hampton Colts. You know you need me against those thugs," Colton said.

The Hampton team is an aggressive team. They had a size advantage, with a defensive line made up of players as big as any college team. They also played dirty.

"Yes, we need you. Show us what you have in practice today, and if you don't look injured, you're in. We need your speed, Colton," said Coach.

The team played a scrimmage with the second team and junior varsity. Colton let no one see that he still had pain in his ribs. He made several very impressive catches and ran for two touchdowns. Everyone cringed when junior varsity tackle, Big Mike, clobbered Colton on a fair tackle. Colton went down, and three hundred pound Mike landed on top of him. He kept saying, "Gee, I'm sorry. Gosh, I'm sorry. Are you OK?"

Colton got up and ran back to the huddle, holding his side. "I'm fine, guys," he grunted.

After practice, Coach told Colton that he was fit enough to start the game. He suggested he use the whirlpool before he left, but Colton didn't want to be late getting home. He had another delivery on Friday morning and needed the rest because he must be ready to play Friday evening.

"Thanks, Coach. I won't let you down Friday, but I can't take the time tonight for the whirlpool," Colton said as he headed out of the locker room. "I'll take a long, hot shower when I get home."

Second Delivery Goes Better

At home, Colton spent half an hour playing with Terry, and then went in for dinner. Dad was home tonight, and the family discussed his new job and the classes he attends at Delta College.

"Colton, tell me how the route went last night."

"Just like you said it would, Dad. I spent a lot of time looking for the boxes. I knew the numbers, but not where to find them."

Adam laughed. "That's what happened on my first night. The second night will go faster. You can speed up the deliver now you know where the boxes are and. Did you put the paper on the side deck for Mrs. Hoffstarter? She's the one north of Main Street."

"Yes, that's a beautiful house. When I got on the deck, I could hear the waves splashing on the beach."

"She's a special woman. Just shy of one hundred, and her mind is as quick as a teenager. If you miss her though, she'll complain. But every month, she puts an extra twenty dollars in your pay as a tip. You know, son. I will miss that extra money. Perhaps you should pay me a percentage of your tips?"

"Only if you do the deliveries, Dad. I have a question: when I do the route, how can I keep from getting bored?"

"Well, I listened to audiobooks. Just download a book on your phone, put your headphones on, and listen to the book," Adam explained.

"Listen to the book?" asked Colton. "You mean someone reads it to you?"

"Yes, actors read the books. They even have sound effects. It makes the time go fast, and you may even learn something."

"Sounds good. Can I borrow one of your books?" asked Colton.

"I have some on my computer."

The two walked to Adam's desk and looked at his list of books. Colton had read a few of them for school, but he settled on the mysteries written by James Patterson and David Baldacci.

"You'll love these. They have a lot of action, and you won't get bored. Which one do you want to try first?" asked Adam.

"Well, Dad, why don't you load a couple you think I'll like, and then I can play Russian Roulette tonight and surprise myself."

The two laughed, enjoying each other's company. Cyndi loved to see them like this. With the rough times past, she hoped they could spend more time together. For the past month, they both worked long hours, and Adam felt bad because he needed his son's income to make ends meet.

"Come on, kids, let's clear the table so we can play a board game," she said.

"Shoot... do we have to?" asked Jason. "Shouldn't Colton be helping? Why doesn't he have to help with the dishes?"

"He did his share when you two were young, Jason. When you're his age, you can skip the dishes. Now get working!"

Colton played one game of Clue with his family and then headed to bed.

Lying on the bed, he called his friend Seth Seamoore. "Hey, Seth, will you be at the game tomorrow night?" Colton asked.

"Wouldn't miss it. Why do you ask? Want to go somewhere after the game?"

"No, I need your help," Colton said.

"You're sounding serious, Colton. I hope it's nothing that will get me beat up like you were."

"I hope not, too. Do you still have that cool professional video camera that your dad gave you?" Colton asked.

"The Sony 2000U?"

"I don't know. Is that the one you said cost almost two grand?"

"That's the one, but why do you want to know?" asked Seth.

"Well, I want you to bring it to the game. The Hampton Colts play dirty, and I think they may try to hurt some of our players on purpose. Last week, they broke a Bad Axe player's arm, and word is, they had it planned. He was the quarterback, and they wanted to stop him."

"Dang, Colton, that's why I don't play football. My bones are too valuable. What will I be recording?"

"The two players doing these ugly deeds are numbers fifteen and eighteen. Two linemen on the defense. I heard they are mean dudes, but if we can catch them red-handed, we might stop them," said Colton.

"Hot damn! I will go undercover. Sure, I'll record them. In fact, I should record more with that camera. It is a professional unit. Maybe if I would use it more, I could become a professional."

"Sure, Seth. I can't believe all the toys your dad buys you. Is there anything you don't have?"

"Yes, more friends like you, Colton. Most of the guys at school just want to play with the toys. You're the only friend I have who isn't impressed with the crap I have."

"Well, I'm impressed with you, pal, and thanks for the favor. Oh, and the answer is... yes. Let's get together after the game. Meet me at my place. We can look at the video and party in the garage."

"Can I bring a girl, or is this just for guys?" asked Seth.

"Who do you want to bring?"

"Stacey Elsworth, the exchange student staying with our family. She's cool, and hot looking."

"I know, Seth. She's in my chemistry class. By all means, bring her and I'll ask Lacie."

"It's a date, Colton. I'll see you then."

Colton texted Lacie, "A go for Friday - Love U."

He set the alarm for one in the morning and slid under the sheets.

When the alarm rang, Colton was wide awake and ready to go. He made sure he had everything he needed and microwaved a mug of coffee before he left the farmhouse. At the storage locker, the papers were already there, and he didn't have to wait. There were no new instructions, so he had to do the same deliveries as last night.

Before leaving the storage building, Colton put his headphones on and checked the list of audiobooks his dad had loaded on the phone. Having never read a David Baldacci novel, he listened to Zero Day. As he drove, he discovered he could listen to the book, and hear road noise and other cars passing. From the start, the book was exciting. A murder mystery featuring John Puller, a military investigator. Colton smiled and knew it would be a great way to pass the time as he made his stops. He had to keep his mind on both tasks. If he lost his place on either, he would have to go back and find it.

Even with the audiobook, by four o'clock Colton got tired. If he would stop at a corner and close his eyes, he knew he could fall asleep, except falling asleep would cause problems with late deliveries and a late arrival at school. He snapped his eyes open, turned up the volume on his book and continued the deliveries. It was four-thirty when he made his last delivery and headed back home. This morning he could sleep again before school. He had completed the route with no problems, and he had read two sixty-minute audio files of his book. A fulfilling evening.

Chapter 10

Cheerleaders Tease The Pirate

Colton woke before the alarm clock rang. He jumped out of bed, ran to the bathroom, and jumped into the shower. Friday is game day, and he didn't want to be late. He searched his closet for just the right pair of jeans — something new, but with that "old" look. He grabbed his Loon Spirit T-shirt and his favorite pair of Nike shoes. A quick shave and splash of Swiss Army cologne finished the job. He looked in the mirror and considered acne coverup to hide the bruising still around his eye. He then thought, I can live with a black eye better than an eyepatch. At least I won't look like a wounded pirate. Today will be a good day!

Time seemed to slip away, so he skipped breakfast and ran straight to the Jeep. It is a quick ride to school, and he arrived twenty minutes early. Not wanting to be too early, he sat in his Jeep and listened to his Baldacci audiobook.

"This could become addictive," he thought.

As the buses pulled into the drive, Colton headed into school. He greeted Lacie in the hallway, and they walked together for a while.

"Do you want me to bring anything for tonight's party?" she asked.

"Mom will pick up pop and chips today. Can you think of anything else we might need?"

"No, that sounds good. I hope you cleaned up the garage. Last time you had a party there, we had to sit next to a disassembled auto part."

"That was my transmission, and it's in my Jeep now. Don't worry, I already cleaned it up. Just the way you like it, Lacie," he retorted.

"Good, I'll bring some of my new CDs, and I invited a few couples," she said as she turned into her classroom. "See you in art class."

Colton made his way to Mr. Dinger's history class. He walked into the room and smiled at the teacher, who seemed surprised to see him before the first bell rang.

"You're early, Colton. I'm glad your new job worked out."

"Thanks, sir. It seems strange being here before the last bell," Colton said.

"Colton. I won't be driving down to the city for the game, but I want to wish you good luck tonight."

"Thank you. We will need a lot of luck. Their team is tough, large, and mean," said Colton.

"I heard they broke the Bad Axe quarterback's arm last week, just for fun," said Ashton Wentworth.

Several other students agreed, and a discussion ensued about how to play against a mean team like the Hampton's, with many students suggesting the Loons should also play dirty.

By the time Mr. Dinger settled the class for attendance, the students had spent fifteen minutes talking. Colton considered that this day may go by quickly, with everyone talking about the game tonight.

The morning went faster because Colton attended a special meeting of the student council during third hour. At the meeting, the group had selected five senior girls to run for homecoming queen. The ten student council members could each nominate one girl, and they placed the names in a basket so five names could be drawn. The lucky five got nominated, and the entire school will vote for homecoming queen next week. Since the queen had to be a senior, Colton couldn't nominate Lacie, but he nominated Kathy Dorsher, Lacie's friend and Aden Carville's girlfriend.

The five girls' names drawn from the basket and nominated were: Kathy Dorsher, Linda Canberry, Casandra Borker, Lucinda Zeller, and Carmin Wadsworth.

Of the five, Colton felt that Linda Canberry, the head cheerleader, or Lucinda Zeller, the principal's daughter, had the best chance of being elected homecoming queen. However, he told Lacie that Kathy would win, hands down.

The rest of the day flew by. Colton's seventh hour class helped set up the gym for a pep rally assembly, and midway through seventh hour everyone filed into the gym. A few members of the school band set up their instruments and played marching music as everyone found a seat in the bleachers. The football team and cheerleaders sat in the first row. Coach Talbert and Mr. Zeller, the high school principal, stood at the microphone in front of the student body.

"I want to thank everyone for being here and for showing their spirit by wearing their team spirit t-shirts today. The band, along with the cheerleaders, has planned a few activities. I give the floor to Coach Talbert," said Mr. Zeller, as he handed the microphone to the coach.

"Thanks, Mr. Zeller. First, I want to introduce you to the team members. Guys, when I call your name, come on up and form a line behind me," instructed the coach.

When everyone finished lining up, Coach asked the cheerleaders to lead a cheer and sing the school song. The band started, and Linda Canberry, the head cheerleader, led the singing.

Linda turned to the football team and said, "Guys, you will win tonight and we'll be on the sidelines cheering for you throughout the game." Turning to the bleachers she said, "We need every one of you to come out for the game and show your spirit tonight. Now, we have a special surprise for one of our team members."

The girls formed a line behind the guys and then ran toward the bleachers. They each had on a pirate hat and an eyepatch. The students roared with laughter.

"Colton, Colton, Colton," they chanted.

Colton gave an embarrassed smile and hit the air with his fist. Linda tossed him a patch, and said, "We can beat the Hampton Colts with one eye shut."

After a few more cheers, and an announcement about the buses taking the team and students to the game, they dismissed the students for the day. Colton shook hands with Coach Talbert and Mr. Zeller, hugged the cheerleaders and then walked with Lacie out the doors.

"You're taking the bus, aren't you?" Colton asked.

"Yes, I would have liked to have driven, but Mom wouldn't let me have the car. So, when we get back from the game, I'll wait and drive to the party with you," she said.

"That's a plan. See you after the game." He leaned toward her and gave her a quick kiss. She smiled and walked to her car.

The Dirty Side Of Football

The football team loaded onto the bus as Coach Talbert called the names of the players and coaches. It was a time-honored ritual for all members of the team to ride the bus to an away game. At one time, the players drove themselves to the game, but many years ago a carload of players had a serious accident and the school board changed the rules.

Once on the road, everyone became somber. Under normal conditions, the team laughed and sang road songs, but tonight the team members spent their time thinking about the monsters they would face on the field. Hampton had always been a tough rival, but this year, with two new linemen who were large, fast, and mean, the team put fear in the hearts of their opponents. The players who would face these two head-on were considering how they could survive the game. Fear and intimidation helped the Hampton team win. Their offensive team was no better than any other in the league, and their defense was strong only because no one wanted to hit them hard, for fear of reprisals.

Last week, when the Hampton team faced a strong quarterback, they ganged up to put him out of the game. During a well-planned tackle, they broke his arm, putting him out of the game and ending his year on the field. The Bad Axe coach tried to get the two players responsible kicked out of the game, but the officials saw nothing wrong. They missed the violations that were occurring every time the quarterback got tackled. An elbow to the ribs, a hard crack to the head, a kick to the groin, and then their full weight on an extended arm. Number 15 kneeled on the quarterback's extended arm, breaking it in two places while the officials were looking the other way.

The bus pulled into the Hampton School parking lot and stopped behind the school next to the entrance to the visitors' locker room. As the door opened, the players grabbed their gear, piling through the door. Colton found a locker and got suited.

"Aren't you afraid those thugs might go after you tonight?" asked Aden, the quarterback.

"It's crossed my mind a few hundred times, but what can we do?" said Colton.

Colton told no one about his plans to video record the two Hampton players' every move, for fear that someone would give away the trap.

Coach Talbert gathered all the players in the center of the locker room for his standard pep talk. Tonight, he gave a reassuring message.

"Guys, I know you have concerns about the dirty tricks the Hampton players use. I want you to think about the fact that they are not talented football players. All they have is the ability to put fear into our hearts. Don't fear them. I want you to hit them as hard as you can. Show them we are not afraid of them, and they will back down. But remember, I won't allow my players to play dirty. If they cheat, I will protest to the officials. If you cheat or play dirty, you will be off my team."

He put his hand across Aden's shoulder and said. "Run as many passing plays as you can. Their line is firm, but their backfield is slow and weak. We can outrun them."

Looking at Colton, he said. "Hold on to that ball. They will use every trick to get you to drop the ball. Don't! I want you to run like the devil is after you. You can do it. We all can do it. We will win this game, and these thugs will know what defeat tastes like. So let's get out there and do it! Put the fear in them by winning!"

Everyone rose with a cheer and rushed out the door. The band played as both teams made their way onto the football field. The announcer called the names of the Hampton Colts as the Lake Huron Loons waited on the sidelines. After the last Hampton player was on the field, the announcer introduced the Lake Huron Loons. When a player's name got called, he ran to the center of the field. Colton looked into the bleachers and could see that Seth with his camera on the top row. He dressed in a team jacket and hat and looked like an official Loons' team member. Seth had mounted the video camera and telephoto lens on a tripod, and he was ready to catch all the action.

The Hampton Colts would kick and the Lake Huron Loons would receive. The ball was set, and the kick was long and good. Colton caught the ball on the fifteen yard-line and began his run. He got tackled on the fifty yard-line. In the huddle, Aden called a pass off play for a run up the center. When the fullback hit the line, it was like running into a cement wall. Absolutely nowhere to go.

It was second down and eleven to go. They were using the "T" formation, and Colton was the right end. Colton reported he had little cover, and a passing game would work best. It became apparent that the thugs who formed the line were the Colt's major defense.

At the snap, Aden faded back and passed to Colton, who was open. Colton pulled the ball close to his side and began his rush down-field. He ran fifteen yards and before he got tackled. When he saw the two guards, number 15 and 18, coming in for the kill, Colton rolled as fast as he could. The two landed face down in the grass. Colton got up and ran back to the huddle. He would be their target tonight. Several times, the two guards pulled back on the play and took off after Colton. He was slippery and fast, playing with the thugs and making them look bad.

Three more passes, and the Loons had their first touchdown, followed by a failed field goal. The guards, Thunder and Lightning, flew through the Loon's line and blocked the kick. Eddy Andrews, the kicker, told Coach that Thunder said, "I'll break your effing leg before the end of the game."

The Colt's offense played a ground game. The two big guards kept breaking through the Loons' defensive line, but the Lake Huron Loons' backfield was there to stop the ball. They gained a few yards and then had to kick. The Loons returned with a twenty yard run and landed on their thirty yard line. A quick pass to the left end, Bill Crawley, ended badly. Bill, who made a good catch, suffered an injury. Thunder and Lightning tackled him, and when they got off the pile, Bill had a broken ankle and was taken off the field on a stretcher, but before he went into the ambulance, he told Coach he felt someone holding his foot in their hands and twisting. "Coach, that bastard did this with his bare hands. Stop them," he said, tears streaming down his face.

Coach protested to the officials, but no one had seen anything. "And besides," said the official, "you're winning the game, what more do you want?"

At halftime, the Loons were ahead twelve to zero. The Colts were furious. On the way to the locker rooms, they were yelling obscenities at the Loons, making gestures and suggesting that in the second half, someone else would go to the hospital.

Coach Talbert congratulated his boys and suggested they keep the same offensive plan for the second half. He told Colton to watch himself and keep a keen lookout for the two thugs. "You can't let them touch you. I would rather see you drop the ball than let them get their dirty hands on you. Having one injury is bad enough; we can't afford another," he said.

During the first half, the Loons' offensive guard, Calvin Rowell, did a great job blocking number fifteen, Thunder. Even though Calvin was a large man, he could stay low to the ground when he blocked. The two thugs were clumsy and couldn't stay low. They kept standing up to see the action and used brute force to get through the line. Calvin just knocked Thunder down and then got away from him as fast as he could. Coach and the team were complimenting him when they were notified that they had to get back on the field.

Bloody Second Half

Both teams returned from the locker rooms as the band marched back to the school. Thunder yelled to Calvin, "Hey, buddy, you're effing dead." The Hampton coach laughed and slapped Thunder on his back. "That's it, Thunder, keep them worried."

Coach Talbert gave Hampton's coach a dirty look, but he said nothing, hoping to use a big win as his comment.

The Lake Huron Loons started the second half with a kickoff deep into the Hampton's territory. They called a fair catch on the twenty-five yard line. They got no further than the twenty-six yard line before they had to punt. The Lake Huron Loons were putting pressure on their offense and holding them. To keep Thunder and Lightning under control, Coach had his line double up on them, and the two thugs seethed with anger because they couldn't do anything.

On the Lake Huron Loons' first-and-ten, Thunder and Lightning ganged up on Calvin Rowell, the guard. Thunder dove low to the ground and forced his elbow into Calvin's right knee, while Lightning hit him on the left side, just a little higher. Calvin could feel his knee give, and he sent a message to Coach telling him the two linemen injured his knee on purpose. Coach called a timeout and argued with the officials. Again, no one saw anything happen.

Calvin said his knee would hold out, and he continued playing. On the next play, the two defensive tackles performed the same maneuver, blowing Calvin's knee out. Coach took him out of the game and had his knee wrapped. The player Coach sent in for Calvin's replacement was neither large nor aggressive, and he didn't want to suffer an injury like Calvin.

By the end of the game, the Lake Huron Loons had won, but by only one point. They made another touchdown in the last quarter, followed by an extra point field goal. Without Calvin in the line, Hampton ran over the Loons' defensive line, and made three touchdowns. The final score: Loons 19 and Colts 18.

After dressing, Colton walked to the bus and pulled his cell phone out of his pocket. When Seth answered, Colton asked, "Did you get anything on the video?"

"Are you kidding, Colton? I got everything. Those bastards did a number on Calvin's knee. From the video I got, I don't understand why the officials didn't catch it. Anyway, I'm getting into my car, and Stacey and I are heading back. We'll be at your place after we stop at home. She wants to pick up something and let my mom know we are fine."

"Great, Seth. I'll see you at the garage," Colton said.

He threw his gear over his shoulder and got onto the bus. It would be a forty-five-minute ride back to Pigeon, and he had a lot on his mind. Somehow, he wanted to get the message out about the nasty antics of Thunder and Lightning. He was sure he would come up with a plan.

During the drive home, the team celebrated. Having two players injured tempered the team's happiness. Colton didn't think the two injured players could continue the season. Also, they would have to face Hampton again in two weeks, during homecoming. A prospect that all the Loons' players dreaded.

Chapter 11

Party Time

The bus pulled into the high school parking lot at ten o'clock, just behind the student bus. Colton took his gear into the locker room and dumped his uniform on the pile for the cleaners. He put his padding in his locker, and as he walked down the hallway, he passed Aden, who had just come in from the bus.

"I hope you and Kathy stop out at the garage party," he said.

"That's what we planned. Kathy was on the student bus, and she is waiting for me outside. Do you need us to pick anything up at the party store?"

"No, we got everything covered. We have lots of snacks and drinks. I have to pick Lacie up at the bus too; so, I'll see you later, Aden," said Colton as he left.

Lacie stood next to the locker room door waiting for Colton.

"Hey, good looking! Want to go to a big party with a small-town girl?" she teased.

"Wow... lady! Like... yes. I like big parties, and you look real purty."

The two laughed and walked arm-in-arm to Colton's Jeep.

Pulling into his driveway, Colton could see that Seth and his girlfriend, Stacey, were already there. Seth had parked on the lawn, and they were setting up the snacks on the garage countertop.

"Hi guys. Let me help you, Stacey. Seth, you can get the cooler open and set up the red cups," Lacie instructed.

The garage was party headquarters at the Blackwell house. Colton and his dad cleaned and remodeled it when they purchased the house two years ago. It's a man cave, with the extras that only a mom could add. Even though you could tear down a transmission in one area, there was a clean counter, sink, stove, and an old refrigerator in another. A plastic cloth covers the table, and there are several leather easy chairs. "Dad's buddies donated these chairs," Colton told his friends. Dad's buddies were the people on The Point who put them out on trash day. They were all in good condition, but no longer needed in the luxury cottages.

As more people drove up, Colton put out folding chairs. The music was soft rock; loud enough to hear, but not loud enough to disturb Colton's parents. Colton also had a "donated" flat screen television set playing ESPN sports. They found the television on The Point. It worked after Colton fixed the speaker outlet and added new speakers. Someone had pulled out the audio cable and broken the plug. Instead of fixing the enormous television set, they threw it away. A lucky break for Colton and his dad.

Colton and Seth were sitting at the table, running through the video. Whenever they found something exciting, they would play it on the big screen television.

"Hey, look at this," they would yell. All the guys groaned because they had interrupted the sports show, and the girls groaned because the guys were watching the sports show.

Lacie turned the TV off, to the dismay of the guys and cheers of the girls. She turned the music up and dimmed the lights.

"Isn't this better, Colton?" she asked as they slow danced next to the table.

"Yes, much better," he replied.

He then turned to Seth and said, "Can you stop by in the morning? I want to edit some of that video."

The party was a success, even though Colton, Seth, and Aden had to prevent three seniors from bringing beer into the garage. They couldn't understand why Colton wouldn't want free beer, but Colton said, "If we let you drink here, and we get caught, Coach Talbert would kick our butts off the football team."

Protesting, the seniors called the partygoers wimps, and left with their beer.

By one o'clock on Saturday morning, Colton and Lacie were the only partygoers left. They cleaned up the garage, and Colton drove her home.

It was a long day, and they both were tired.

"Thanks for the party, Colton," Lacie said.

"Trust me, Lacie, you made it a wonderful party by keeping things going. Next party, I won't let anyone watch the sports channel on the TV."

"Perhaps I could bring a nice chic-flick to watch?"

"Love you, but not that, please." Colton said as he gave her a big kiss. They kissed for a few minutes, and then she opened the car door and started toward the house.

"Lacie," Colton yelled out the window, "if you get a chance, stop over tomorrow. Seth and I will edit the video of the game, and I want to post it on Facebook and YouTube. The world needs to know what Thunder and Lightning have done."

"I'll try," she said.

Colton sat alone, considering how lucky he was to know Lacie. He started the Jeep, eager to get home and into bed. He was sure that tonight he would have only pleasant dreams.

Thunder And Lightning On YouTube

Running with the ball, Colton saw Thunder and Lightning coming at him. They had huge fangs, and fur covered their faces. Like wolfhounds, they caught his scent and were nipping at his heels. An arm caught his

ankle and pulled him down to the ground. "Don't let go of the football,"
the coach yelled. Colton hugged the ball as the wolves dragged him off
the field. His legs bundled with a rope, they lifted him to the rafters,
hanging him upside down. "Oh God," he cried. "They plan on gutting
me like a deer." He screamed as he saw the knife coming at him. The
rope let go just in time, and he crashed down to the ground.

Colton hit his head on the floor as he fell out of the bed with his
legs wrapped in the blanket. He was wet with perspiration and had
to get to the bathroom. Unwrapping his legs, he crawled across the
floor, and into the hallway. He stood and ran naked to the bathroom,
only to find a locked door. "Hey, I have to go," he yelled. The door
opened, and Terry ran back to bed.

At seven in the morning, Colton was eager to get busy. After doing
his bathroom business, he dressed and ran downstairs. His mom was
up and had a pot of coffee on the burner.

"How was the party last night?" she asked.

"Great, we had six couples show up and three idiots we kicked
out for bringing beer. It was fun," he said. "Did you catch the game
on the radio?"

"Yes, congratulations on the win, and I'm sorry about the injuries.
Hampton must be a mean team."

"They play dirty, Mom, and we have proof on video. We plan on
posting the video on YouTube."

"Colton, be careful," she advised. "You don't want to make too
many enemies. You know what happens when you do that."

"Yes, I get my face beaten," he laughed, and took his coffee out
to the garage.

Seth drove up in his new red Dodge Charger at eight-thirty.
Already in the garage, Colton worked on the video. He attached his
computer to the large television and started cutting and pasting the
video.

"How's it coming, Colton?" asked Seth as he walked up to the table. "Did I get enough footage for you to work with?"

"You sure did. I'm trying to get the best video segments separated into one file. I think I have enough, and now I need to add a narrative," Colton said.

The two watched the video that Colton had assembled. It showed the two Hampton tackles doing everything they could to hurt the Lake Huron Loons' players. A closeup showed Thunder holding Bill Crawley's ankle in his hands and twisting it, followed by Bill being taken off the field on a stretcher. In the next two scenes, Lightning and Thunder were hitting Calvin's knees, and then Calvin was being carried off the field on a stretcher.

"Wow, that is a powerful video. What do you want to say in the narrative?" asked Seth.

"It should tell the story," said Colton. "And I want to talk about how important football is to high schools, and how idiots like these ruin the sport. If they allow this to go on, the sport will soon get banned. Even without these thugs, people want to ban the sport because of head injuries."

"Well, why don't you talk while the tape is running? I'll record it, save the file, and then I can help splice the audio onto the video," said Seth.

"You make it sound so simple," laughed Colton.

After twelve attempts, Colton said he was satisfied with the recording. Seth merged the files and ended up with a four minute MP4 video recording.

"Now we need to send it to my YouTube account, and then I want to post a link on our Facebook pages," said Colton.

Seth worked with Colton, taking turns posting on Facebook. When they finished, all of their friends had the video. They also sent copies to five radio stations, three television stations, four newspapers, a dozen websites, and Seth emailed it to a list of high school athletic directors and football coaches. By noon, they had finished the entire project, and over four hundred people had already viewed the YouTube video.

"This could go viral, you know," said Seth. "It's a big story and people will spread the word and pass it forward."

Since the video was done, and it was Saturday, Colton could relax so he would be ready to do the Sunday delivery of the Metro Press by eleven o'clock.

Seth left his camera equipment with Colton for safekeeping because he intended to drive to Bay City. He had shopping to do, and would stop by Sunday afternoon to see how many people viewed the YouTube video. Colton started toward the house, and his cell phone rang.

"Hi, Colton," Lacie said. "I'm sorry I couldn't get over there; Mom had a list of things I had to do."

"I understand, Lacie. Seth and I got the video finished, and we posted it all over the web."

"Yes, I saw it. Do you know TV 5's news broadcast it on their noon news program? They played excerpts from the video and showed some of their own video of Thunder and Lightning. They questioned why there hadn't been an investigation."

"Wow! That was fast. I will see if I can find a re-broadcast on their website."

"I wanted to let you know I can stop over Sunday afternoon. How would one o'clock be?" she asked.

"That's fine. Seth and Stacey are also stopping by. We can go over the results of our video campaign, and play cards or, better yet, we can watch one of your chic-flicks."

"Aren't we funny? Bye, Colton. See you tomorrow."

"Bye." Colton put the phone in his pocket and walked into the kitchen where his mom had just served burgers and fries to Colton's brothers and sister. She pulled out another plate and set it for him.

"Wash your hands first," she instructed.

Chapter 12

Uninvited Guests For Sunday Brunch

Colton did a few chores around the yard. He helped his mom bring in produce from the garden so she could can, and picked apples with his brothers, Terry and Jason. Terry played in the trees more than he helped.

It was late afternoon when Colton's dad came home with two large Little Caesar pizzas. The family gathered in the kitchen, eating and talking about the past week. Colton listened intently as his dad told about his new job and college classes. Dad was happier than he had ever been, and Colton considered how important work was to a father's self-image. He thought about himself and wondered what he would do when he was his dad's age. Would he have four kids? Would Lacie still be in his life? What kind of work would he be doing? He put those thoughts out of his mind and excused himself. Getting up at eleven o'clock Saturday evening for his Sunday morning deliveries would require his getting sleep.

Colton had difficulty falling asleep in the early evening. He kept checking the alarm, and eleven o'clock kept getting nearer, but he wasn't sleeping. The alarm rang, and he jumped out of bed. When he went downstairs to get coffee for the route, he saw his dad sitting at the table.

"Colton, I want to give you some advice about your Sunday delivery," he said.

"I'm listening," said Colton.

"You will have over fifty extra deliveries. I marked them as Sunday only on the sheet I gave you."

"I saw them."

"It's important to get the store deliveries done before they open at five a.m., so you should do everything before The Point deliveries. By doing The Point last, you will have the stores done, and you can take your time getting all those houses delivered. You don't want to get the stores delivered late, because that is where you'll make your money for the week," he explained.

"Thanks, Dad. I'll do the route your way. My count shows over seven hundred papers. I hope I can get them all in the Jeep."

"You will; Thanksgiving is the only time you have that problem. That paper is huge."

"Well, I have to get going," Colton said. He grabbed his coffee mug and headed out to the Jeep.

The deliveries went as Colton expected. The papers were on time, and he delivered the papers before midnight. Because of the increase in the number and the size of the Sunday paper, it took over six hours to get the route completed. Since Colton didn't sleep Saturday evening, he grew tired. Listening to the Baldacci novel helped, but there were a few times he got so involved with the novel, he lost track of where he was. He had to backtrack to make sure no customers got missed. He drove for a while in a trance, subconsciously doing the work.

Colton delivered the last paper at seven o'clock on Sunday morning. When he got home, his mom had breakfast on the table. Colton wasn't hungry, so he went straight to bed. He told everyone to leave him alone until noon. He would have lunch and then his friends were stopping over. Even Terry said he wouldn't disturb him. He remembered the times Dad got mad at him for waking him after the Sunday route.

Several times, Terry ran up the stairs and looked in on Colton to see if he was up yet. The two brothers always played after church, but today Colton didn't go with the family to church. Terry wished that his big brother would wake up so they could throw the football.

When Colton heard him coming up the stairs for the last time, he hid behind the door. As Terry peeked into the room, Colton jumped out and yelled, "What do you want?"

Colton broke out laughing, and Terry ran at him and punched him in the leg.

Terry cried, "You shouldn't scare me like that, Colton."

"Sorry, Terry. You wouldn't want to go outside to throw the ball, would you?"

"Sure would. Wow, can we go now?" Terry was so excited. They ran downstairs, yelled "hi" to everyone and went out the back door.

When Terry got tired, Colton suggested they get lunch, provided their mom still had leftovers.

By one o'clock they had finished lunch, and Colton noticed Seth's Charger drive up to the garage.

"I'm going out to the garage, Mom," Colton yelled. "And when Dad gets done with his studies, tell him where I am, and that everything went fine on the route last night."

Colton took his laptop with him to the garage to check the video he had posted on YouTube. Seth was alone, standing next to his shiny red car.

"I thought Stacey would be with you," Colton said.

"That was her plan, but her parents called from England, and she wanted to visit them. Mom might drop her off later," Seth said.

"Did you see the newspaper today? The Metro Press had an editorial on the sports page about our video and the game with Hampton, and they even had still images from our video," Colton said as he booted his computer.

"I didn't see that, but the TV news had a story about the video. We've created quite a buzz. It looks like your plan is working," said Seth.

"I sure hope so. Like I said in the video, we need to clean up football before the schools ban it."

As the two were talking, Aden Carville drove up in his old Camaro.

"Hey, guys. You sure did a number on the Hampton Colts. Why didn't you tell me what you were doing?" yelled Aden as he walked into the garage.

"We didn't know what would happen, so we kept it to ourselves. Besides, you have a big mouth, Aden," Seth said.

"True, but I still wish I had known ahead of time. I got a call from some newspaper reporter, and I had to tell him I had nothing to do with the video. I'm the team captain, and I should know about everything involving my team."

Seth laughed and handed Aden a can of Coke. "Aden, have a drink and relax. You know, you could have taken the time to look at the video when we were working on it Friday night, or you could have looked at the finished video on YouTube. Then you would know what it's all about."

"Oh, I saw the video, Seth. Better yet, I was there. Those Hampton boys were two mean S-O-B's."

"That's why I wanted to do the video, Aden. I wanted to let everyone know what those guys were doing," Colton said.

Thunder And Lightning Attack

A large black pickup screeched down the driveway and slammed on its brakes, just missing Aden's car. Dust filled the garage, and the truck doors flew open. Out jumped Thunder and Lightning. Their faces were red and their fists clenched, ready to hit the nearest person.

"You bastard, Aden. What gives you the right to ruin our lives? Damn it, we wanted to get scholarships to State, and now our pictures are all over the freaking internet. What the hell were you thinking?" Thunder yelled.

"Me, I did nothing... Colton is the one you want," Aden said, moving behind Seth as Thunder marched into the garage. Seth reached across the worktable and turned the video camera on, aiming it into the center of the room where the Hampton players were standing. He set the lens on wide angle, so all the action would get caught.

With his finger pointed at Colton, Thunder walked up to him and said, "So, it was your idea?"

"Yes, someone had to tell what you guys were up to. You can't go into a game intending to injure your opponent. It's wrong, Thunder," Colton said. He would not back down and had his fists ready in case Thunder came any closer.

In a flash, Thunder threw his right fist into Colton's left eye. Colton fell back onto the table, his hand rushing up to his injured face.

"Why does everyone want to hit me in that eye? I'm getting pissed. Get out of my garage!" Colton screamed.

Seth ran to Colton and tried to shield him from any more hits. He turned to Thunder and said, "Leave while you can. If you want a fight, you will fight all three of us."

Aden was as far away from the action as he could get. "I'm not getting involved in this. You two made the video, so you can handle these guys."

Lightning rushed up to Seth and swung his fist toward his face. Seth ducked and hit Lightning in the abdomen. The only pain he caused was to his hand. Lightning laughed and punched Seth in the nose.

From outside the garage, Colton's dad, Adam, ran toward the door. On his way to his son's aid, he stopped and pulled the keys out of the intruder's truck. As Adam entered the garage, he grabbed a baseball bat from the corner, and yelled, "I suggest you stop now. You have no right to come here and assault these boys."

Thunder turned and said, "No, right? They ruined us. We'll never get a football scholarship now."

"You did that," Colton yelled. "We didn't make you break the rules. You two need to put the blame where it belongs, on your own shoulders."

From the distance, police sirens grew louder. As the sound drew closer, Lightning turned to Thunder and said, "Let's get the hell out of here. The old man must have called the cops."

"Damn right I did. And you're not going anywhere," Adam said, holding the truck keys for the boys to see.

Thunder started toward Adam, but he held his bat up, ready to swing. "Try me, boy. I wanted to be a professional baseball player, and I have a good swing."

Thunder turned and hit Colton in the stomach. As Colton fell to the ground, he kicked him and then swung at Seth, hitting him in the side of his head. "It's your fault, you pinheads."

The State Police car slid into the driveway and stopped behind the black pickup. Two troopers rushed out, both with one hand on his gun holster.

"Sir, put the bat down," the smaller trooper said.

Adam set the bat down and said, "I called you. This is my house, and these two came in and assaulted my son and his friends."

As the troopers came in to talk, Thunder rushed them and hit the larger officer in the face with his fist. "Get out of my way, creep. We're leaving and you're not stopping us." Lightning just watched as the second trooper drew his Taser gun and gave Thunder, a little lightning. Twitching on the floor with his eyes rolled up, Thunder could go nowhere.

The officer turned to Lightning and said, "If you don't want to be next, get down on the ground, with your hands over your head.

Without hesitation, Lightning did as instructed.

The smaller trooper put handcuffs on Lightning and then put cuffs on the still incapacitated Thunder.

Adam rushed to his son and Seth. "Aden, get some washcloths from under the sink and wet them."

Aden did as instructed. Now that everything was secure, he regained his courage. He brought the wet cloths over and helped Adam move the two teenagers to the chairs and clean up their bloody faces.

The troopers led Lightning to the back seat of the police car, dragged Thunder to the car, and returned to the garage to talk to the boys.

"I have called for help from the County Sheriff, and they'll be here in a few minutes. When they do, they'll take your intruders to Bad Axe. Are the two of you OK, or do you need me to call for an ambulance?"

Adam turned to the trooper and said, "They'll be fine. It looks bad, but I'm sure nothing got broken. Looks like a bloody nose, two black eyes, and bruised ribs."

"I'm OK," said Colton. He looked outside and could see Lacie standing next to his mom, brothers, and sister. A county sheriff's car parked next to the state patrol car.

The state trooper turned to Adam and said, "I'm Trooper Steve Emery and my partner over there is Trooper Gary Brown. I need to take statements from each of you regarding the events that transpired here today." As he was talking, the county deputies walked in.

"We will be right back," said Trooper Steve as they turned and went back to their cars to talk.

"Guys, just tell the truth. Hide nothing about the video, or why those two got mad at you," instructed Adam.

"Dad, I'm not ashamed of what we did."

"Me neither," said Seth.

"Mr. Blackwell, I had nothing to do with any of this," said Aden.

Chapter 13

Cleaning Up A Bloody Mess

Adam stepped outside and talked to his wife, Cyndi. He explained to her what had happened and reported that Colton and Seth's injuries were not serious. She understood the reason she couldn't go into the garage until the troopers left. It was the scene of a crime, and the officers must interview everyone involved.

Lacie listened to the conversation and asked if the assault was because Colton and Seth had posted the video of the two Hampton football players on YouTube. It didn't come as a surprise when Adam confirmed that the video was the reason for the assault on the boys.

"I wasn't sure what would happen. I think it was the right move, though. Something had to be done," she said.

"Yes, but Colton and Seth are lucky. If those Hampton boys had come here with a gun instead of their fists, this could have been deadly," Adam said.

Trooper Steve Lithowski put his hand on Adam's shoulder and said, "Let's talk. I'm not sure if your boys are in trouble or not, but I need to know what they did to get those Hampton guys so upset."

"Sure, but I'll let them explain it," said Adam as they walked into the garage.

Colton, his dad, Seth, Aden, and Trooper Steve all took a seat around the garage table.

"Colton, why did you make a video of those two players Friday night?" asked Trooper Steve. "Don't you think you may have violated their rights?"

"Seth and I made the video because we knew they intentionally tried to hurt their opponents. We wanted to prove it, and making the video was the best way to achieve that goal. We violated no one's rights any more than an eyewitness news reporter would. In fact, TV-5 also had a reporter with a camera at the game."

"Well, it sounds like you were being sneaky. You should have just reported it to your coach."

Seth interjected, "Sir, they are the ones who tried to hurt our football players, and when they got caught, they came here to hurt us, because we showed everyone what they did. We are the injured party, not them."

Trooper Steve gave Seth a dirty look and turned to Colton. "When they came into the garage to talk, did you hit them first?"

Again Seth interrupted. "No, we hit no one." He reached for the video camera and set it in front of Trooper Steve. "I did a video of the action, and it begins when they came into the garage."

Colton plugged the camera into the wide-screen television and hit play. Seth caught the entire fight in excellent detail, and when the video stopped, Trooper Steve turned to Colton and said, "Ok, I guess you were telling the truth. I need to take this to Bad Axe with me as evidence."

Seth said, "I will put a copy of the video on a DVD. I would rather the camera stayed here," said Seth. "My dad bought it for me, and it cost a couple grand, and he wouldn't be happy if it got broken by the police."

"Fine, make a copy, but don't take all day," grunted the trooper.

Colton handed the trooper the DVD and asked who would take care of Thunder's pickup truck.

"Unless you want it left here until someone comes from their family, I suggest taking it to the Sheriff's office in Bad Axe and leaving the key with them. We will question the two Hampton boys, and then they will face the district court judge in the morning," said Trooper Steve.

"Seth, will you follow me over to Bad Axe?" asked Colton.

"Sure. We can get something to eat at McDonald's, my treat," said Seth.

The state troopers got in their patrol car and left. Colton explained to Lacie what had transpired and asked her to come with him and Seth to Bad Axe. She used her cell phone to let her mom know where she was and when she would be home.

Before leaving, Colton went to his room, showered, and changed out of his bloodstained clothing. He needed to put something on his swollen eye, and he ached from the punches and kicks and wore the pirate's patch and skinny red jeans his sister had given him.

When he came downstairs, Lacie laughed. "The pirate has returned."

"Don't laugh, Lacie. It's the only pair of jeans that doesn't hurt my side."

Seth had used the downstairs restroom to clean up. He said he felt fine, because didn't get hit anywhere other than his face, which was swollen and bruised, but not bleeding. Colton and Lacie jumped into the black pickup, and Seth followed them to Bad Axe.

On the ride over, Colton told Lacie that he would try to keep away from trouble for a while. At least until he healed, but she insisted it was impossible and he would be a pirate.

Colton And Seth Are News

While sitting at the Bad Axe McDonald's, Colton's phone rang for the fifteenth time. Everyone wanted to ask him what had happened, how he and Seth were doing, and would they would be back in school?

"Aren't you going to answer it?" asked Lacie. "You know, it could be important."

Holding the phone up, he said, "Well, it's not a number I recognize, but I'll see who it is. This is Colton Blackwell."

The caller, a TV-5 news reporter, wondered if Colton and Seth would do an on-air interview regarding the Hampton Colt's antics. Colton asked Seth, who was in favor, and then told the reporter, "Yes, can you come to my home this afternoon?"

The TV reporter would be in Pigeon within thirty minutes. As they left the restaurant, Colton noticed that the TV-5 news van was in the parking lot next to Seth's red Charger. They had stopped at the police station and had been trying to reach Colton for the last hour. Colton walked up to the news van and surprised the driver, telling him to follow them back to Pigeon. The driver agreed.

Colton, Seth and Lacie discussed what they should say as they drove back home. Lacie felt they should play down their personal feelings.

"Don't show your anger," she suggested. "Let them know you did this professionally as a concerned citizen and felt the truth should be told."

"Sure, Lacie," said Seth, "I can just about see Colton not getting on his soapbox and telling the world how he feels. I think we should just let the reporter ask the questions and then be honest with our answers."

"Seth, when did you get so smart? That's how I feel. But I want people to know thugs like Thunder and Lightning could destroy football."

"There he goes," said Lacie, "preaching again."

The TV-5 news van parked in the driveway behind Colton's Jeep. The reporter and camera operator followed Colton into the garage. They set up their camera and lights. Lacie said she didn't want to be on screen, but Seth became excited about the prospect of being on television.

Colton did not preach, but he explained why he wanted to save football, and Seth smiled a lot. The reporter told them the story would be on during the late news and perhaps again Monday morning since the story had grown in importance, now that the two Hampton players were in jail for assault.

The TV crew left, and Colton suggested they all head for home. He was sore and tired, and Seth conceded he was also sore. Lacie gave Colton a quick kiss and congratulated him on doing a good job with the news.

Seth asked, "What about me? Didn't I do a good job?"

"Yes, Seth, and you smiled nicely, too," she said.

Colton took a nap and then spent time with Terry. At the dinner table, everyone talked about the big fight.

Colton's dad suggested it would be wise if Colton kept away from controversy for a while.

"You know, Colton, a lot has happened this past week," he said.

"Dad, I'll be careful not to have any more visits with the police. At least they aren't after me for doing something illegal," Colton said.

"And you better keep it that way," his mom chimed in. "I didn't raise criminals."

Colton had a restful evening. He didn't have to do another delivery until Tuesday morning, so he could get plenty of sleep, except his aching ribs and sore eye kept him up most of the night.

Chapter 14

Still The Hero

As he dressed for school, Colton considered buying more elastic skinny jeans. It would seem that they were the only pair that allowed enough stretch to keep his bruised body from aching. If only I had a pair that looked more like jeans instead of red tights, he thought as he looked at himself in the mirror. It is these pirate jeans or my pajama bottoms; he considered.

With the patch again on his left eye, the bright red jeans and a white t-shirt, Colton joined his family at the breakfast table.

"My, don't you look nice," his mother jokes.

"I think you look hot, Colton," added his sister, Steph.

"Yes, Colton, you look like a hot dork," his brother Jason said.

"I like it, Colton. Mom, can I get a pair of those tights?" asked Terry.

"They are not tights. They're skinny jeans. The Bieber wears them, and they're the latest fad," said Steph.

"Son, don't listen to your brothers and sister," said Colton's dad. "You look silly, but comfortable. I wouldn't be caught dead wearing something like that."

"Well, now that I feel great about myself, I think I'll head to school. I'm sure my fellow students will make me feel appreciated," Colton said.

Heading out to his Jeep, Colton grabbed his egg sandwich. After he got behind the wheel, he checked his phone messages. A message from Trooper Steve requested a return call.

Colton called and said, "Hello, Trooper Steve, this is Colton Blackwell, and I got the message saying you wanted to talk?"

The trooper informed Colton that he and Seth were to report to the district attorney's office at nine o'clock this morning. A plea bargain must be in the works.

"Do you want me to call Seth?" asked Colton.

"No, we already talked to him. He will meet you at the school. We called the school, and they know you will leave for the meeting. Just make sure you're not late. The D.A. doesn't appreciate being held up," trooper Steve said.

"We will be there, sir. Do you know what kind of plea bargain they offered?" asked Colton.

"No, but that's not your concern," said the trooper. "Just be there."

Colton was amazed at the number of people who knew about Sunday's fight. It appears more of his friends watch and listen to the news than he suspected. As he entered his first hour class, the entire class stood and applauded. Colton felt embarrassed and told them it wasn't anything. The class spent most of the hour discussing whether football should be banned because of the high number of head injuries. Being a history teacher, Mr. Dinger had to tell the history of the game, and how protective uniforms and helmets have advanced safety.

During second hour trigonometry, Colton met Seth in the office and left school to meet with the District Attorney in Bad Axe. On the ride over, the two discussed what type of plea bargain they would be offered, the Hampton teenagers, and why Colton and Seth had to be a part of it.

Walking into the courthouse, Colton found the office directory and headed to the D.A.'s office. The secretary, a young blond woman, directed them into the conference room where a large man sat with

Todd Hernandez and Cory Borman, also known as Thunder and Lightning. Two men, who appeared to be Todd and Cory's fathers, sat next to the boys. Across from the two thugs sat a well dressed, dark skinned man in his forties. The man turned to Colton and Seth and said, "I take it you are Colton and Seth? I am the District Attorney, Mark Bagley, and you know these two gentlemen."

"Trust me, sir, there's nothing gentle about them," said Colton.

"Perhaps, but we're here to resolve this matter," said the D.A. "I have seen the tape you made of the game, and also the tape of the incident at your home on Sunday. Todd and Cory regret their actions and have asked for leniency from my office. Not wanting to leave a dirty mark on these teens' legal record, I have suggested that if they drop out of football for the rest of the season and apologize to the two of you, all charges will be dropped."

"That's crazy, sir," said Seth. "They broke the law and should be punished."

"I agree with Seth," Colton added. "These guys have broken players' arms, legs, and knees, and then, they beat us up because we reported their crimes. And you will give them a slap on the wrist?"

"Sorry, boys, you have no say in this. My decision is final. Todd and Cory, please apologize to these two," said the D.A.

In unison, the two thugs said, "Sorry for hitting you."

The D.A. then added, "Colton, if you and Seth you are free to sue Todd and Cory in civil court, but your odds of having the court hear your case or winning would be very slim."

Before Colton could say anything, Trooper Steve led them out of the room. "Well, boys, as you can see, your little prank didn't result in anything. Was it worth all the trouble?" he asked.

"No, but it was an excellent education on why our legal system sucks," said Colton.

"Yes, they should have thrown the book at them," added Seth.

"Boys, get back to school, and keep your damn opinions to yourself," said the state trooper. "You teenagers are more trouble than you're worth. For your own good, learn to keep your nose out of other people's business."

The Calm Before The Storm

Colton and Seth pulled into the school parking lot at ten fifteen. They sat for a few minutes talking about how unfair the legal system seemed.

"You know, that woman state trooper I met last week suggested I go into law enforcement after I graduate. Perhaps I should. Maybe I could fix the system," Colton said.

"That would be unlikely. An individual has a limited ability to change the system. Hell, even a group of people has a hard time making changes," said Seth.

"Perhaps you're right. What class do you have this hour?" asked Colton.

Seth said he had a study period, but he had nothing to do, so he asked if he could go down to the media center to help on a video project they were doing.

"Well, I have art class, and I have to get my project finished," said Colton.

They walked into the school and went their separate ways.

Colton and Lacie talked during art. She consoled him about the plea bargain and reminded him that at least Thunder and Lightning couldn't play football.

"Isn't that what you wanted?" she asked.

"Yes, you're right again, Lacie," he said.

The day seemed to fly by, and it wasn't long before Colton ran out to the football field. The coach told the players what had happened with the Hampton players and reminded his team that cheating is never an option.

"I would rather lose the game than resort to playing in an unsports-manlike manner," he said.

Everyone agreed as they formed two teams for a scrimmage. A lot of work had to be done to get ready for the next game. Two of their players were now on the injured list, and in a few weeks, during homecoming, they would have to face a strong Bay City team.

After practice, Colton headed home for some rest. He would deliver the Tuesday paper and needed to be on the road by two a.m. Tonight, Colton looked forward to doing the route and listening to the Baldacci novel, loaded with action and violence. Something that Colton didn't have enough of in his life.

He spent part of the early evening on the computer, but he was fast asleep by eight o'clock. He had no trouble falling asleep.

Deliver Me From Evil

The ship rolled back and forth with the sea. Water rushed over the sides as it listed. Colton knew that in a few minutes the ship would be underwater. Screams from other passengers rang in his ears. Children were crying for help, and their parents could not reach them. There was water everywhere, with no land in sight. Colton ran to the highest point on the ship and looked out across the ocean. He saw a wire extending out from the ship. His eyes followed the wire, and it led to a telephone booth, with a man standing inside. Colton grabbed the telephone wire and began the long and treacherous ride down, his hands sliding along the line, burning as he slid toward the phone booth. He could see that the standing man was himself, and the phone kept ringing, and ringing, and ringing.

He was now one with himself, safe on land, looking out at the sinking ship, but the phone would not stop ringing.

Colton reached across the bed and turned the ringing alarm clock off. With tired eyes and his mind confused by his dream, he got up and headed toward the bathroom. He got dressed, grabbed his cell phone and earphones, and headed downstairs. Colton reached into the refrigerator for a large Coke to help keep him awake. It seemed strange that he should be so tired after getting almost six hours of sleep.

The cool September air was refreshing, yet chilling. He jumped in the Jeep and headed for the storage facility, wishing that the heater would begin its job quicker.

The papers were not at the storage shed. Joe, one of the other drivers, sat in his old Plymouth Voyager. Colton walked up to the van, and Joe opened the window, allowing a cloud of smoke to escape.

"Hey, Colton, I heard about your adventure Sunday afternoon. It was all over the news. Seems like you're always getting into some kind of trouble," said Joe.

"It happens. Things will quiet down soon. Any idea why the papers are late?" Colton asked.

"I called, and they said the driver left an hour ago; he should be here soon."

Colton waited half an hour before the truck arrived with the papers. He kept his audiobook playing as he counted and loaded the papers in the Jeep. There were several customers on The Point who requested vacation stops. Many of The Point residents were summer families who returned to the city in the fall. Colton's dad had warned him he could lose at least thirty customers during the winter. Colton marked the stops on his list, which he seldom looked at anymore. He had the entire route memorized and rarely missed a customer.

"Thank you, Joe," Colton yelled as he left.

Listening intently to the audiobook, Colton became mesmerized. An entire family murdered, and John Puller, a military investigator in the U.S. Army's Criminal Investigation Division, tried to solve the mystery. The West Virginia adventure had Colton on the edge of his seat. There were even sound effects, explosions, and gunfire. A local female homicide detective joined forces with Puller in the investigation. She reminded Colton of State Trooper Laurie, the officer who had helped him when he got beaten last week at the dairy. And Puller could be an older Colton. Calm, unafraid of danger, and determined to get to the truth.

By the time Colton delivered on The Point, the sky was clear with a huge full moon. He considered that this may well be the harvest moon he had read about. Farmers used the moonlight to finish harvesting their crops.

The back roads of The Point got darker as the overhead trees kept the light out. Being careful not to hit any deer, Colton kept delivering, with his window open and his arm reaching for the newspaper tubes., and he thought about how chilly it was and how cold it would be this winter. At the end of Sunshine Lane, Colton stopped and closed his eyes. There was gunfire on the audiobook, which startled him. His eyes were tired, and he wished the route was done. Half done, he thought, *Oh well, this is still better than the farm job.*

When Colton reached Mrs. Hoffstarter's home on the north shoreline, he stopped the Jeep, opened the door, and walked up the sidewalk to the side door. He pulled the earpiece out so he could enjoy the sound of the waves. As he gazed out toward the moonlit lake, he noticed three men standing next to the water, talking. Curious, Colton tried to see what they were doing. About twenty yards from him, one man kneeled on his knees while the other two kept talking and pointing shiny objects at him. The two men standing were heavyset, and the kneeling man was smaller and younger. With a flash that could only have come from a gun, the man on his knees fell forward. Colton realized he had been shot in the back of his head... his face now gone... blown away.

"What the hell," Colton considered, *"Is this real?"* Like the investigator John Puller, he kneeled down to avoid being seen. He had just witnessed a murder. Shaken with fear, he studied the two men's faces as they wrapped the dead man in a tarp and loaded his body into a small boat. Colton took his phone out of his pocket, unhooked his earphones and dialed 911.

"There has been a murder on The Point. I'm at Mrs. Hoffstarter's home, and I witnessed two men murdering a third man. They were standing next to the lake on the beach."

"Give me your address, and your name," the dispatch woman said.

"I'm Colton Blackwell, and I am a newspaper delivery person. My location is 1630 Point Drive, on The Point," he said, as he continued to watch the men.

"They have a small motorboat and put the dead man into it. I think they are about to leave. Can you get here quickly?"

"Are you in danger? If you are, please move to safety if you can," she instructed.

"I don't think they know I saw them," Colton said. "I hid as soon as I saw the murder."

"Two state troopers are in the area and on their way, Colton. Do nothing foolish. Go back to your car and wait for them. Do you understand?"

"Yes, I understand. I will be in a yellow Jeep," Colton said.

Chapter 15

Trooper Steve Isn't Happy

As Colton snuck back to his Jeep, he heard a boat motor start, and saw a small, expensive looking SUV drive away. Colton tried to catch the license number, but could only see part of it. He wanted to jump in the Jeep and follow the SUV but knew the police would get upset if he did.

It took another fifteen minutes for a blue Michigan State Police car and a white Huron County Sheriff patrol car to pull up behind Colton's Jeep. Colton stayed in his vehicle as Michigan Trooper Steve approached him.

"Is that you, Colton?" the trooper asked.

"Yes, sir. I witnessed a murder down by the water. I stopped to deliver a paper to Mrs. Hoffstarter's home, and I saw two men shoot a third man in the back of his head."

Colton pointed out Mrs. Hoffstarter's home, and Trooper Steve Emery and his partner, County Deputy Derk Former, took their lights and walked toward the lake. Colton got out of the Jeep and walked around to get a better view of what they were doing. As he stood in the road, another Michigan State Patrol car drove up to the scene.

Trooper Laurie Claybern, Colton's favorite state trooper, walked up to him and said. "Well, Colton, what are you involved in now?"

"Murder, Ms. Laurie. I saw a murder, and it was awful. It was the most horrible thing I've ever seen," said Colton.

"It always is. I'm going down to the scene. You had better stay in your vehicle, Colton."

Trooper Laurie started for the lake as Trooper Steve and Deputy Derk were coming back from the beach.

Steve approached Laurie and whispered, "There isn't anything down there. I think the kid is lying about this for attention. He has been doing a lot of crazy stuff, and I'm convinced he's unstable."

"Did you take you a close look? We have to do a thorough investigation even if it is a false alarm," Laurie said.

"Hey, look for yourself. There is no blood, and there are footprints all over the beach from the weekend vacationers."

Deputy Derk chimed in, saying, "He's telling the truth, Laurie. I saw no signs of a murder. We can check it out in the morning, but I don't think we'll find anything."

Trooper Laurie walked to the beach. The two county deputies followed her. With their flashlight guiding them, they walked along the shoreline. Trooper Laurie shined her light into several windows of the cottages and then returned to the road, and told the deputies, "Guys, I want to canvas some of these homes. We need to ask the homeowners if they saw or heard anything."

There were now five officers at the scene. All but Trooper Steve went door to door, asking if anyone heard or saw anything suspicious. They told Colton to sit in the back of Trooper Steve's patrol car… making him feel like a criminal.

Trooper Steve sat in the front seat and questioned him about what he saw. Colton repeated what he had told the 911 dispatcher and then gave every detail he could think of. Steve asked if he had a history of mental illness, family problems, or problems with his girlfriend.

"Look, I saw a murder. I am not crazy, and my family is just fine. Why don't you do your job and investigate? The killers are getting away as you question me. Did you try to trace the license I gave you? I think he was the second killer. The first one took the dead guy in his boat," said Colton. "You passed the killer in the SUV as you were driving here."

"Kid, listen… there was no murder. You told me you were listening to that audiobook thing... perhaps you got confused or you're lying to get attention. You guys are all alike."

"What do you mean, us guys?" Colton asked.

"Teenagers. You think you know it all, and you are all smartasses," said Trooper Steve.

"Well, that's your opinion. And now I have a new opinion of the State Police, Sir," Colton said.

Growing tired of the questioning, Colton asked, "If you won't investigate this murder, can I at least finish my paper route? I have another hour to go, and then I have to get to school. You know what school is, don't you, Sir?"

"See, you are a smartass. I can't let you go until I'm sure you haven't broken the law. If you called in a false report, you could be liable for costs incurred."

Colton shuddered. As a good citizen, he did what is expected; he reported a crime, and now he is the one in trouble. No wonder people keep saying they don't want to get involved. Colton didn't want to get involved either. It wasn't his plan to stop just as two men were killing another man. Colton sighed. If only this were a dream.

Not Guilty

Trooper Laurie opened the back door of the patrol car and asked Colton to step outside. She led him to her vehicle and said, "We have to talk, Colton. Only two neighbors were at home. Most of the homes belong to summer people. Of the two we talked to, neither heard a gunshot nor saw anyone near the lake, and they didn't hear a boat leave the beach."

Colton looked down at the road, leaning against the hood of the patrol car. He looked up at the Trooper and asked, "Do you think I made this up?"

"I don't know. Before I arrived, you told Steve that you got tired and you had been listening to a murder mystery on your MP3 player. You could be mistaken, or perhaps you are lying?" She looked past Colton and saw Steve approaching. "Steve thinks you called 911 because you wanted attention. Trooper Steve thinks every teenage boy is out for attention. But, that's Steve." Laurie held her hand up, showing Steve that he should stay back.

"Ms. Laurie, I saw a murder. I saw the murderer's faces, I saw the victim's face get blown away, I saw the boat, and I saw them wrap the victim in a plastic tarp and put him in the boat. I also saw a luxury SUV drive away. Its license number started with RUE-7. I didn't get the rest of the number. I also heard the boat drive away. You can be assured I'm not lying."

Colton could feel tears welling in his eyes. This event reminded him of the time his dad had accused him of taking money from his pocket. Adam didn't believe him when he said he hadn't taken it. His mom didn't believe him either. The next day, his dad came to him and asked for his forgiveness, because he found the money in his jacket pocket and was sorry he didn't believe Colton. That hopeless feeling came rushing back.

"From what I know of you, Colton, I don't think you're lying. I have requested a crime scene team investigation, and they will go over the beach to see if there is any evidence. In the meantime, you can finish your newspaper deliveries and then get home and to school."

Colton was relieved at Trooper Laurie's comment. He liked her and realized that she reminded him of Lacie — tough, but understanding. He smiled and said, "Thank you, Trooper. I know they will find the evidence because I know what I saw."

Colton walked back to his Jeep and got behind the wheel. Troopers Laurie and Steve walked up to his open window, and Steve said, "Colton, I still think you called 911 for attention."

"I know you do, sir. I also know a man got killed, and if you were as interested in finding the truth as you are in making me look bad, you would get your job done correctly."

Trooper Laurie could see that Colton's comments were getting to Steve. Holding Steve's arm, she guided him away, talking to him as she led him to his patrol car.

Colton knew his comments were harsh, but he hated the way Trooper Steve badgered him. Colton knew there must be a deep-rooted problem in the Trooper's head that made him so angry with teenagers. Perhaps a traumatic childhood, or, God forbid, he had a teenage boy of his own who didn't mind him. Whatever the reason, the friction between the two was obvious, and Colton felt it clouded the Trooper's reasoning.

As Colton drove off, he decided not to listen to his Baldacci novel. There had been enough murder for one night.

Getting Back To Reality

It was past six o'clock when Colton drove up his driveway. He could see that someone was up already as the light was on in the kitchen. Running up the steps, Colton went into the kitchen, where he saw his dad sitting at the table, listening to the local radio station.

"What's this I hear about a murder on The Point last night?" Adam asked.

"When I stopped to deliver Mrs. Hoffstarter's paper, I saw two men kill a younger man on the beach. I called 911, and the police came and said I was nuts. They couldn't find any evidence, but Dad, I saw it. I saw a man get killed. Oh, God! Am I crazy?"

Colton's voice got emotional. The evening's events came rushing at him, and pent-up emotions welled. "Why won't they believe me? You know I would never lie about something this serious. Dad, they think I'm just looking for attention." His emotions turned to anger as Colton discussed how Trooper Steve talked to him.

"I believe you, Colton. Calm down and have breakfast with me. We can talk about what you saw. I'm sure they will find evidence to support you." Adam grabbed two bowls and pulled a box of cereal from the counter.

Colton walked to the refrigerator and took out a gallon of milk. Setting it on the table, he said, "Thanks, Dad. I know I can always count on you. I don't think you realize what a great feeling that is."

"I know because it's how I feel about your mother," Adam said as he filled the bowls. "I never knew my dad, and my mom kept busy working. Perhaps that's why I try so hard to be there for my family."

The two talked and laughed as they listened to the morning radio host, Johnny Burke, tell his silly jokes and banter with his sidekick, Blondie. Colton felt better and got ready for school even though it was still early.

With the events of the evening filling his mind, he spent a longer time than usual in the shower. Perhaps he was trying to wash off the death he witnessed. The only other time he had faced death was when Grandma Blackwell died. She had been ill, and Colton and his dad stayed at her side when she passed. That was such a gentle death compared to this morning's brutal killing.

Chapter 16

An Investigator Is Born

Colton's brothers and sister were pounding on the bathroom door, demanding that he let them use the room. He realized how long he had been in the shower and relented. Walking out in a towel, he let the snide remarks fall on deaf ears. He understood why they got upset, and he apologized for using all the time and hot water.

It was great to dress in normal clothing again. His wounds now healed and he could see with both eyes. Now, he wished his eyes had been shut earlier this morning. Then, he wouldn't have been able to see the murder. But he saw it. It was not a dream, and he made his mind up; he would find out who the killers were and who they killed.

Once he was in the Jeep, he checked his messages and dialed Lacie. He wanted to talk to her today, to share what he was feeling. Lacie was one person who Colton trusted to give him an honest opinion. After several rings, the call went to Lacie's voicemail. Colton just told her he would see her in art class. He decided that the entire story would take more than a quick message.

It was a leisurely drive to school, and since he wasn't late, he took the time to study the countryside, something he often missed. The farmers were taking crops off the field, and he passed several enormous trucks with their heavy loads of sugar beets. Giant wind turbines dotted the landscape, and today they seemed bigger and more plentiful. Colton wondered when so many of them got built since he remembered just a few years ago. *It is amazing*, he thought, *how much you miss when you have to speed to get to school on time.*

History class with Mr. Dinger flew by. There was a pop quiz, and even though Colton didn't study, he knew all the answers. One advantage of having a photographic memory is that you can remember the books you read in grade school and the movies you saw. When added together, most of the history that Mr. Dinger's class covered had already soaked into Colton's mind. He only needed to pull them out and put them on the paper in the correct order.

As he walked to trig. class, he wondered if the police investigated the crime scene, or if they had a good laugh at his expense. He could see Steve and the CSI men discussing his crazed mind. Joking about the boy who cried wolf one too many times.

"Hey Colt, why so glum this morning?" asked Seth as he caught up with him in the hall. The two stopped next to the lockers and Colton, for the first time, didn't know what he wanted to say. Seth was his best friend, next to Lacie, and he wanted to tell him everything. But now wasn't a good time.

"Seth, some crap has happened and I need to talk, but it's too much for the hallway. How about the study period?" he asked.

Seth knew this was serious, just by the tone of Colton's voice. "Does it have anything to do with the Hampton boys?"

"No, this is way beyond them. This is murder. Gunshot... blew the face off... murder!"

"Holy crap, man. I want to know now!" Seth insisted.

"Later, I have art class this morning, and I need to tell Lacie. I'll talk to you fifth hour. OK?"

Seth relented with, "Sure, Colton. See you in the study period." He knew he would die trying to figure out what murder Colton meant. Was it a joke? Colton had pulled a few jokes on him, but no... Colton was serious and upset. The fifth hour seemed like such a long way away. How could he have waited that long?

Colton continued in silent mode throughout trigonometry. Aden commented He seemed a little off today, but Colton remained silent. He didn't want to talk to anyone. He felt like he was in a slow-motion movie, and he wasn't sure why. Perhaps he was in shock, or he had post traumatic stress syndrome. *Isn't that what a soldier comes home with after seeing too much death on the battlefield?* He wasn't sure, but he felt down. If this were a dream, he would be in an enormous swimming pool... sinking to the bottom... like a stone.

The ringing bell startled him, and he walked to the door. Mr. Sellerman stood next to the door, and he put his arm out and stopped Colton.

"It looks like you're troubled, Colton. Your fire is burning dim today," he said.

"What?"

"Is there anything I can help you with? If so, please let me know," the teacher said.

"OK," Colton said as he walked past Mr. Sellerman.

Colton's fire continued to burn out during chemistry class. He kept watching his phone for messages from Trooper Laurie, but there were none. Deep down, he knew the police investigation was dead. They did not believe him, and he would never know the truth. This realization made him feel alone and angry, and he didn't want to talk to anyone... he needed to think.

Heading down the hall toward art class, Lacie walked up to Colton and held his hand as they walked. She said nothing, sensing he was deep in thought and would talk to her when he was ready. This wasn't the first time she had seen him in this condition. Every so often his mind needed rebooting. Like a hard drive, in looking for answers to a complex puzzle, he had to search all the data in silence.

"Hey Colton, you looked better in the pirate outfit," said Jerry.

"Don't bug him, Jerry," insisted Lacie.

Colton looked at her and smiled. "Hi Lacie, when did you get here?"

"Man, can I have the stuff you've been using? It must be powerful to put you away like that," said Jerry.

"Jerry, my man." Colton smiled at the tie-dyed shirt and jeans Jerry wore. "You look great."

"Now I know something is wrong, Colton," said Lacie. "What the hell's going on? Tell me now, please."

Colton drew her close to him and whispered, "I saw a murder last night, and I think I could have posttraumatic stress syndrome. I felt good this morning, but I feel down now, and all I can think of is how bad I feel inside, and how stupid the cops are."

"Tell me about the murder. Was it in one of your dreams?"

"No, it was real. I even called 911, but Trooper Steve says I'm a crazy teen who's seeking attention."

Jerry worked on his abstract painting while he listened to the conversation. "Colton, you're not crazy, man. You're the most sane guy I know."

"Jerry's right. If you say you saw a murder, then that's what you saw. So, get out of this funk and give us the details. We can help you solve this."

"Yes! We can be your CSI team… like on TV, man," said Jerry.

Colton smiled again. "You know, Jerry, you're the man. Thanks."

Lacie grabbed Colton's wrist and pulled him around, so he faced her. "Now, tell us what happened, and don't leave out any of the details." She could see the spark return to his face. The hard drive was reformatted and ready to work.

No Police Investigation

Before Colton could tell his tale of murder and mayhem, his cell phone vibrated. He pulled it out of his pocket and saw Trooper Laurie's number. Even though it was against school rules, he answered the phone.

Standing, he walked out of the classroom and said, "This is Colton, Trooper Laurie. What can you tell me about the investigation?"

"Colton, the CSI agents spent all morning on the beach. There was no evidence of a murder. They checked the house, and it belongs to an old woman in Roseville, Michigan. She says they closed the house up on the first of September, and only she and her caretaker have a key. Colton, I'm not saying you didn't see something, but the County Sheriff and the State Police will not be looking any further into this. You're not being charged for calling 911 because I think you saw something."

"I sure did... I saw a murder!" insisted Colton. "So what do I do now? Just forget about this and let the murderer get away with it?"

"Colton, do nothing to get yourself in trouble. You know what happened the last time you took matters into your own hands. Those Hampton guys could have shot you with a gun instead of giving you and your friend a good beating." Laurie felt Colton might try to do his own investigation. She liked Colton and wanted nothing bad to happen.

"Well, thank you for the news. I have to get back to my art class. Oh, I will try to find out who got killed, and who the killers are. But if you are correct, I won't have any luck. So unless you think there is a killer out there, don't worry about me. OK?" He disconnected the phone before she could answer.

Lacie and Jerry eagerly waited for Colton to return and fill them in on all the events of the previous night. When he came back into the classroom, the teacher was at the door.

"Problems at home, Colton?" he asked.

"No, sir. But if you want to hear the story of the murder I witnessed early this morning, you're welcome to join us. It looks like I will have a mystery to solve."

"Now you've piqued my interest. What murder are we talking

about?" Mr. Swansear asked.

During the next half-hour, Colton told the entire class about the murder. His classmates and teacher listened as he described the killers and gave detailed accounts of what the police said.

"Man, that's sick. Why won't the police investigate this?"

"He told us, Jerry," said Beth Lawser. "They think all of us teenagers are lying scum."

"I didn't put it like that, Beth. The police couldn't find any evidence of a murder, so they can't justify spending money on an investigation."

"Like, it's always about money, isn't it, Lacie?" Jerry said.

Lacie had been listening to the conversation without making many comments. Colton knew she was holding her opinion for later, when they were alone, but he wanted to know what she thought. "So, Lacie, any ideas what I should do next?" he asked.

"I think we need to start an investigation on our own. You know, Colton, until those guys get caught, you won't give up, and I can't stand to be around you when you're like that. So, if everyone here agrees, I think we need to do what the police won't," she said.

The class applauded in full agreement with Lacie. Colton's smile grew, and he reached around and hugged her. "Damn, you always know what to say to make me feel better."

Mr. Swansear said they could discuss their investigation during class, but only if they got their artwork done. "I don't want to be a spoiler, but I can't let your work slide. Do the artwork and I will look the other way if you need to use class-time to investigate. But remember, your safety is important. If there is a killer out there, and you step on the wrong toes, you could be in trouble. Be careful, Colton. Since you have yourself and now your classmates to think of."

"Agreed, sir. No one should get into a situation they can't handle. Our goal is to find the killers and learn who their victim was," Colton assured. "If we do that, perhaps we can convince the police to do their job."

Chapter 17

Assistant Detective Seth

Colton sat with a few members of the football team during lunch. Bill Crawley had his crutches, and everyone wanted to see if they could walk with them. Bill described how the Hampton boys had sprained his ankle by twisting it with their bare hands. When asked if he could play again this year, he insisted he would be back for homecoming, Friday of next week. This week, he will be on the bench rooting for the team.

Not wanting to take time away from Bill, Colton didn't tell the guys about his murder investigation. Last week, everything revolved around Colton, and today Bill deserved a little fame. The boys decided that Bill's crutches looked cool, but it would be easier to walk without them. Bill enjoyed having a great excuse to have others carry his books, and now when he was late to class, no one questioned him. Aden suggested that the entire team come in next week with rented crutches, but everyone said it was a dumb idea.

Seth rushed up to Colton as the bell rang for the fifth hour. "So what the hell is this murder stuff? I've been trying to figure it out, and all I got was what Jerry told me in the media room. He said you saw a murder, but the cops don't believe you. Well....?"

"Let's find a table out of the way of prying ears," said Colton, as he walked to the back of the lunchroom. The multipurpose room is now being used for a study period, and Miss Walker, the instructor, allowed students to work together as long as they remained silent.

"Last night, while doing my route on The Point, I saw two men standing on the beach pointing a gun at a man on his knees. I couldn't believe it when the men shot the guy in the back of the head and blew his face away. I hid while I was watching and called 911. The men wrapped the dead guy in a plastic tarp and loaded him into a small boat. One guy took the boat out onto the lake while the other guy got into their SUV and left. This happened before the police arrived."

Seth sat with his mouth wide open in amazement. "God, Colton, they would have killed you if they knew you were there. Weren't you afraid? I would have wet my jeans if I had been there."

"No, you wouldn't, and yes, it scared me silly. I have been listening to some Baldacci murder mysteries on my MP3 player and took a cue from the lead detective, John Palmer. I remained calm and tried to study every detail of the crime scene. You know, I can play back the entire scene in my mind. Their faces became engraved in my memory, and I wish they weren't. This morning I was in a real funk. I thought I suffered posttraumatic stress syndrome, but Lacie said my mind was trying to figure out my feelings. God, I hate it when she's right."

"You're wandering, Colton. Back to the murder," Seth insisted.

"Well, when the police arrived, there was no evidence. That state trooper Steve insisted I wanted attention. He's such an ass. Trooper Laurie was nice, but there wasn't anything she could do, because the CSI team found no blood, bullets, or tracks. They said the beach and house didn't show that anything had happened." Colton watched as Jerry and two other students from art class came up to the table.

"Man, when are we investigating?" Jerry asked.

Seth looked surprised. "Investigating? Don't tell me you plan to look for the killers yourself."

"That's my plan, Seth. During art class and study period, we will be the Loon's Investigation Service. Doesn't it sound good?"

"Sounds crazy, but can I be an assistant detective?" asked Seth.

"You sure can, Seth. We need to plan out our investigation, and all we have to go by is what I witnessed; so it will be a hard job," said Colton.

Jerry approached Colton and Seth. "Colton, I got Kelly Ryder here. She's... like... the best portrait artist in class, and she's willing to help draw the killers for us," said Jerry. He had a huge grin on his face and was excited about the new task he had. Jerry was never a part of Colton's antics, but now he enjoyed being a member of the group.

Colton studied Kelly for a moment. "Wasn't some of your work in the art exhibit last year, and didn't you win an award, or something?"

"I won first place for the portrait of my grandma. Thanks for remembering, Colton. I always felt you were a stuck-up jock, and you still may be one," Kelly said with brutal honesty. "So when do you want to start? It'll take time, but if you go through Google Images, you might find a picture similar to the men we are trying to identify. I can then change the images so they match what the men looked like."

"That's a great idea, Kelly. I'll do that tonight and print them. Is it OK if we start during art class tomorrow? The sooner the better," Colton said. He wanted to get started now, but he knew it would take time.

"That would be fine," said Kelly. She turned to Jerry and said, "Well, Jerry, let's get back to the art room. If we hurry, we can check the pottery kiln. I want to check out that outstanding bowl you finished last week."

"OK. I'll meet you in art, and man, we'll solve this mystery, just like that Sherlock Holmes guy did in the movie," said Jerry.

Miss Walker approached Colton and Seth and asked, "Colton, what's this I hear about your seeing a murder last night? Is it true... or is it gossip?"

"It's true, Miss Walker, but the police found no evidence and they won't continue the investigation. So, in art class, we will investigate for ourselves. We don't want the killers to get away with their crimes."

Colton then added, "Will you mind if we work on the investigation during study period?"

"As long as you have your other work done and you don't disturb the class, I have no objection. But be careful. One thing about killers, if they killed once, they don't mind killing again. I don't want you to get so involved that you become their next victim. So be careful."

"We will, and thanks," said Seth.

The Day Ends Better

During gym class, the football members did their workouts in the equipment room. Colton ran through his routine and got psyched for football practice, and ten laps around the football field would make him forget his problems.

Coach Talbert told Colton that he had been doing a great job clutching the ball after his catches. "You've come a long way. I thought you would never get the knack of keeping the ball secure, but you've got it down now. I want you to improve your footwork by performing agility drills."

The team would play Bad Axe on Friday, and a new player would fill in for Calvin Rowell, whose knee got blown out by the Hampton boys. The new player, Kyle Waters, was a powerful player, and the doctors told Calvin he could play in the homecoming game.

Everything is coming together for a great football season. The Lake Huron Loons were undefeated, and they might just win it all, provided there were no more injuries.

Colton had the evening free to do what he wanted. He had no route to do, no homework, and no special jobs to do around the house. Terry was at a friend's for the evening, so he asked his brother, Jason, if he wanted to play football tonight.

"No, that's a lame sport. I'll play a video and watch a movie later," Jason responded. "But thanks for asking."

Colton helped his mom with the dishes and then went to his room to find pictures that might match the killer's. He spent hours combing through photographs. When he found an image that resembled one man, he downloaded and saved it with a comment of what he saw that caught his eye. He had images labeled: killer one's smile, lips, ears, hair, or skin tone. By bedtime, he had collected close to fifty images, divided into three groups. One for each killer and one for the victim. He also found the SUV and had a rear view of the black Lincoln MKX.

Before getting ready for bed, he called Lacie.

"Hey, I got the images to use in art class. Is there anything else we need?" he asked.

There was silence as Lacie considered the question, then she said, "We should use Google Earth and print out pictures of the houses where the murder occurred, and we should interview the woman to whom you delivered a paper. She might have information about her neighbors. We also need to know who the other neighbors are, and what they said to the police."

"That sounds good. Lacie, you would make a good detective," Colton said.

"Yes, but I'm sure you would have come up with these ideas. Colton, please be careful."

"I will. I love you, and I'll see you in art class."

"Love you too, Colton," she said, making a kissing sound.

Alternate Murder

I'm Detective Colton Blackwell, and tonight I'm casing out the home of Big Mike, noted hitman for Anthony Bungalow. I have been in this pine tree for over fifteen hours, watching Big Mike through the window of his lake condo. All I've seen tonight is a parade of scantily clad girls entering Mike's bedroom. It's a shame. The poor girls don't know what a loser they're messing with. Big Mike kills people just because they don't dress well.

It's eleven o'clock in the evening, and Robo Jones, Mike's partner in crime, drives up in his shiny black Lincoln MKX. Jones drags a small Latino boy behind him. The young boy begs for his life, and I feel bad things are about to happen. I get down from the tree and sneak around the house. The two hitmen walk to the beach, with the girls looking out at them from the window. Big Mike points his gun at them, and they scatter like flies, knowing Big Mike doesn't want them watching him do his business. The business of murder.

I have to save the boy. No one should die at the hands of these creeps, let alone a teenage boy. I pull two guns from my holster and run toward the men. The boy gets loose and jumps into the lake. With their guns pointed at me, I shoot the guns out of their hands. With blood dripping from their fingers, the stupid thugs cry, asking for mercy. The young boy screams, "Kill them, Señor. Kill them now!"

"No, kid. Killing is for cowards. These men will spend the rest of their lives in jail."

"Bravo," the boy yelled. "Bravo, Señor!"

I used an old rope and tied the two thugs up, and when the police car arrived, I told Detective Laurie what the men had done. She charged them with attempted murder, and we threw them into the back of her patrol car.

"Laurie, let's get a root beer after we do the paperwork on these men?"

"Sure, dollface. Then you can come to my apartment for a while." She smiled, and I smiled, and I could see young Tony smile, too.

Colton woke with a big smile on his face. He wasn't sure what his dream was about, but today looked brighter than the last few days, and he was eager to get on with the murder case.

Chapter 18

Getting The Picture

W ednesday morning looked good. Rested, eager to get to school, and ready to launch a full scale investigation, Colton could see no obstacles. Perhaps that is why he had that uneasy feeling again. You know, "When things seem too good to be true, they usually are."

It surprised Colton that so many of his classmates had heard about the murder, and they all wanted to give him their theories about who did the deed. A few students suggested it could be a mafia killing, or perhaps a gang war. Someone even suggested that the killers were federal hitmen killing a Canadian spy who had snuck into the USA by crossing the lake. Colton liked the spy theory.

In art class, the detective team talked through their planned attack. Colton would sit with Kelly, telling her what he saw, so she could do a sketch of the killers. Lacie would gather as much information about the owners of the homes on The Point as she could from computer records. Jerry and Betty Lawser searched for information about similar killings in Michigan, and they also checked for missing persons, because someone must have known the dead man.

The art teacher, Mr. Swansear, liked the way the students organized their investigation. He told Kelly that if she needed help doing the police sketch, he would assist her. She felt she could do it herself. Mr. Swansear sat back and watched the action.

Colton and Kelly went through the photographs of the two killers. They both were heavyset, but the tallest man, at about six foot, had curly black hair; cut on the long side, but not an Afro; an unshaven look as if he cut his beard with a clipper; and dark olive skin, perhaps Mediterranean or Middle Eastern. The other man was about five-foot-ten and had thin light brown hair and a clean-shaven face. Colton could only guess his eye color as it was night, and the area was lit only by the full moon.

Kelly took the picture that Colton considered the shape of the first man's face and drew it on a larger paper. Then, she asked which picture had the best eye shape and eyebrows. As they continued following this process, the image came to life. When she finished, Colton exclaimed, "That's him! Damn, Kelly, you're fantastic!"

"You're the one who's good, Colton. I can't believe you have the memory that you do. I bet you would have remembered how large his pimples were if he had any."

"He didn't have a pimple, but that reminds me, there was a mole on his right ear."

"What?"

"Just kidding, let's do the other killer," Colton said as he arranged the photographs he had selected for the second man.

At the end of the hour, Kelly suggested she come to fifth hour study period and continue working with Colton. Lacie and Jerry reported they had found a few leads and would also meet fifth hour. The entire team seemed pleased with the progress they had made in such a short time.

As they left for lunch, Mr. Swansear congratulated them on a job well done and reminded them that tomorrow they had to get back to their artwork. One day was his limit for investigations.

Colton spent lunch with the football guys again. He would have rather been with Lacie, but team camaraderie was important, since they were on a winning streak and on Friday they would face their archrival, Bad Axe. There were several questions about the murder case, but Colton tried to pass over the subject with a single comment, which sounded like a police officer talking to a group of reporters.

"We're looking into it. I'll let you know when we have more details."

The investigative team gathered during fifth hour study period. Seth, Lacie, Jerry, Kelly, and Beth joined Colton at a table in the corner of the multipurpose room. Colton had asked Miss Walker if they could meet, and she approved, but for only fifteen minutes.

Lacie and Jerry reported: Mrs. Hoffstarter lives next to the home where Colton saw the murder. A Mrs. Alberto Torengia owns that home. She is 89 years old and lives in St. Clair Shores, Michigan. My guess is she only uses the house during the summer. Her husband has been dead for twenty years, and she has two daughters who live in the Detroit metro area.

The neighbors on the other side of Mrs. Torengia's home are year-round residents, Mr. and Mrs. Stone. The couple are in their late seventies and are the parents of Lake Huron High School English teacher, Mrs. Betty Castle.

"We haven't talked to any of these people, including Mrs. Castle," said Lacie.

"Man... like I could talk to them. I could get them to talk, you know... squeal on the bad guys," suggested Jerry.

"That's OK, Jerry," said Colton. "I'll talk to Mrs. Hoffstarter this afternoon after practice, and I have Mrs. Castle for sixth hour."

"If there isn't anything else to report, I need to work with you, Kelly. I would love to get the drawings done today so we can put posters up," Colton said.

Kelly enjoyed Colton's company. She was not a popular girl in school because, with spiked hair, black stretch tights, a tight halter top, and sarcastic comments, students thought she was *odd*. It surprised her that Colton never made a single derogatory comment about her appearance. He was kind, and not at all what she had expected.

It surprised Colton that she was brighter than he had expected. He knew her artwork was excellent, but he expected her to be an airhead. She turned out to be bright and easy to talk to. They made a good working team.

"Are you sure he had blue eyes?" She asked as she added color to the second killer's eyes.

"No, but since he had light hair, and must be of Northern European descent, he either had blue or hazel eyes. I guessed blue. But you could go with blue-green. That might work better."

"How can you remember these details, Colton?"

"I don't know; what goes in just sort of stays there, I guess," Colton replied, as he looked through the pictures he had selected for the victim's drawing.

"Do we have time to work on the third drawing?" asked Colton.

"Only if we can work together later. What do you have seventh hour?"

"Gym, why? Are you free seventh hour?" Colton asked. He considered Coach Talbert would let him skip gym class for one day.

"No, but if you can get out of gym, I can get out of English class. The teacher likes me, and I often leave to work on my artwork. I'm her best student, and she lets me do whatever I want. Besides, I work with her on the school paper."

"OK, see you in the art room. I wouldn't have taken you for an English lover. Art yes, but English too? That's cool, Kelly." Colton finished his sentence just as the bell rang. He took the two finished drawings, and Kelly gathered the pictures of the victim.

"Bye, see you later," she said.

The First Interview

When Colton arrived for English class, he approached Mrs. Castle and asked if she would have time to talk on a personal subject before the end of class.

"I planned a half hour of silent reading. If you like, you can come up to my desk then. Is this meeting about the incident last night on The Point?" she asked.

"Yes. Is that OK?"

"That's fine, we can talk later, so sit down now and let me get the class started," she said.

The class discussed The Grapes of Wrath for half an hour, and then Mrs. Castle told the students to finish reading for the rest of the hour. There will be a quiz on Thursday, and they must have read the book by then.

Colton raised his hand, and Mrs. Castle called him forward. He pulled up a chair and sat opposite her at the large oak desk. "Tell me, Colton, what happened last night?"

Colton explained the entire evening to her. When she asked what the police were doing Colton said, "They will not continue the investigation, because they found no evidence and they don't know I witnessed a murder, and I will investigate the murder myself with the help of some friends," Colton added.

"What is your important question?"

"I understand your parents live next to Mrs. Alberto Torengia's home. The murder happened on the beach behind her home. I'm not sure what your parents told the police last night, but I wondered if you know or if I may ask them," Colton said.

"My parents live in a nursing home, Colton. The house on the point is empty. My brother and I might sell it next summer."

"I'm sorry, I didn't realize. Did you live there when you were young?"

"No. I grew up on a farm near Caro, Michigan. When my dad retired ten years ago, he sold the farm and bought that monster of a house for Mom because she always wanted to live on the lake. Because of their age, they now live in a small assisted living apartment in the village."

"Do you have any information about Mrs. Alberto Torengia and her family?" Colton asked. It disappointed him that his questions brought forth no new information.

"I met her once, many years ago, and I'm aware she has a lot of money and her husband is dead now. I know nothing that would help you. Do you think she is involved in this?"

"I'm not sure. I have her name, your parents' names, and what I saw. It's looking like I have a lot of investigative work ahead of me."

"Colton, this is good practice for you. Approach this investigation like a newspaper reporter; find the who, what, where, why, and when of the story. You must dig deep, and be tenacious," she said with a smile. "But remember, a big smile will get you further than a tough demeanor."

"Thank you, Mrs. Castle. I will keep you updated on my progress. Heck, I might just write a paper about this adventure when I find the killers."

"Sounds good, Colton. Class, the bell is about to ring. Remember to read tonight and prepare for the quiz tomorrow." The class was already halfway out the door when she finished her sentence. "Bye, Colton."

Coach Talbert let Colton skip his workout in the gym to go to the art room. Colton said he had an important project that needed his attention. He didn't tell the coach it wasn't an art project. By the end of seventh hour, Colton and Kelly had finished all three drawings.

"Now I have to make copies to put around school and the community," Colton said.

"Let me take these drawings home. I'll scan them and make a letter size poster with all three pictures in it. Trust me, Colton. I can do the graphics. Give me your email, and I'll send you the file when I'm done. OK?" she asked.

"Sure, Kelly, based on your work so far, I trust you. But I need a copy of them tonight. I'm seeing a woman who lives on The Point, and I want to show it to her. Can we take them to the office and scan them?"

"Why not scan them here? We can use the art room computer and printer," Kelly said.

After printing the copies, he wrote his email address on a piece of paper, gathered the three pictures and handed the originals to her. "Here you go, and I'm looking forward to seeing your completed poster."

They headed back to their classes before the seventh hour bell rang. Colton stepped into the locker room to change for football practice. The room was dark, empty, and silent. He sat on the bench, considering the day's events. He still could not understand why they had murdered that man, but now he might discover the truth. *It's been a busy two weeks*, he considered, *and it looks like this week will be busy, too.* Remembering the last two weeks' events, he chuckled. *If this were an audiobook, I'm not sure I would believe it happened. So much crap in so little time. But it happened to me.*

Football practice proved invigorating, and Colton felt that his stamina and agility were better. Coach Talbert had the team doing sprints and foot drills again, and he could run through the line of 20 cones... hitting none. Some other runners stumbled on the cones, making Colton look even better. At the end of the exercises, the team ran through their playbook, making sure they knew every play by heart. Aden did a great job explaining the plays when a player didn't understand the coach.

Chapter 19

Mrs. Hoffstarter Likes Colton

Colton called Lacie and let her know Kelly had completed the drawings. He said he would send her an email before he went to bed, provided Kelly sent them to him.

"Where do you think the posters should go, Colton?" Lacie asked.

"Let's begin in school, and the bulletin boards around town. I talked to Seth, and he's buying a cheap cell phone with a new number we can use. I don't think we want to post our personal numbers all over the county. He said he would call Kelly and give her the number."

"Great idea. Did you talk to Mrs. Castle during English class?"

"Yes, but it's a dead end. Her parents own the house, but they haven't lived there since they moved into an assisted living apartment. I'm on my way to Mrs. Hoffstarter now. I called her before sixth hour, and she sounded happy that I intended to visit. Dad says she is quick-witted, but I don't know. She sounded old to me."

"Well, if she offers you a cookie, be careful. You know old women; they can be twisted. My great aunt used to put rat poison in her husband's lunch box. She spent time in the mental ward. Her husband was the one who drove her crazy. I would have just shot him."

"Nice one, Lacie. Now I have to worry about poison and more gunshots. Thanks for the encouragement."

"You're welcome. I have to get going, so good luck, Colton. I love you, bye," she said.

It felt funny driving along his newspaper route in the daytime. It all looked different. When he got to Mrs. Hoffstarter's house, he felt panic. *Not fright*, he thought, *but dread*. He wanted to look at the beach where he had seen the man being killed, but he didn't know if he could.

He rang the doorbell, and a thin woman with silver gray hair opened the door.

"Colton, you look so much like your dad. He told me you were doing the route for him. Your father is the finest newspaper carrier I have ever had. Such a kind man," she said.

"Thank you. I think he's special, too."

"Well, come in! Or will you be standing there all afternoon?"

The house was enormous. Colton loved the huge windows overlooking the lake. He stood and watched a sailboat in the distance, and two elderly women walking along the beach. The room was light and modern. It reminded Colton of a bank lobby with stone and iron and rich wooden trim.

"This is beautiful, Mrs. Hoffstarter. I wanted to see you because of what happened last night. I'm not sure if the police told you I was the one who called them."

"No, they didn't say who called them. They asked if I had seen a man being killed? You know what I told them; otherwise, you wouldn't be here, and they would be investigating."

"You're sharp, Mrs. Hoffstarter. What clued you I'm investigating?" Colton asked.

"Call me Trudy. That's my name. I'm Mrs. Hoffstarter to strangers, not friends. Oh, sit down over here and I'll get us some cookies and milk. Or would you prefer coffee?" She said as she walked toward the kitchen counter.

"Coffee, Trudy. Thank you for making me feel so comfortable."

"Well, I don't think you know this, but I graduated from the U-M

Department of Psychiatry when I was 24. I had a private practice in Pontiac for over forty years. All that time as a psychiatrist, and I still don't understand people." She set a tray of homemade cookies on the oak table as she continued to talk. "I enjoy talking to young people, though. You know what I miss the most?"

"I would guess, people to talk to. It must get lonely in a huge house like this," Colton said.

"My, you are like your father, very perceptive. Yes. It gets lonely. I try to attend as many community functions as I can, but it's so hard to get around, and people don't like to be bothered with an old lady. Even my children are old, and my grandchildren only want to come here when there is a party in Caseville; holidays and festival time is when I see them. And what do they do when they get here? They stay as far away from me as they can get. I know my grandchildren would be more willing to visit with me if I didn't criticize them, but I have strong opinions and it's too late to change now."

"They've missed a great opportunity if they don't spend time with you. I wish I could have spent more time with my grandparents. They are gone now, and I miss them."

"Aren't you sweet? Well, Colton, what do you need to know for your investigation?" Trudy put her cup of coffee down and dunked a cookie into it.

Watching her every move, Colton said, "Trudy, I know what I saw last night. I'm not a person who makes things up, and I am not delusional or an attention seeker. I saw two men on the beach, and they shot a younger man in the back of his head. They used a tarp to keep the blood off the beach and to wrap the man up. The one man drove a Lincoln MKX. Do you know anyone who lives in this area who might have done this?"

Trudy thought for a few moments and then said, "From your description, I would say it had been a planned murder. It's a style that the mob or a gang would use. If it were emotional, it would have been haphazard and sloppy."

"I brought three drawings of the killers and victims so you could look at them."

"You have police drawings? How on earth did you get that?" Trudy asked.

"A girl in my art class helped me pull together the images. I saw the guys in the moonlight, and I remembered every detail. The pictures look close to my memory, but we haven't made a wanted poster yet. Kelly, the girl who did them, will send me the poster via email."

Colton handed the folder with the three pictures. "Do you recognize any of these people?" he asked.

Trudy put on her glasses and studied the images. She laid them on the table and walked into the kitchen. When she returned, she picked up the pictures and studied them again.

Setting them down, she looked at Colton and said, "These two men look familiar. I know I've seen them before, but I don't know where or when. The younger man is not familiar."

"He is the victim, and the other two are the killers."

"The darker man with black hair looks like the Torengia family. They all have olive complexions and dark hair. But I couldn't be positive, and I don't have a name to give you."

Trudy sat down and said, "I'm sorry I can't help you more, Colton."

"You have helped me, Trudy. Now I know the two killers had been in the area before. Now I have to find them," Colton said.

"Can you tell me about Mrs. Alberto Torengia, the woman who lives next door?" Colton asked. "Perhaps someone in her family is involved."

"Cora is a lovely woman. I've known her for many years. Her husband is dead, and she has two daughters and a son living somewhere in the Detroit area. I only see them once a year when they have a family get together over July Fourth. Other than that, she never has company. Cora lives here only for the three summer months, June through August, then she leaves in September and goes to St. Clair Shores. During the winter, she is in Arizona and Mexico. She has a lot of money and several homes. Her only friends are her housekeeper and cook. She has three people who travel with her."

"Wow, what a life," said Colton.

"Well, I will tell you this, Cora may be rich in money, but she is not a happy person. Her children hate her; she tells people that her money is going to her servants, a charity for animals, and her only grandson. No, money doesn't guarantee happiness," Trudy said, shaking her head and dunking another cookie into her coffee.

"I wouldn't mind trying it with money. My family is always on the short end of the cash line. We are happy, so you may be right." Colton dunked his cookie, and it fell in his coffee. He and Trudy both laughed.

"There is a trick to it, you know," Trudy said. She gave Colton a spoon. "Here, this will help." As Colton found his soggy cookie, Mrs. Hoffstarter pulled out a picture album. She slid several pictures out and handed them to him. "Here are pictures of Cora's family members. They are from four years ago, at her eighty-ninth birthday party. I received an invitation but couldn't attend. They sent me these photographs as a memento. Take them with you; they may help."

Colton looked at the pictures. He noticed that several of the men looked similar to the olive-skinned killer, but the killer was not in the picture. Turning one photograph over, he noticed a sticker with Cora's name and several telephone numbers.

"Are these Mrs. Torengia's phone numbers?"

"Yes. If you want to call her, use the St. Clair Shores number. She doesn't go to Arizona until after Christmas," Trudy said, pointing out the number.

"Do any of Cora's family come up to the lake when she isn't here?" Colton asked.

"Not that I know of. But you have to remember, Colton, my house is large, soundproof, and I don't have windows overlooking the Torengia home. So if someone snuck in at night, I wouldn't see them."

Turning very serious, Trudy said, "Colton, you need to know Alberto Torengia may have had mob ties. The police questioned him in the Jimmy Hoffa case, but they never charged him with any crime. I want you to promise to be very careful. If his family is into something like murder, they won't stop at the man you saw killed. Please be careful. I like you, and I don't want any harm to come to you or your family."

Colton stood and put his arms around the frail woman. "I like you too, Trudy. And I will be careful." As he walked toward the door, Colton continued to assure her he would be cautious.

"Good luck, Colton. And please come back soon. I enjoyed our visit."

Thursday Morning Deliveries

As Colton drove home, Seth called. "Hi, Seth. Did you go to Bay City after school like you said?" Colton asked.

"Sure did, and you should see all the goodies I got. I went to Security Tool Supply. Dad has an account there; so I put everything on his company's bill."

"Won't he be angry?" Colton asked, knowing Seth's dad would do anything for him. Seth is an only child, and his parents have tons of money.

"No, but he will wonder why the hell I need security cameras, listening devices, and night vision goggles." Seth chuckled. "I think I'll tell him I started a security company, or I will become a private eye, or an undercover detective. That's what we've become, isn't it?"

"Sort of," said Colton. "I talked to Mrs. Hoffstarter and got pictures of the neighbors. She doesn't know if anyone stops there at night.

Do you still want to set the cameras up tonight?"

"Sure do, we need to see if anyone uses that house at night, don't we?"

"Yes, I'll pick you up at two thirty tomorrow morning. You want me to call and wake you, or can you get up on your own?"

"Call me, and I'll bring school stuff so we can go to school from your place," Seth said.

"That's a plan, pal. See you in the morning."

Colton ended the call and dialed Lacie's number. The call went to voicemail, so he told her he loved her and would see her in art class. He decided it was too complicated to tell her everything Mrs. Hoffstarter said, and what he and Seth were planning. And texting while driving kills! Voice mail... that works. He thought.

Kelly sent Colton the wanted poster a few minutes after seven o'clock. He printed out a color copy of the file, and her professional work amazed him. Across the top, the headline said, "Do You Know These Men?" in large letters. She placed the three men's pictures across the center of the page. Underneath the pictures in large letters it read, "Two Of These Men May Have Killed The Third." Under this, in smaller letters, it read, "If you have any information, please call this number." Seth must have given her the new cell number because Colton didn't recognize the number that she listed.

Colton avoided telling his family about the events of the day. He knew they would worry, and his mom would freak out. It wasn't like him to avoid talking to them, but this was not an ordinary event. He felt they believed him when he told them about the murder, but he could see that sliver of doubt. His mom kept asking if he was sure he was OK. "You know, dear, they hit you in the head a lot this past week, what with football and that other stuff. Perhaps you should see a doctor to make sure something didn't break. They could do an MRI scan, you know," she said. Terry and Jason believed him. At least they said they did. And his little sister didn't seem to care because she was busy talking to her girlfriends.

Almost falling asleep at the computer, Colton made his way to bed. Thursday's delivery was just five hours away, and with Seth going with him, Colton didn't know how many extra hours the route would take.

Chapter 20

Undercover Eyes

At two-thirty Thursday morning, Colton sat in his Jeep trying to reach Seth on the phone. It took three calls to wake him. When Seth answered his phone, he promised he would be ready. Seth only lived a mile out of the way, so Colton wouldn't lose any time tonight.

Driving into the parking area at Seth's family home, Colton wondered what exotic cars his dad had parked in the five car, two-story garage. Seth's dad loved collecting unusual cars and pickup trucks. His collection reminded Colton of Jay Leno. He had seen a television special about his cars, and several of Jay's cars looked like Mr. Seamoore's.

Before Colton could finish his thoughts, Seth opened the back of the Jeep and placed a large box of spy goodies on the floor. "I'm ready," Seth said as he jumped in the passenger seat. "Where do we start... The Point or Caseville?"

"We have to pick the newspapers up in Pigeon, at the storage unit, then we do the rural homes south of Bay Port." Colton pulled out of the parking lot, and headed toward Pigeon. "I noticed you have the toys. Did you get the poster Kelly did?"

"Sure did. She did a great job. Do you think they resemble the guys you saw?" he asked.

Colton considered, and then said, "Absolutely! Her drawing is so close to what I saw that anyone who ever saw those men should

134

recognize them. I hope we don't have to wait forever to find someone who recognizes them."

Colton had fun letting Seth stuff the newspapers into the tubes. When he delivered the papers himself, he had to slide over to the passenger side to deliver papers on the right side of the road, but tonight he had two extra arms. Seth kept complaining that Colton drove too fast. "That last stop, you almost tore my arm off! You drove away before I pulled it out," Seth said.

"Stop complaining, and move faster. I rarely even stop when I deliver the papers. I drive by, throw it in, and keep going."

By the time they reached The Point, Seth's arm was sore. He was relieved when Colton told him most of the papers would now be on the left side. Colton now drove on the wrong side of the road, but as long as no other cars were driving on the roads, it wasn't a problem.

When they reached Mrs. Hoffstarter's house, he turned off the lights and engine. Colton walked a newspaper to Trudy's door, while Seth arranged a camera in the shrubs along Cora Torengia's driveway. The camera was solar powered and Wi-Fi equipped. They came with a Wi-Fi service plan that would allow Seth to access the camera online. Whenever someone drove or walked onto the drive or garage, the camera would record and send the images to Seth's computer.

Colton watched for cars as Seth set up the camera. He tucked it in the bushes and made sure that nothing blocked its view. Using a penlight, he adjusted the settings and made sure the unit worked.

The next stop was the house next door. Mrs. Castle's parents were not living in the house, but Colton and Seth put a spy camera in her shrubs too. "I'm sure Mrs. Castle's family has nothing to do with this, but someone might use their driveway," reasoned Colton.

"Can the cameras record in the dark?" Colton asked.

"Let's get into the Jeep and see. I have my laptop here, and there should be images of us installing them," he said as he lifted the screen of his computer to show Colton.

"Wow! That looks good, Seth," Colton said.

The recordings had already downloaded to Seth's account, but Colton noticed the color was a misty green. "What are they — night vision cameras?" he asked.

"After dark, they use night vision technology. Cool, aren't they?"

"I bet they're expensive too," said Colton.

"They sure are... nothing but the best," Seth said.

The route didn't take long to finish, which surprised Colton. He thought having Seth with him would slow him down, but Seth was a good worker, and he learned to get the papers in the tube without losing his arm.

Since there they would have time to get sleep, Seth asked Colton to drop him off at his home. He left the spy toys in Colton's Jeep for safekeeping. "I'll talk to you in school," he yelled as Colton drove away.

Do You Know These Men?

Colton arrived at school twenty minutes early. He went into the media room and put one poster into the color copy machine. When he hit print, fifty copies spewed out. He knew he could get into trouble using school property, but figured he could plead insane, if caught.

Using tape he brought from home, he plastered the wanted posters on the walls of both the high school and middle school. It took fifteen posters to cover the entire school. As he put the posters up, several students stopped and asked if these were the killers he had seen on Tuesday.

"You tell me. If you tell me who they are, I'll tell you what I know," he said.

The entire school talked about the new posters. At the end of the first hour, Mr. Dinger got a phone call on his classroom phone.

"Colton, you're wanted in the office," he said.

The students whispered, wondering if he was in trouble again. "I bet it's because of those posters," said Connie Jackson. Several other students agreed.

When Colton entered the office, Ms. Downer pointed toward the conference room. The principal, Mr. Zeller, leaned against the door smiling.

"Do you have anything to tell me about your posters?" he asked.

"Posters? You mean the wanted posters on the school walls?" Colton said, pointing to one poster.

"Yes. Those posters. I talked to the art teacher, and he told me what you and your friends did. Do you think the men on that poster are killers?" Mr. Zeller asked.

"Just the two older men; the younger man is dead. I saw his face getting blown off with a bullet. I know it's farfetched, but, Mr. Zeller, it's the truth."

"Remove them, Colton. You can't put posters up on school property without permission," Mr. Zeller said. "What you can do is leave one on any of the five bulletin boards throughout the school. Those are there for student use, provided they have permission. Just take down the ones on the hallway walls and let me know if you get any responses from your posters. And tell Kelly Ryder, the artist, that I want her to do a picture of my wife and kids. She's a fantastic artist, isn't she?"

"Yes, sir, and thank you," said Colton as he turned around and walked to the receptionist's desk. "Ms. Downer, can I get a pass to get into Mr. Sellerman's trig. class?"

Ms. Downer gave Colton a pass, and he walked down the hall, removing the posters. Mr. Zeller's reaction surprised him. At least he gave permission to leave five posters up. *Perhaps I need to change my view of the principal. No, not yet,* he thought. Many students feel Mr. Zeller is spiteful. It may be just the view of the students who had problems with him, but it is still the common view of the students.

The detective team met in art class. Seth got out of his class so he could be there for the meeting, where the posters were the first item of discussion.

"Like, man, Kelly did an outstanding job, don't you think, guys?" Jerry said.

Everyone agreed, and when Colton told them that even Principal Zeller liked them, they were impressed. Kelly was proud, and the glow on her face grew even brighter when Colton told her that Mr. Zeller wanted her to see him about doing a portrait of his family.

She smiled and said, "Thank you, Colton, I enjoy being on your team."

Seth said there were seven calls on voicemail, and he answered another ten calls. "How are we going to handle the crank calls from the poster? So far, it's just a bunch of students trying to figure out who put them up on the school walls. No one has any idea who the men are."

"We have to listen to each one," said Lacie. "We don't know who will recognize these men, so if we miss the one caller who knows, we lose."

"That's true, but I think we need to get these posters out into the towns. We will not get much from the students, but someone in town might know something."

"I'll go during lunch and post them in Pigeon," said Beth. "I have a dentist appointment and I can put them in the hospital, library, grocery store, and any store that will let me."

"Great, can everyone take some and put them up after school?" Seth asked.

They all agreed, and then the teacher ended their conversation, and artwork was again on the agenda. Colton took his watercolor out and set his brushes on the table while Lacie signed her mosaic piece. She handed it to Mr. Swansear for a grade.

"This looks great, Lacie. The colors are in balance, and you gave the piece a three-dimensional appearance," he said as he marked an A- in his grade book. "Now you can start your watercolor project, and remember, it's due in two weeks."

Road Trip Planned

Colton asked Mr. Swansear for permission to use the restroom. He went into a stall and took his phone out, along with the number of Mrs. Alberto Torengia, in St. Clair Shores.

"Hello, is this Mrs. Torengia?" Colton asked.

The woman who answered told him to wait a minute; she had to adjust her hearing aids. "Yes, this is Cora."

"I got your number from Trudy Hoffstarter, your neighbor on The Point. I am looking for the two men who broke in and used your cottage," Colton said, knowing he told only part of the truth.

"Oh my, would that be why the police called the other day?"

"Yes, did you tell them anything?" Colton asked.

"I told them that the house is empty nine months out of the year, and my caretaker and I are the only ones with a key."

"Can I send you pictures of the men who have been messing with your house?"

"You need my mail address?"

"No, I have your address on Jefferson Ave., but I need your email address."

"Email? If you mean that computer thing... well... I don't own a computer," she said.

"If I drive down Sunday afternoon, would you have time to look at them?"

"Sure, be here at one o'clock, and use the west side door."

Colton said thank you when someone came into the restroom.

He flushed the toilet and hurried back to the art room.

Back in the classroom, Colton watched as Lacie talked to a student he had seen around school, but he didn't know her name. He walked over to them... noticing the girl had tears in her eyes.

"What's up, Lacie?" Colton asked.

"This is Rosa Washington. She came here because she recognized her uncle in the poster."

"He's the one that Lacie said you saw being shot. I can't believe he could be dead, but he hasn't been home since Monday and that guy," she pointed to the heavy set dark skinned man, "came to our house to talk with him. They left together."

"Do you know the man's name and why he was talking to your uncle?"

Rosa sobbed... her face in her hands. "Drugs!"

She got up and rushed out the door. Colton started after her, but Lacie grabbed his arm. "Let her go, Colton. She needs to compose herself, and she's in our study period, so we can talk to her there."

"What did she tell you?"

"She said there are problems at home. Her parents are into alcohol and drugs, and she thinks her Uncle Bobby is the man in the picture. He has been selling drugs." Lacie put her head down and looked as if she were about to cry.

"What do you tell a girl who has to live in that kind of environment? I had never talked to her before. She always acts shy and keeps to herself, does her homework, and seldom talks in class. I feel so sorry for her, Colton. How do we help her?"

"I'm not sure, Lacie. Perhaps we should have considered the side effects before we started this investigation." Colton added a few more dabs to his watercolor and then cleaned their area. The class rushed to the door as Mr. Swansear yelled, "Sit down until the bell," and then a mad rush to the lunch room started. Colton, Lacie, Jerry, Kelly and Beth ambled behind the crowd, discussing Rosa's situation.

Chapter 21

He Sold Drugs On The Side

No one in the group knew the Rosa Washington family. Jerry thought they were from the Sebewaing area, but he wasn't sure. When Colton asked Jerry if he knew anything about the drug dealers in the area, Jerry became upset.

"Hey, man. Just because I dress like this, doesn't mean I would do drugs," he snapped.

"Sorry, I didn't mean it that way. You know more students than I do. You have tons of friends, and you're always going to the bigger parties. I thought you might have heard something," Colton said.

Kelly said, "I dated a boy last year until I found out he used drugs. He used weed and crack cocaine he got from a dealer in Sebewaing. It could have been Rosa's uncle."

"I've tried weed," Seth said. "I know it's illegal, but I was at a party last summer in Caseville, and they passed a joint around, and I tried it. All I got was a sore throat and the munchies. It wasn't something I wanted to repeat, but I think a lot of kids see it as an escape from their problems. Trust me, your problems will always follow you, and drugs will only make them worse."

Colton turned to Lacie. "Well, Ms. future doctor, it appears we know who the dead man was, but how can we prove he is dead? How do we prove the other two men killed him? And what can we do to help Rosa?"

"I want to be a small town nurse. You're the big time detective.

You solve the mystery and come up with the answers," she said.

"Seth, do you want to make a road trip to Detroit on Sunday? I set up a meeting with Mrs. Alberto Torengia, Cora, for short. She owns the house we are monitoring."

"Yes, sounds good. Want me to drive?" Seth offered.

"The Jeep will be fine; I wouldn't want your nice new car to get stolen in the big city."

"Great thinking. Dad would have to buy me a new one, and after paying for our spy toys, he might get upset," Seth said as he finished his lunch. "Anyone want me to take their tray back?" he asked.

Seth carried most of the trays, while Colton walked with him, carrying his own tray. "Seth, I would also appreciate your helping me on the route again tonight. I'm not sure why, but I have this feeling that something might happen."

"Crap! It better not be anything like Sunday. I don't want to get my ass kicked again," he said.

"I hope not, but the two of us can deal with trouble better than just one." Colton used his pleading look on Seth. His lower lip rolled down, and his eyes were as sad as a puppy dog.

"Damn, you're good. Pick me up, and don't forget to call," said Seth, as he slapped Colton on the back. They walked together to their lockers, discussing the spy gear and how they could use it in Detroit.

Helping Rosa

Concerned about Rosa, Lacie talked with her uncle Ned Wood-dell. Ned is a Huron County deputy and former military police officer. Lacie often confides in him. He has never broken her trust, and she considers him a friend.

Miss Walker excused her so she could go to her locker, but she walked into the girls' restroom to make her call, instead.

"Uncle Ned, I have a problem, and I need your advice," she said.

"I hope it's not a ticket, because I can't get you out of paying for it."

"No, it's Colton's murder case. I told you we planned to look for evidence. Today Rosa Washington, a girl here in school, identified the man Colton saw killed as her Uncle Bobby. She said the last time her family saw him was Monday morning, and he was with the killer that Colton identified."

"Lacie, I told you messing with this could be dangerous. It's a job the police should do, not a bunch of high school kids."

"Have the police started their investigation?"

"No, they dropped the investigation for lack of evidence."

"We are digging up the evidence they need. If we don't, no one will."

"OK, so this Rosa girl saw the killer and thinks her uncle is dead?" Ned asked.

"Yes, the problem is, her uncle was a drug dealer, and her mom and dad are alcoholics with a drug habit. What can I do to help her?"

"Damn, Lacie, that's a tough one. Let me think for a minute. Oh, did your dad tell you I beat him at poker the other night? If we were playing for real money, I could have a new sixty-inch television for my apartment."

"Uncle Ned, I'm at school and have little time. Rosa will want to talk, and I need help," she insisted.

While he was stalling, Ned checked his laptop for information on Rosa and her family. "OK, her name is Rosa Washington. I will have her parents checked out, and if they use or sell drugs, we can help her. We can't just ask them, because we need probable cause, and according to my computer, they have no criminal record," Uncle Ned continued. "I will give you a number for her to call. It's for the County Help Center. Talk to Brenda Sampson. She is an expert on substance abuse, and she works with children of users. We have to help Rosa. They can help her even if her parents don't want to save themselves."

"That sounds good. Will they keep her information private?" Lacie asked.

"Yes, they're like a doctor or lawyer. Talk to Rosa and tell Colton to be careful. If he needs help, have him call me," Ned added.

Lacie walked back to the multipurpose study room and sat next to Colton and Seth.

"Colton, I called Uncle Ned," she confessed.

"How much did you tell him?"

"Don't be angry. I told him who we think the dead man is, and that someone saw the killer with the victim on Monday. He will not stop us from digging for the truth, because he understands that if we don't investigate, no one will," she said.

Seth could see that Colton was upset with Lacie. He said, "I think it's smart to talk to the police, Colton, and Ned Wooddell is the most honest deputy I know. If he says he won't interfere with you, you can trust it's true. Besides Colton, the cops will know about this when they see all the posters."

Colton considered Seth's words. He sat down and took Lacie's hand and said, "I guess I should thank you. Like Seth said, I trust Ned's opinion. Tell us what he said we should do to help Rosa."

Lacie explained the plan to get help for Rosa, and when she saw Rosa coming toward them, she asked if she could talk with her in private. Seth and Colton walked back to their table, smiling at Rosa as they passed her.

Rosa and Lacie talked for the rest of the hour. By the time the bell rang, they were both exhausted. Lacie told Colton later that Rosa was relieved to have someone to confide in. She hates her parents' lifestyle and would move out if she had any money or family to live with. "I think she will get help from the woman at the County Help Center. She took the phone number and seemed very interested."

Seth asked if Rosa had told them where she lived, and if she knew who the killer was.

"She lives near Sebewaing, and Monday evening was the first time she saw the killer. She didn't know the second man, but the killer drove a large black SUV."

It pleased Colton that the investigation was going so well. He told Lacie he wasn't angry at her for telling her Uncle Ned. "The police should do this investigation, so if Ned can help us, that's fine, as long as he doesn't talk to Trooper Steve. That guy would put me in jail for doing detective work without a license."

"Didn't you get the license when I asked you?" Lacie jokes.

Mom, I'm A Detective Now

The football team became excited when Coach Talbert told them a major college scout would be at Friday's game at Bad Axe. "Seniors, this is your chance to shine, and remember, juniors, they will also watch you. If you show them you have talent now, they will mark you down as a player to watch. So, put your best game forward."

"This is my chance, Colton," said Aden. I need a scholarship to attend college, and I would love to play at that level.

"Have you thought about where you want to attend school next fall, Aden?" Colton asked.

"Man, like I said, anywhere I can get help with the money. My parents don't have crap, and I've only been able to get jobs as a short-order cook in Caseville. It's a wussy job that doesn't pay much, and I ended up spending everything I earned last summer on my crappy car."

"Aden, keep throwing that ball and I promise I'll make both of us look good. You're a great quarterback, and you deserve a spot on a college team."

Colton could see that Aden liked his comments. Aden had his flaws, but Colton wanted to overlook them for the sake of the team, because together, they could impress the scouts, and perhaps land themselves a scholarship.

After practice, Colton headed for home to tell his parents what had been happening. He didn't like keeping secrets from them and decided that they needed to know about the investigation.

As he pulled into the driveway, Terry rushed his Jeep and pulled the door open. "Colton, I did it. I made quarterback. That brat, Jimmy Seawart, hit me when he found out coach picked me instead of him, but I don't care, because I'm the man."

"Good job, Terry. See, all that practice paid off. Now, keep working and remember that as a leader, you must listen to your players. Don't do it all yourself. Being a quarterback is like Dad's new job. You're the supervisor of the team, and Coach is your boss."

"Whatever! Want to play football before dinner?" Terry asked.

"No, sorry. I have to talk to Mom and Dad."

"OK, I will throw the ball awhile."

Colton walked into the kitchen, and both his mom and dad were at the table, cleaning vegetables from the garden. On the counter were rows of canned tomatoes, salsa and pizza sauce.

"Tomatoes for dinner again?" he asked.

"Yes, we're having BLT sandwiches and mac and cheese, not from the box, but the genuine stuff. It's in the oven now," his mom said.

Adam looked up and said, "How was school? Word is, you and your friends are now detectives? Care to tell us about it, or do you plan to keep us in the dark?"

"I planned on telling you now, but I guess you beat me to the punch. I saw the murder, and so we've been trying to dig up evidence.

Lacie's uncle, Ned Wooddell, will help us. He's a Huron County deputy."

Colton figured that having a police officer involved would make his parents less apprehensive about his investigation.

"Well, he's the one who told me, and I wouldn't call him involved. He said, however, that he thinks you guys are being careful and, from what he said, you appear to be getting results."

"We sure are. We know who died, but we can't prove he's dead. I think the killer might have tied a rock to Bobby Washington's leg and dumped him into the lake. Any idea how long it would be before the leg would fall off and the guy would float back to shore?"

"God, Colton, not while I'm cooking supper. That's gross," his mom said.

"Let's go into the den, Colton. We don't want Mom getting upset."

"Great. And do you know anything about drug dealers? The guy who died sold drugs and ..."

The conversation moved into the den, with Colton doing most of the talking. Adam reminded him he could get into trouble if he messed with the killers. "If you learn who he is, call Deputy Ned Wooddell. Don't take matters into your own hands. It's bad enough that you and your friends are now *detectives*. The least you can do is use common sense, and be cautious," Adam warned him.

Chapter 22

Nasty Dreams

The waves were crashing on the beach as Detective Colton Blackwell sifted through the sand looking for evidence of murder. The coroner, Lacie Wooddell, bent down and whispered, "Do you want to go out for drinks after we finish?"

"Sure, Lacie. How about The Riverside in Caseville? I hear they have great food, and working on a murder investigation always makes me hungry."

"Sounds good."

Pointing at a shiny object in the sand, she yells, "What's that?"

"Good eyes, Lacie. It's a bullet. Must have come out of the victim's face and then it went into the sand. Nice catch. Hand me an evidence bag. This could break the case."

As the lovely coroner handed Detective Colton a plastic bag, two enormous arms grabbed her from behind. A knife was at her throat, and she screamed. Colton went for his gun, but realized that he could cause her to die. An ugly, scar-faced man looked from behind Lacie and smiled, showing brown stubs of broken teeth.

"Don't be silly, boy. Give me my bullet, and no sudden moves."

Seth came up behind the thug and put his revolver at the back of his head. "Don't move, I have you covered, and I would love a reason to blow your head off like you did to that young boy yesterday."

Before Colton could warn him, the thug's fat, sandy-haired assistant hit Seth on the head with a shovel. "You're all dead now," he yelled. "We have a boat coming to get you bastards, and you'll be fish food in no time."

Colton cried when he saw Lacie's neck being cut open. "Oh, God. Stop.... PLEASE STOP!"

He sat up in bed, perspiration running down his face, and realized he was in the middle of a nasty dream. He ran to the bathroom, did his business, flushed the toilet and ran cold water over his face. Looking in the mirror, he wondered, *Could my actions cause my friends' deaths? Oh, God, what have I gotten us into?*

It was two-thirty Friday morning, and time to get ready for the route. Remembering he needed to pick up Seth, Colton made his first of seven wake-up calls. No answer.

The nights were getting colder, so Colton grabbed a black hoodie and ran out the kitchen door. The Jeep started, and he could swear he saw a black SUV drive past the driveway. *Damn my imagination,* he thought. *I hate having nightmare dreams. Why can't I dream of nice stuff? Like hot girls playing volleyball on the beach. Or...* His imagination was now in overdrive as he sped towards Seth's place.

The seventh call woke Seth. He told Colton that he would be ready when he got there, but Colton had to wait ten minutes before Seth jumped in the front seat. "I made breakfast for us," he said, handing Colton a chocolate power-bar and a bottle of Coke.

"Last night I was hungry all night, so I brought food." Seth said, munching on the bar. "I had the strangest dream last night, Colton. I dreamed that you someone shot you in the head on the beach. Lacie was there, and so were those killers. Man, it was sick."

Colton decided he wouldn't mention his dream. *Two similar dreams during the same night... way too much to handle,* he thought.

Are We Being Followed?

As Colton and Seth did the newspaper route, Seth kept his laptop on. He checked the wireless cameras they had set up at the two lakeside homes. Since the installation of the cameras, no one has entered or left the house. The camera caught two dogs sniffing each other, several raccoons, a skunk family, and so many deer that Seth lost count.

"What's with all the deer on The Point?" he asked Colton.

"Dad says the deer people can't hunt them here because it's a residential area, so they send invitations to all their relatives to move to The Point."

"I get that, but how do they mail the invitations?"

"See all these mailboxes? Deer know how to use them, too."

The two laughed and then started toward the wooded south section of The Point. As Colton turned, he noticed the black SUV again. He pulled over and stopped, turning off his lights.

"You got to pee?" asked Seth.

"No, I saw that black SUV again. I didn't tell you, but I saw it driving past my house when I left to get you. I haven't gotten a good look; it's an SUV or a pickup."

Seth checked the laptop again. "Colton, look at this."

The views of the two cameras was both on the screen as the cameras streamed live video. The black Lincoln MKX pulled into the driveway, and a heavyset man with light brown hair got out and walked up to the back door. He opened the door and returned with a cardboard box. The Lincoln pulled away, and the screen was still again.

"Wow! I knew it. They're using Mrs. Torengia's house for some kind of drug drop," Colton speculated.

"But, Colton, that wasn't the Torengia home; that was Mrs. Castle's parents' house. Someone is using her parents' house as a drug drop."

Seth turned to Colton with a strange look on his face. "Could our English teacher be into drugs? Holy crap, Colton, this looks bad for her. Wait 'till we tell the other guys. This is amazing. Mrs. Castle is a drug dealer!"

Excitement filled Seth's voice.

"Hold it, Seth. No one said Mrs. Castle is a drug dealer. Her parents' house is involved, but we don't know if it's drugs, and we can't say anything until we know for sure. Understood?"

"Understood, but it sure is a good story," Seth said.

Colton started the Jeep, heading to the only house on the wooded street. He looked behind him, and could see the headlights of the black vehicle.

"Damn, look around, Seth. We have to get out of here," Colton said as he sped ahead. He threw the paper on the driveway and turned the Jeep around. Now pointed at the vehicle sitting at the other end of the road, he realized it was a black pickup truck, not the Lincoln MKX.

"What's the plan?" asked Seth. "Hey, that's a pickup, and look, the guys getting out are the Hampton boys. What the hell are they doing here?"

Colton drove forward and stuck his head out the window and yelled, "What do you guys want? I thought we were through with you."

"Not yet, dumbass." Thunder opened his door and got out. He pointed a gun at the Jeep and fired a shot, missing the Jeep. He was weaving around, and Colton could tell that the two of them were drunk. "Stand still, Mr. Dumbass Colton, I'm killing you."

Lightning laughed and fell down. Colton put the jeep in gear and started toward the pickup. The two Hampton boys jumped back into the truck and drove toward the Jeep. To avoid a crash, Colton turned into the woods. He had all four wheels engaged, and drove between the trees, avoiding any damage.

The pickup was a few feet behind, and there was another gunshot. Colton noticed a canal ahead and drove straight for it.

Seth yelled, "Stop, Colton. There's a big ditch ahead."

Colton turned at the last minute and headed back toward the road. The pickup didn't turn. Flying over the edge, the pickup flew into the air, did a forward flip, and landed upside down in the canal.

Must We Save Them?

Colton and Seth got out of the Jeep and walked to the edge of the canal. The pickup truck sat in the center of the canal with its tires poking above the water. There was no sign of life, only steam bubbling from the engine compartment.

"What do we do if they don't come out of the pickup?" asked Seth.

"I guess we'll have to go in the water and get them out."

"Can we wait an hour before we go in the water?" Seth said. He looked at Colton and giggled. "You know, this is hilarious. Did you see the way Lightning fell on his face? They're so freaking drunk."

"Look, there's Thunder." Colton could see Thunder gasping for air as he clung to the side of the pickup truck.

"And there's Lightning," said Seth. "Now what do we do? They look furious."

"Help!" yelled Thunder. "I can't swim."

The two Hampton boys clung to the pickup, alive and deathly afraid of the water. Colton took his phone out and dialed Trooper Laurie's personal number. He didn't want to call 911, because every time he did, he got into trouble.

"Laurie, this is Colton. Are you working, or did I wake you?"

"I'm in my patrol car, working. What's the problem, Colton?" she asked.

"Well, the Hampton boys are in the canal on Wooded Drive at The Point. Their pickup is upside down, and they are drunk. They tried to shoot Seth and me while we were delivering newspapers. Can you get here? They can't swim, and I don't want to go into the water."

"Are they injured?" Trooper Laurie asked.

"No, but I think they might sober up soon. The water looks freezing. You'll need a wrecker to get the pickup out, and perhaps a rowboat to get them out."

"Be there in five minutes, Colton. Don't move... do nothing," she said.

"Thank's Trooper Laurie," Colton said. "Oh, do you have to tell Trooper Steve about this? I would rather he didn't know, because he might try to put me in jail again," Colton said.

"He's not on duty tonight, but I have sent a message to the County Sheriff, so they may get there before me. Like I said, do nothing unless you have to save their lives," she said.

Seth sat on the edge of the canal watching the two Hampton boys, who now sat on the bottom of the pickup. "I take it Laurie is coming to save the day?"

"She's coming, but Trooper Steve isn't around tonight."

"Lucky us."

In a few minutes, there were two county patrol cars and Trooper Laurie's dark blue vehicle along the wooded road. Five officers, Seth, and Colton stood at the edge of the canal, wondering how they would get the boys off the pickup and into a patrol car.

Laurie yelled out, "Are you sure you can't swim?"

There was no response. The two just hung their heads, looking like drowned rats.

Trooper Laurie decided the tallest county deputy would walk out and lead the two boys back. The water isn't over their heads, and the boys just needed to coaxing.. It took two officers to bring them to shore, and by this time a tow truck was pulling the pickup to the edge of the canal.

"I can't lift it out; that will take a crane," yelled the truck driver.

One of the county deputies pulled two guns from the upside down pickup. He called up to Laurie, "Trooper Laurie, I have the guns. Want me to tag and bag them as evidence?"

"Yes, and put them in the front seat of my car," she said.

While the county officers took Thunder and Lightning into custody, Trooper Laurie stood next to Colton's Jeep, recording his and Seth's statements. She wasn't condescending like Trooper Steve had been and was laughing with them.

"Will we have to testify?" Colton asked. "Or will they get another plea bargain freeing them to come after us again?"

"Trust me, Colton, they are in deep trouble. Any weapon's charge is a felony, and so is attempted murder. Add drunk driving and a minor in possession, and they will be behind bars for a long time," Trooper Laurie said.

"Well, guys, you are free to get back to your route," she said. "Oh, I wanted to ask if you learned anything from those posters you plastered all over town?"

"We have leads," said Colton.

"Are the state police ready to investigate the murder?" Seth asked.

"No, not yet. I don't like you kids trying to be detectives, but I can't stop you. Just be careful, and if you need help, call me," she said.

"Thank you. It's comforting to know you would be there for us," Colton said.

Chapter 23

Now What?

Colton and Seth returned to the route. It was past four o'clock, Friday morning, and both had become tired. Between deliveries, the two discussed the investigation, the SUV at Mrs. Castle's parents' home, the Hampton boys' fiasco, and filing the police statement.

"You know, Colton, everything is getting complicated. I keep trying to figure out why they killed Rosa's uncle, and where his body is because without a body, there is no crime."

"I saw it, Seth; so there was a crime. But I agree. It's getting complicated. Perhaps we can learn something from Mrs. Torengia in St. Clair Shores. And now we will investigate Mrs. Castle's parents' house. I wonder if one of her relatives uses drugs. Perhaps she knows the second killer."

Colton was rambling. He looked over at Seth and saw that he had fallen asleep. Instead of waking him, he continued doing the deliveries himself. In the morning's silence, he studied the murder case, seeking answers.

Colton dropped Seth off and returned home. It was five o'clock, and he had time to take a quick nap. Falling asleep was not a problem; getting up at six thirty was.

"Colton, if you don't get up now, you will be late," his mom called up the stairway. "Your brother and sister are already up, so get moving."

"I'm up Mom, I'll be down in a minute." Colton made his way

to the bathroom and remembered that today was Friday. He jolted awake. This is game day at Bad Axe, with college scouts in attendance. Now rushing, he got dressed, and ran down to the kitchen.

"No time for breakfast, Mom. I'll get something at school." Colton gave his mom a quick kiss, and then said, "Oh… you know those Hampton guys, Thunder and Lightning? They tried to shoot Seth and me last night, but they ended up in the Wooded Drive canal, and the police saved them and took them to jail. Bye."

He ran… knowing his mom would be upset… but he thought, *At least I told her what happened.*

When Colton got to school, he had to run to history class to avoid being late. The second bell rang as he sat down. It was nice to see half of his classmates dressed in the team spirit t-shirt. The administration had been pushing the students to show more school spirit. Students could now even win prizes for participation in pep rallies and game attendance.

"Hey, Colton," whispered Barry Goodell, "are we going to win tonight's game?"

"Yes!" Colton answered.

"Good, I have a ten-dollar bet with my friend in Bad Axe."

"It's a safe bet."

This year, Bad Axe and Lake Huron High both were undefeated. The game tonight is important for so many reasons. Only one team will remain undefeated. There will be college scouts at the game, and it will be Bad Axe's homecoming. As Coach Talbert told his team, "No high school football team wants to lose its homecoming game; so Bad Axe will fight hard for their school's honor."

During the lunch hour, Colton went to Mrs. Castle's classroom and asked if she could talk to him during his fifth hour study class. Since she doesn't have a class that hour, she agreed and gave Colton a hall pass to come to her room. He returned to the lunchroom and sat with Seth, who had just finished eating.

"Seth, I'm talking to Mrs. Castle during fifth hour. Do you want to join me?"

"Sure do. Can we grill her about being a drug dealer?"

"No, we can't grill her. What's wrong with your head, man?"

"I'm just kidding. I know it's not her house, and her parents don't even live there now. But why her parents' house? There are too many questions without answers in this investigation, Colton."

"I know, but we have to be careful about what we say to Mrs. Castle. Let me do most of the talking, and you can take notes," Colton suggested.

"OK, Mr. Detective. I will behave."

Seth put his tray away and got his books. "Let me put these in my locker. I have to use the restroom, and then I'll see you in front of Mrs. Castle's room."

Colton told Miss Walker where he and Seth would be during the hour. Since he had a hall pass from Mrs. Castle, she excused them.

Before they left, Miss Walker asked, "I see the posters are still on the bulletin boards here at school and in town. Have you students solved this matter?"

"It's a murder, Miss Walker, and we have clues, but no evidence," said Seth.

Seth and Colton walked into Mrs. Castle's room and stood at the door. She noticed them there, and waved them in, even though she was on the telephone. When she finished, she asked, "Now what is so important that the two of you need to see me? You know, this is my free time."

"Yes, thank you for the time," said Colton. "I need you to look at these people on the poster and tell me if any of them look familiar."

Taking the poster, she said, "I've seen these posters around school, and the only person who looks somewhat familiar is the light-haired man. I don't know where I've seen him, but he looks familiar. You know how it is. He could be a former student, an old co-worker, or someone I've seen in town."

"I ask because I saw him murder the man at the beach in front of your parents' lake home. And then we saw him here." Colton opened Seth's laptop and started the video, showing the man walk into the back door of her parents' house, and walk away with a package. "We recorded this video at your parents' house on The Point last night. We don't know what the man took from the house, but we have information that the man killed is involved with drugs. Could your parents' home be a drug drop?" Colton asked.

Mrs. Castle laughed. "That's a good one. Is this a joke?"

Seth chimed in, "No, Mrs. Castle, we are serious. As serious as the Hampton boys were early this morning when they shot at us on The Point."

"They did what? I saw on television that two teenagers from Bay City that they arrested for drunk driving and assault with a weapon. Is that what you're talking about, Seth?"

"Yes, but that has nothing to do with our murder investigation, and his video does. The man on this video is a killer, and he was in your parents' house last night," said Colton.

"I do not know who he is, or what he is doing, and I think we should stop now. Be careful, Colton. You can't make accusations about your teachers. I have done nothing wrong, and besides, the police said there was no murder. Please leave. I have more important work to do than to listen to your jokes."

Mrs. Castle stood up and walked to the door. She had become upset with Colton and Seth and turned away as they walked out of her room.

As soon as the boys left, she closed her door, and walked to her desk. She picked up the phone and dialed.

"Peter, Betty here. We have a problem that concerns Mom and Dad's house. It could become serious, so we need to talk."

"What's the problem?" Peter, her brother, asked.

"Not over the phone. Can you stop over Saturday morning?"

"Yes. I can stop in after I visit Mom and Dad at the nursing home. Is there something I should tell them?"

"No, they shouldn't be told anything," she said. She put the phone down and put her face in her hands. She wasn't crying, but she was upset.

In the hallway, Colton and Seth looked at each other. They hadn't heard her conversation, but noticed that she shut and locked the door.

Seth said, "And you told me not to grill her. Man, you did a number on her."

"No, I didn't. I asked her a few questions, but now I wonder if she is hiding something. It's strange that she got upset and then kicked us out like that."

"Sure is. Hey, do you need me to bring something for tonight's party?"

"Got it covered. Is Stacey Elsworth, your exchange girlfriend, coming?" Colton asked. Seth had been dating the exchange student, who was spending the year living with his parents.

"She will be there, but she has a date. I told them they could come. I'm bringing Linda Canberry, the hot cheerleader."

"Damn, she's the woman of my dreams, Seth." Colton laughed and slapped Seth's back. "Congratulations, man. Hope it works out for both of you."

"Me too! She's nice. We dated last year a few times, but we never met up again. This could be our time. You know, I'm older now, and wiser too," Seth said, with a swagger in his voice.

The bell rang, and the two headed to their sixth hour class. During sixth hour English class with Mrs. Castle, Colton noticed she was avoiding him. She would look at him, and when he looked up, she would look the other way. This game went on the entire hour, and it made Colton feel creepy, and he did not know what she was hiding.

Only One Team Can Win

The seventh hour pep rally was fun. They honored Aden, the quarterback, for his four years on the varsity team. He couldn't have been prouder, and he told everyone that his team members were the reason for his success as a quarterback. Colton considered how much Aden had changed since he had settled down with Kathy Dorsher. The cheerleaders were in great form, performing exciting demonstrations. They worked the entire student body into a frenzy.

Imagine what homecoming week will be like, Colton thought.

The excitement of game day allowed Colton to push the murder investigation to the back of his mind for a while. He still kept thinking of the murder, but he felt relaxed. He thought to himself, *What could happen that would be worse than being shot at by the Hampton boys?* What could be worse?

Lacie and Colton walked out of the gym together. Colton promised to drive her home after school since her dad had driven her mom's car to work.

"You know, Lacie, you need a car of your own. It seems like you never get to use either of your parents' cars," Colton said.

"If I had a car, then I would have to buy gas, pay to have it fixed when it fell apart, pay for insurance, and I would have to make payments. Trust me, having you drive me is no problem."

"Agreed, I'm more than happy to drive you."

"Did your mom get food and drinks for the after game party tonight?" she asked.

"Yes, but they have to pick up pizza after the game. That will be the only food other than chips."

"Be sure to get one with cheese only; you know that is my favorite,"

Lacie said with a big grin.

Colton knew Lacie liked any kind of pizza, with or without meat and vegetables. They had planned a small party with only a few friends being invited, and tonight there would be no ESPN sports on TV, or video to edit. It would just be a time to relax and celebrate the victory over Bad Axe.

Sitting in Lacie's driveway, Colton talked about the adventure of the previous night. He had told her during art class, but she wanted more details, now that Colton seemed willing to talk about it.

"Weren't you scared?" she asked. "I know if someone shot at me, I'd be in shock."

"I didn't have time to think about it. When Thunder shot the gun, and the bullet went high into the air, I knew they were drunk. Before I could see what he hit, we jumped into the Jeep and I planned our escape."

"And they ended up in the canal. That is so funny," Lacie giggled.

"Sure was, Seth, and I sat laughing our heads off after it was all done."

"Colton, stop getting into these situations. Having one relative who is a cop is enough. I don't need a boyfriend who is a crazed detective."

"So now I'm a boyfriend?"

"Well... yes."

"Hot damn! I'll see you tonight, girlfriend," Colton said. He gave her a quick kiss and got out to open her door, but she was already out before he reached her door.

"Bye, dear," she said, walking toward the house.

Chapter 24

The Game

Neither the Bad Axe Kings nor the Lake Huron Loons has lost a game yet this year. Last year, Bad Axe was the district champion, and the Loons came in second place. The rivalry between these two schools goes back to the 1960s, when several small schools combined to form the Lake Huron Community School District. Bad Axe, the largest city in Huron County, has always been the Bad Axe Kings, but over the past forty years Lake Huron Community School has developed into a powerhouse in sports. The school has won districts and regionals in both boys and girls' sports and has been state champions many times.

This year, both football teams want to be the champions, but only one team can win tonight, and Coach Talbert intends to make sure it's his Loons who end up the winners. The Loons' coach drilled his boys relentlessly, built them into strong athletes, gave them the drive for victory, and taught them how to win with honor. Bad Axe's Coach Stevens has done the same with his team, and tonight they will face each other for the first of two times this season.

In the locker room, Coach watched his boys as they suited up. The team appeared to be in great spirits, but several of the seniors were fidgety because two major college scouts would be on the sidelines watching them play. Like an actor going on stage knowing a major critic would be in the audience, the seniors wondered if they would be up to performing their best. Could they win a scholarship and compete at the college level? Aden and Colton knew they were talented enough, but they knew tonight they must prove themselves. A football scholarship is their ticket to an excellent education, perhaps their only opportunity.

Sitting on the locker room bench, Colton tried to clear his mind of the crazy events of the past two weeks. To play good football, his mind must be on the game, not the murder case, not the evidence that seems to point in every direction. Like Coach often said, "Leave the girls, the problems, and the doubts at home. Football takes all your concentration."

Colton turned to Aden, the team quarterback and team captain, and said, "Remember, Aden, keep the ball coming my way and I will make us both look good." He pulled his jersey over his shoulder pads and stood up, adjusting himself.

"I'll try, Colton," Aden said. "God knows I'll try. Do you think we will get noticed?"

"Oh, we'll get noticed. I hope they like what they see."

"Me too. I want this so badly, Colton."

"Don't worry, just play like you always do. You're a great quarterback, Aden," Colton said. Colton wasn't under the pressure that Aden was. If he doesn't get a football scholarship, he will still get help because of his grades. As an all A student, he will be up for several big scholarships. What he wants, though, is a full ride scholarship, the kind that only goes to superior athletes. Since he is a junior, not a senior, he will have time to improve his game.

"Men," Coach called out to the players, "gather around. Let's have a moment of silence." The team members bowed their heads; some prayed, and the others were silent out of respect. "Bad Axe is looking for a victory. It's their homecoming, and you know how hard we fight for a victory when it's our homecoming. I want you to spoil their party. I want you to make them a second-place team, like they did to us last year. We are better, we are stronger, we have more talent than Bad Axe, and we will be victorious tonight. Remember what your coaches have taught you. Stay focused on the goal and don't let anyone intimidate you. Do your job like I know you can, and you will come out winners. So let's get out there and make those Bad Axe boys the most unhappy team in the county!"

The team jumped up, doing a high-five with the coach. They yelled, hooted and began the long walk out of the locker room, patting each other on the backs, eager to meet the opponent. As they neared the field, they could hear the band, the announcer, and the fans being worked into a frenzy. A team banner was at the center of the field. Coach told them to run as a team through the banner when the announcer called their names.

"And now," said the announcer, "The Lake Huron Loons!"

The fans were standing as the Loons ran onto the field and through the white banner. They lined up facing the Loons' fans and cheerleaders as each player's name was called. Once the entire team was in line, they huddled and the captains walked to the center of the field to meet with the officials. They had already decided that Bad Axe would kick off and the Loons would receive, but for the crowd, a traditional coin was tossed.

Colton and Aden were deep, and the Bad Axe kick was long. Aden caught the ball at the ten yard line and started down the field, with Colton running at his side. Aden isn't the best sprinter, but tonight he sidestepped and jumped over two players. The crowd was on its feet as he passed the fifty yard line. There were now more Kings players behind him than there were ahead of him. His skin tingled as he realized that with a little harder, and he could do it! Colton, seeing two guards closing in on Aden, threw himself in their path, and they stumbled and fell on him. It was enough to give Aden a path to the end zone and a touchdown on a ninety-yard-run.

The coach was standing with tears of joy running down his face, and the crowd became hysterical. Colton ran up to Aden and hugged him.

"Good beginning, Aden. Now let's get down to business."

During the first half of the game, there were no other touchdowns. The two teams were so well matched that it was a constant back and forth; each side made a few yards and then ran into a brick wall. Colton caught several nice, quick passes, but before he could break out, he was down. The Bad Axe defense was on him like flies on roadkill.

During halftime, Coach discussed the situation with his boys. "Aden, I know you like throwing to Colton, but you have to switch gears. Bad Axe is guarding him more than your other receivers. During the second half, I want you to throw to them. When they become convinced that you won't throw to Colton, then pass to him, and make it a longer pass. He can run through their defense and make yardage better than anyone."

The team was excited. They were leading by one touchdown, and if the defense holds Bad Axe down, like they have been, the Loons will win. Through the open locker room door, they could hear the band playing, and the announcer introduced the Bad Axe Homecoming Queen and King. Colton didn't know either, but several of the guys said she was a nice girl. Not beautiful, but with a friendly personality.

It felt like the longest half-time ever, but the call came and they headed back to the field to warm up for the second half. The team ran to the field, filled with energy and eager to win. The Bad Axe team was already on the field. They were out during much of the homecoming halftime activities. The Loons kicked off, and Bad Axe ran the ball back to the fifty yard line. The first two plays were runs around the end. No yardage was gained, and the quarterback ran a pass on the third down. It was a good pass to the wide receiver, who snuck past the Loons' defense and made a twelve yard gain. After several failed passes, and an attempt to run up the middle, the ball was back in the Loons' possession. The Loons worked the ball down the field, and on the twenty yard line, Aden decided it was time to pass to Colton again. He ran the play as if he were setting up to throw to the wide receiver on his left, but stepped back and threw to Colton. The pass was good, and Colton took off. Like in his dream last week, he sidestepped the defensive players, dodged being tackled, and made the twenty yard dash to the end zone. The Loons' fans were on their feet, and the Bad Axe fans felt defeated. Even though there was the rest of the second half to go, Bad Axe never made a point. They held the Loons to two touchdowns and blocked the extra points. The Loons, however, were victorious and remained undefeated!

Garage Party

After the game, Coach Talbert led two men in their thirties into the locker room. He asked Colton, Aden, and three other players to join them after they got dressed.

"Colton," Aden said, "those guys are the college scouts. I saw them walking on the sidelines with their laptops and cameras. Are they going to talk to us?"

"I think we'll find out in a few minutes, Aden. The way you played tonight, I know they will give you good news. Me, I'm not sure. One touchdown, but only twenty yards, not a big deal."

The team showered and dressed. Carrying their bag of gear to the bus, Colton walked over to Coach and the scouts. Aden and the other senior boys were already there, waiting for him.

"Guys, this is Albert Sweitzensine and Carl Gage. They are the college scouts I told you about. Gentlemen, they're all yours."

Albert looked across the eager faces and said, "Carl and I represent several colleges. We contract with the schools to search for and recommend athletes we feel meet their standards. We have an above average of accepted recommendations. That means that if we suggest you to the schools, you have a ninety percent chance of getting a scholarship."

Carl took a sheet of paper from his folder and handed it to Albert, who said, "Coach asked that we look at the five of you. Based on the way you played tonight, your past performance, and your current grades, we are sending the following recommendation to the colleges we represent. Gary, Steve, and Alex, we recommend they offer you a partial scholarship. Colton, we recommend that someone should watch you again next year, with a strong recommendation to offer a full scholarship. Aden, we recommend you should receive a full scholarship."

Aden almost fainted with joy. He shook the scouts' hands until they pulled them away to avoid injury. All five players celebrated, and Coach stood there with the biggest grin and a twinkle in his eye. Colton could tell that this meant a lot to Coach. He put so much effort into getting his boys ready for this event, and they made him proud.

A happy team climbed onto the bus and started back to the high school.

Chapter 25

Party Time

When the bus pulled into the school parking lot, the student bus had already dropped off its passengers. Lacie stood next to the locker room door, waiting for Colton. Colton ran up to her and gave her a huge hug.

"Guess what?" he asked, not intending to let her guess. "Aden will get a scholarship. They don't know which school, but they told him he would get a full ride."

"That's great, Colton," Lacie said. "What about you?"

"I won't know until next year, but it looks good, but if I keep going at the rate I've been, I could be in jail, or dead."

"Don't even joke about it, Colton. It's not funny! You'll just have to be more careful. No more getting shot at, promise?"

"Promise," he said, giving her a quick kiss. "I'll be back. I have to turn in some equipment and put a few things in my locker." Handing her his set of keys, he said, "I'll meet you in the Jeep."

When Colton and Lacie reached the garage, only Seth was there, alone.

"Hey, what happened to your date?" asked Colton.

Lacie said, "Linda said she would be here. She seemed excited about coming with you."

"She hurt her leg at the game. Nothing serious, but her mom wants her to keep ice on it tonight, so she can't be here."

"Sorry, pal. That's what happens when you date an athlete or cheerleader," teased Colton.

As the three organized the garage for the party, setting out cups, ice, and bottles of Coke and Mountain Dew, more cars pulled into the driveway. Before long, six couples plus Seth stood around, talking and drinking. The party was on its way.

Colton's mom and dad drove up. They walked into the garage carrying several large pizzas from the Bay Port Hotel. Mr. Blackwell yelled, "Pizza delivery for the winning football team." He handed the pizzas to Colton, who handed them to Lacie. She put them on the counter and set out paper plates.

"Thanks, Mom and Dad. I wanted to tell you, the college scouts said I should be able to get a scholarship next year."

Aden walked up with a huge smile and said, "And they told me I could get a full ride scholarship this year. I'm going to college! Isn't that awesome?"

"Sure is, Aden! With the way you played tonight, I'm surprised the Lions aren't after you. That opening run of yours was inspired," said Mr. Blackwell.

Mrs. Blackwell put her arm around Aden and said, "It almost looked like God picked you up and carried you down the field, Aden. It was wonderful."

Colton asked his mom, "Are Terry, Jason and Steph still at Aunt Sally's?"

"Yes, dear. I'll pick them up in the morning. They were at the game and had a lot of fun with their cousins. Have a wonderful party!" she yelled to the teenagers. "Come along, Adam. Let's get into the house and let these kids have fun."

Adam turned to Colton and winked. "Don't stay late, and you all know the rules."

"Thanks, Dad."

About an hour into the celebration, a car pulled up that no one recognized. Seth said they better not be from Hampton, or he's moving to another town. It was Rosa Washington from school.

Lacie ran up to the car and said, "Rosa, I'm so glad you could come tonight. Did you see the game? It was awesome!"

"Yes, Taylor and I were there. Lacie, this is Taylor. He goes to Sebewaing High School. Taylor, this is Lacie, the girl from school who helped me. She gave me the number of the County Help Center. I told you about Brenda Sampson, the woman who is helping me deal with my parents."

Lacie invited them into the garage and introduced them to the rest of the group. Around midnight, a few of the teenagers announced they had another party to go to, and they left. Rosa and Taylor were talking to Colton about Rosa's missing uncle when her phone rang. It was her father, and from the conversation, Colton could tell he was drunk and angry. Rosa became nervous and said, "OK, Daddy... I'll come home soon... I'm sorry, Daddy... No, I'm not on a date, I'm with friends... No, you can't come, Daddy, please..."

From the conversation, Colton and Lacie could tell that her father intimidated her.

"Taylor, we have to go. Lacie, thank you for everything, and Colton, I hope you find out what happened to my uncle."

The two left for their car, and when her phone rang again, she said, "Yes, Daddy, I'm on my way home now."

She turned to Lacie and said, "The sad part is, he won't even remember calling me, and Mom will be out cold already."

After they left, Seth let out a sigh. "Man, I will never get upset at my parents again. I have it so good compared to Rosa. That's got to be a hard life."

"I can't imagine, Seth," said Lacie. "You would have to live it to know it."

After everyone had left, Lacie and Colton sat in the easy chairs, talking about the future. They both agreed that they are now boyfriend and girlfriend, but that's only a step above good friends. They agreed they could tell their friends about they are in a relationship... with limits.

Mrs. Castle Confesses

Colton spent the night dreaming of football. In one dream, he was a college all-star player, being drafted by the Detroit Lions, then he attended the Rose Bowl in Pasadena while playing for The University of Michigan. It was no wonder he woke with a backache and sore knees. He thought to himself, *is it possible to injure yourself in a dream? Or is this from last night's game?* He guessed the aches were from the football game. He had several heavy guys drag him down to the ground and fall on him. It didn't hurt then, but today's another story.

He worked his way to the bathroom, where he found Magic Ice, which gets hotter than hell after it freezes your skin. *Dad swears by this stuff,* he thought. *Too bad it stinks.*

Today, I'm not doing anything except helping around the house and yard. No detective work. There will be enough of that in Detroit tomorrow, he thought while hobbling down to the kitchen where his mom was frying eggs and bacon.

"The pancakes and hash-browns are warming in the oven, and the eggs and bacon will be done in a second. Would you call everyone, Colton?" she said.

"Can I call them after I eat? That way I'll get more." Colton didn't wait for an answer. yelling up the stairs that breakfast was on. There came a thunder of footsteps clamoring down the stairs, and in seconds, the entire family was around the table.

Adam walked to the coffeepot and poured a cup. "Anyone else want a cup?" he asked. Colton decided that milk might help his bones today. Besides, he would drink a ton of coffee and cola to keep himself awake this evening.

As the family enjoyed breakfast, Colton explained what they had discovered about the murder. Terry and Steph were excited to have a brother who is now a big time detective. Jason thought the whole thing was dumb.

"You're not a cop, Colton. Cops carry guns and shoot people," he said.

"I never said I was, Jason. I want to prove that I saw the murder. The cops think I'm lying, and they're wrong."

"I don't think cops can be wrong, Colton," Jason said.

"Just be careful, Colton," said his mom. "I'm not happy with your going to Detroit tomorrow."

"It's St. Clair Shores, not Detroit," insisted Colton. "I studied it on Google, and the homes are just like the ones on The Point. Seth and I won't get into trouble, and I promise to call you when we start for home."

After breakfast, Colton helped his dad bring in vegetables from the garden, mow and rake the lawn, trim shrubs, and then the two worked on their cars. It was oil changing time, and Adam had enough oil and grease for each of their cars.

"Your Jeep needs more work now because you're doing this route," Adam said. "Are the brakes still good?"

"I think they're fine, and they seem to work when I need them."

"Well, we should check them," Adam suggested.

It took the two two hours in the garage before they completed the work. Colton's stomach growled, and he thought about lunch. His mom yelled out the back door for him, and he put his head out the garage door.

"What do you need, Mom?" he yelled.

"Mrs. Castle, your teacher is on the phone. She wants to talk to you."

"I wonder what she wants," Colton said as he rushed past his mom and grabbed the phone.

"Mrs. Castle, this is Colton. How can I help you?" he asked. It surprised Colton that his English teacher would call him at home since she didn't want to talk to him in school after he insinuated that her parents' house may be involved in drugs and a murder.

"Colton, we need to talk. I may have misled you yesterday regarding my parents' house. Could you come over to their house on the point? My brother will also be there," she said.

Colton sensed she was ready to confess. Her words carefully chosen, and she didn't act like she was under any stress. He wanted to play with Terry, but this could break the investigation wide open.

"I'll be there in fifteen minutes. I would like to bring Seth with me if you don't mind."

"That's fine. Come to the back door," she said.

Colton called Seth, and when he answered, he said, "We have to talk to Mrs. Castle at her parents' house on the Point. I'll pick you up in five minutes. Be ready. Bye." He didn't leave time for Seth to say no. "Mom, I have to run. Tell Dad I'll be back soon. Love ya."

Now running, Colton jumped in the Jeep, spun the tires on the gravel, and headed to Seth's house. Time was ticking, and he didn't want to keep the teacher waiting. Seth was ready, with a digital sound activated voice recorder in his pocket.

"Do you think she had anything to do with the murder?" Seth breathlessly asked.

"God only knows, Seth," said Colton. "I don't think she is a murderer or drug dealer, so it must be something else."

Colton and Seth pulled into the driveway of The Point home. The remote camera remained hidden in the bushes overlooking the drive, and Seth looked to make sure the camera next door was still there. Colton knocked, and Mrs. Castle's brother, Peter, opened the door. Peter Stone, a handsome man in his forties, stood over six feet tall, and had thinning blond hair.

"Come in boys, my sister is in the kitchen." The beautiful home had large windows overlooking the lake. The main floor had a kitchen, dining room, and family room. Standing at the window, Mrs. Castle said, "Would you boys like something to drink? We have coffee or soda."

Colton and Seth took the cola and walked over to Mrs. Castle.

"It's a beautiful view, isn't it, Mrs. Castle?" said Seth.

"Yes, but I prefer farm scenes. You know I grew up on a farm in Caro. My parents bought this house a little over a year ago. Let's sit at the table. We have to talk," she said.

"Our father was a farmer, and Mom was a teacher in Caro. I wanted to be a teacher like Mom, and Dad hoped my younger brother, Peter, would take over the farm when he got out of school," she said.

Peter added, "I hated farming, and told Dad I wanted to be a teacher as well. He got upset, but Mom calmed him down. Dad had people working the farm for him for many years, and then two years ago, he announced he sold the farm."

"That surprised us, but since Mom and Dad were in their late seventies, we figured they would go into an assisted living apartment. Instead, Dad took half a million dollars and bought this house for Mom. She always wanted a lake cottage, but she felt he spent too much money without asking her."

Colton and Seth sat, wondering why the two needed to tell them these details. Colton said, "May I ask where this is going?"

"I'm getting there, Colton. Please be patient," she said.

"Over the past year, Mom and Dad have been getting sick. They became ill, had to be hospitalized for a few weeks, and then they spent two months in a nursing home. We thought it was just their age, but the two had the same symptoms. Then the pattern repeated several times. They would come home and then get sick again. The last time they got sick, Dad told someone at the nursing home that perhaps his kids were poisoning them because he spent their inheritance."

"Poison? Is that why they got sick?" Colton asked.

"Yes. The nursing home notified the State of Michigan, and an investigation began. There is concern about elder abuse, and when a senior says anything about abuse, they have to investigate. Peter and I got upset because the authorities accused of hurting our parents. Even our parents knew we would never hurt them. The State, however, had to continue investigating," Mrs. Castle said.

Peter added, "Through blood tests, they found out that our parents were being poisoned. Now the investigation is getting serious, and we could be in deep trouble if we can't prove we didn't poison them. When you showed the picture of the man coming into their house to my sister, she recognized him as a delivery man, and we think he may be the one trying to poison our parents."

"Any idea how he poisoned your parents?" Seth asked.

"Yes, the drinking water," she said, pointing to the water cooler sitting next to the counter. "He delivered water every two weeks, and I think he put something in the water. The police investigators looked everywhere, but they didn't find a trace of the poison."

"How did he get the poison into the water?" asked Colton.

Peter said, "Our parents gave him a key so he could come in when they were gone. My dad is an old-fashioned countryman who trusts everyone."

"Any idea why he would want to poison your parents?"

"No," said Mrs. Castle, "that's why we want your help. We figure that as you investigate the murder you witnessed, perhaps you will come across some evidence that will help us. If they bring charges against us, both of our careers are over. No school would want a teacher being charged with attempted murder."

Colton and Seth assured Mrs. Castle and her brother that they would try to help. Colton suggested they call the state police. He gave Mrs. Castle, Trooper Laurie's personal phone number and suggested she call her.

Colton told Mrs. Castle, "Show Trooper Laurie the picture of the man you recognized. If you tell her you suspect he is entering your home to hurt your parents, she may search the state database for his identity."

"In the meantime, Seth and I will talk to Mrs. Alberto Torengia in St. Clair Shores. Perhaps she has useful information."

"Thank you, Colton. Peter and I will have the locks changed as soon as we can," Mrs. Castle said.

"No, don't do that," said Seth. "I will put another camera inside your house to see what he does. This is evidence we will give to the police when they arrest him."

On the way home, Colton asked Seth, "Do you think they told us the truth?"

"Yes, they seemed concerned. And now I understand why she got so tense when we talked to her at school."

"I agree, and I hope she calls Trooper Laurie. I would love to get the name of that guy, then we might find the other killer," Colton said.

Colton dropped Seth off and left for home. It was getting late, and he wanted to take a nap before his Sunday morning delivery. *I sure hope there aren't any more problems on The Point tonight. But then* he thought, *I have been hoping there wouldn't be any problems all along. It doesn't seem like my hopes worked out too well.*

Chapter 26

Sunday Morning

Colton jumped out of bed, ready to start the Sunday route at eleven o'clock Saturday evening. He ran downstairs to get coffee and chips for the route. His dad sat at the kitchen table waiting for him.

"Hi, Dad. Did you say you wanted to do the route tonight?"

"No, I want to have a chat. I didn't have time to congratulate you on the game last night. You made me proud. You worked so hard to make Aden and yourself look good for those scouts."

"Dad, Aden won't be able to go to college without a football scholarship, and I was glad he impressed the scouts. That run he made was awesome. I never saw him run that fast... ever!"

"You did great too, and you had several fantastic plays plus a touchdown," Adam said. "Anyway, I won't be able to go to your homecoming game next Friday. Your mom and I have to go to a special meeting at Delta College. It seems I'm getting an award for the paper I wrote. My teacher entered it into this contest, and I won first place. Your mom is so proud of me."

"Congratulations Dad. I knew you would do great in college," said Colton.

"I'll let you read it when you're not so busy," added Adam. "Are you sure about tomorrow? You know it can be dangerous in the city, and you will mess with people who may not want you snooping into their private lives."

"Dad, I promise I will be careful. I have to get going, but trust me

177

when I say there won't be anyone driving into the canal, or shooting at me, tonight."

The newspaper route was painless. Colton finished a Baldacci audiobook, and he started another one. He enjoys these murder mysteries while mentally occupied with figuring out who the killers were on The Point and who's trying to kill Mrs. Castle's parents, and why.

At six o'clock on Sunday morning, Colton drove up to the garage. Tired, he wanted to rest before driving to Detroit. Even though his mom was in the kitchen, Colton skipped talking to her and ran to his room. It was only minutes before he was in dreamland.

Colton opened his eyes and thought he saw someone standing next to his bed. Squinting to block out the sunlight streaming through the window, he could see the shape of his little brother Terry, standing with a football in his hands.

"You snore a lot, Colton," Terry said.

"No, I don't! I never hear myself snore. I bet you want to play football this morning? Well, I'm sorry, kid, but I have to get up and go over to Seth's house. We're going on a road trip to Detroit."

"A football game? Can I go too? Please. I'll be good," Terry begged.

"Not this time, but I'll be back later and we can do something fun," Colton promised.

He jumped out of bed and ran to the bathroom to clean up. It was already close to nine o'clock on Sunday morning, and he told Mrs. Torengia that they would be at her house in St. Clair Shores by one o'clock. It was a three-hour drive, so they couldn't waste any time.

Colton called Seth, and his mother said he was on his way. *That will save time*, Colton thought. *Now, a quick bite to eat, check the Jeep's oil, stop for gas, and we're ready to go.* Colton checked to make sure he had enough cash. Since his dad had refused to take any money for the last two weeks, and Colton had received his last paycheck from the dairy farm and his first delivery check from the newspaper route, he felt rich. He put over five hundred dollars into his savings, and he still had more than a hundred dollars in his wallet.

Seth's Dodge Charger pulled into the driveway as Colton finished checking his Jeep.

"All ready to go, Seth. Did you bring more spy tools?" Colton asked.

"Yes, another camera with a super sensitive microphone, and I brought my video camera, in case we see something we want to record... like another murder," Seth said.

"Don't even talk like that. One murder was enough to last a lifetime. But it's a good idea to have the camera. Hop in and let's get on the road."

Seth threw his gear in the back seat and jumped into the passenger seat. "I brought the GPS from home. My car has one built in, but I thought we could use this in the big city."

"OK, the address is in my notebook. You can set the GPS up, but I want to drive down M-53. So, make sure you plan to take that route. I hate those things when they want you to go another way, and the creepy voice keeps telling you to turn around and take the next exit; you are going the wrong way."

"Yeah, the GPS lady can be dumb," Seth said.

After stopping for gas at the Village Qwik Stop, the two were on their way. Colton felt good about the trip because it would give him and his best friend time to talk about football, girls, and murder suspects. The two talked non stop through Marlette, Imlay City, and Romeo. They only had to make one pit stop at a party store before reaching the Van Dyke Freeway, near Romeo. The GPS did great. She only got upset once when Colton made the pit stop. He could swear she scolded him for taking her out of the way.

Both Colton and Seth had been in the Detroit area many times with their dads, going to baseball, football, and basketball games.

Neither of them had been to the St. Clair Shores area. The GPS had them drive M-53 to Fifteen Mile Road, to Utica Road, to Masonic Boulevard across to Veterans Memorial Park on Jefferson Avenue. The lakeside area was beautiful, with huge homes on large waterfront properties.

"You're right, Colton. These houses look just like the homes on The Point. No wonder so many people from here like moving up to the Thumb," Seth said.

"The house we're looking for is a little south of the park. It'll be on the left side. There it is. Wow! Look at that. It's huge and even has a swimming pool."

Colton turned into the driveway, past the pool, two tennis courts, a guest house and enormous parking area, next to a massive garage.

"She said to come in the back door on the north side. That's the door," Colton said as he turned the Jeep off and took out the keys. "Now, do you have the camera and recorder hidden in your pocket?"

"Sure do, and the recorder is running," Seth said. "Let's go see what the old lady knows."

Before they could ring the doorbell, an elderly woman with long black hair pushed the door open and yelled, "You the boys from up north?"

"Yes. I'm Colton and this is Seth."

"Come on, damn it, get in here. I don't have all day for this fool-ishness."

The boys walked into the large house, and Mrs. Torengia asked them to sit down. There was a large table in the entryway, with several wooden chairs around it. Colton sat down and took the poster of the three men out of his notebook.

"These are the men I saw at your home on The Point, Mrs. Torengia. Do you know any of them?" he asked.

"Let me see." She grabbed the pictures and strained to see them.

Reaching for her glasses, she put them on. "Don't know them. Nope, never saw them in my life. Well, if that's it, you can leave now." She snapped.

"But don't you want to know what they were doing?" asked Seth.

"Nope, I don't care. The house is insured, and if they did something to it, I would just get a little more money. I don't care, boys. So, bye now." She seemed to be in a hurry to get them out of the house. Pushing them to the door, she opened it and said, "Be careful, now. I wouldn't want you getting yourself hurt trying to find those two men," she said.

As Colton and Seth walked out, Seth took the camera from his pocket and stopped by the sidewalk. He pretended to tie his shoes as he placed the camera in a flower bed. He pointed the camera and the sensitive microphone at the doorway.

"Well, that should catch anyone coming and going," he said to Colton.

Climbing into the Jeep, Colton said, "I can't believe how eager she was to get rid of us. And she hardly looked at the picture."

"And what's this about finding those two men? There were three men on the poster," added Seth.

"I think something is fishy in St. Clair Shores, Seth," Colton said as he started the Jeep and turned around toward the highway. When they got to the end of the driveway, Colton turned right, toward Veterans Memorial Park. He drove into the parking lot and stopped the Jeep.

"Let's have a candy bar and Coke while we watch the video of her doorway.

"Do you think anything will happen?" asked Seth.

"I hope so. Otherwise, we drove a long distance for nothing."

The words had barely left Colton's mouth, and the video started. The two killers walked out the doorway with a large duffel bag, and the olive-skinned man turned around and yelled. "Thanks, Grandma, for covering for us. I owe you one, but at least those creeps won't be back again to pester you."

From inside they could hear, "That's OK, just keep working hard on the business, Joey. Make your dead grandpa and me proud."

"Come on, Donny, let's get going. We've got business to take care of, and they don't enjoy waiting for their money."

Joey opened the garage door, and they jumped into the black Lincoln MKX. Colton started the Jeep and drove out to the Jefferson entrance of the park. He watched as the SUV left Mrs. Torengia's driveway.

"I'll try to follow them, like they do in the movies, but I hope they don't spot us," he said.

"Spot us in a bright yellow Jeep? How could they spot us?" Seth said, half joking.

Colton knew the Jeep could be a little conspicuous, especially in the city, but he felt comfortable driving it, and knew how it handled in emergency situations. "We'll pretend like we're not yellow, and perhaps they won't notice either," Colton said.

The Lincoln drove south on Jefferson Avenue, and Colton tried to keep several cars behind. He would let them drive further ahead as Seth watched to see if they turned unexpectedly. At Eight Mile Rd. and Jefferson, the Lincoln exited onto Eight Mile. Colton was not familiar with this part of Metro Detroit and needed to rely on the GPS for some idea of where they were. He could see Eastland Mall on his left, expecting perhaps that the Lincoln would stop there. It didn't. For another several miles they continued on Eight Mile Road.

Chapter 27

No Exit From Hell

A s they continued on Eight Mile Road, Seth asked, "Colton, do you think we could meet the rapper Eminem today? He is from this area, isn't he?"

"No, he was from this area. I'm sure he has moved to a better neighborhood. Can you believe how many buildings are empty? They talk on the news about how bad it is in Detroit, but this is worse than anyone said."

The Lincoln stopped at a red light at the Van Dyke Road: M-53, but it didn't turn. They continued on Eight Mile Road, another two miles. Colton felt uncomfortable. He didn't think the Jeep had been spotted following the Lincoln, but there was no way to know for sure.

"Perhaps Joey and Donny will lead us into a trap, Seth. They would know what we were driving because they would have seen my Jeep in their driveway when they stopped in St. Clair Shores."

"Great time to think of that, Colton. They turned into that alley. Go around the block; let's see where they went," said Seth.

Colton drove beyond where the Lincoln had turned. It was an abandoned medical office, covered with gang tags and drawings. At the next corner, about a half block away, stood an old auto repair building. Colton turned, and when they came up to the alley on his left, he could see the Lincoln parked behind the abandoned office building. Another car, a white Cadillac Escalade, parked next to the

Lincoln. Two black men and a white man gathered in the parking lot next to a huge trash dumpster overflowing with garbage. Next to the alley was a row of pine trees and a steel fence with abandoned buildings on the other side. Colton parked in a spot at the end of the alley where he thought he would be out of their view.

As Joey and Donny got out of the Lincoln, they walked toward the other three men, carrying a duffel bag.

Colton whispered, "I wish we could hear them."

"We can. Here, put these headphones on and point this toward them. It amplifies their voices." Seth gave Colton a pair and put a pair on himself.

"Wow, it works," said Colton as he listened in on the conversation.

"So, you got all the money?" said the largest black man. He appeared to be the leader.

"Yes, even the money they stole for us up north," said Joey.

"And you have the stuff? I trust it's the same quality as what we've been getting, so I won't ask for a look," Joey said, setting the duffel bag on the pavement, next to a cardboard box.

"So, Joey, what did you do with that dealer up north after he stole our money? I hope you didn't make too much of a mess. We don't need publicity, you know."

"I took care of it. He's at the bottom of the big lake with all the fish. We have kids poking around looking for us. Somehow one of them saw us do the dealer on the beach," Joey said.

Seth kept the camera on and continued to film the conversation while recording their voices for evidence.

"Hey, did you see that reflection?" the black man said, pointing toward the Jeep. "What was that?"

The group looked around for the source of the reflection. Colton could feel their gaze reaching the end of the alley when Donny yelled. "Hey, it's those kids. What the hell, they followed us!"

Donny took a gun out of his holster and shot at the Jeep. It bounced off the bumper, and Colton jumped. The Jeep was still running, so he turned his head to back out of the alley, but there was now a truck parked behind him and he couldn't move backwards.

"What can we do?" Seth yelled.

"The only thing we can," Colton said as he put the Jeep in drive and hit the accelerator. The Jeep jumped forward and raced down the alley toward the drug dealers. Seth ducked under the dash, holding his head in his hands. There were three shots at the Jeep; one blew a hole in the side mirror, and the others grazed the fenders, but did no damage. As Colton raced toward the men, they scattered to the side. To miss the parked vehicles, he had to drive around them and over the duffel bag and box in the center of the alley. There was a bumping, crashing sound, and white powder flew into the air.

"Oh, crap," he yelled. "We drove over their drugs. That's gonna make someone pissed."

Colton looked to his left, and two black men had their guns pointed at him. He heard the shot, saw the fire coming out of the gun barrel and felt the bullet pass the back of his head, as it went through Seth's open window. Colton didn't hear the angry swear words the two men uttered. Everything was like a slow motion film, passing frame by frame, until he realized he would crash onto Eight Mile Road.

The Jeep jumped the curb and flew onto the road. Cars hit their brakes to avoid a collision with the Jeep, and Colton turned right on Eight Mile Road. He weaved in and out of traffic and drove as fast as he could. The drug dealers argued and tried to pick up the pieces of their drug deal. The pieces that Colton and Seth had just destroyed.

Under The Influence

Colton watched the rear-view mirror, and he listened for gunshots. Every few minutes he asked, "Are they still behind us?"

"No! How many times do I have to tell you, I don't see them coming! Let's get out of here," Seth said. "I thought we were goners back there. Damn it, we got shot at two times in one week. I don't think I should play with you anymore, Colton, because you're bad for my health."

"Thanks, pal. You are aware I have the whole thing recorded. You're just chicken… afraid of a little action."

"Me? You should have seen how white your face got. You looked like you would mess your jeans, but I was the cool one under fire," Seth insisted.

"Under fire? You spent the whole time under the dash." Colton turned onto Van Dyke and headed north.

"Can you believe this is the same road that drives through Bad Axe and ends up in Port Austin? It sure starts out in hell, doesn't it?"

"Yes, but it ends up in paradise," Seth said. "And don't change the subject. I think we were both scared."

"I agree, and I hope we don't get stoned driving around with all of this white powder in the Jeep. What do you think it is?" Colton asked.

"Well, I bet it's not flour, baking soda, or sugar. You want to snort some of it?"

"No! Do you think it's cocaine? I wonder how much we destroyed? That sure was funny, though, wasn't it? That dope flew into the air when we hit it with the Jeep. Sky high dope." Colton laughed so hard his eyes welled up with tears. Seth was also laughing. To keep from getting into an accident, Colton drove into a McDonald's and parked.

"You want a burger with your dope?" Colton said while laughing. He felt high, and he didn't enjoy being out of control; it was a strange sensation. One he had never felt before… not even with alcohol.

"Seth, do I appear stoned?" he asked.

"No, but you look all wavy and fuzzy. See if you can adjust your picture because it's out of focus."

It took over an hour before the two were close to normal. The steady rain that started while they were sitting in the McDonald's lot helped to wash the drugs off the Jeep. Seth used a cloth and wiped down the interior.

"We have to get back home, Seth," Colton said. "Did you still want a burger or not?"

"Not here; we better get going before the cops see the white stuff on the parking lot, or the dealers drive by and find us. I won't feel safe until we're home."

Colton pulled out of the parking lot and returned to Van Dyke. The traffic was still heavy, but there was no sign of Joey and Donny. Colton and Seth discussed what they should do with their additional evidence.

"If we go to the police now, perhaps they will believe us and help find the killers," Seth said.

"But if they didn't believe us, then we might get into trouble for spying on people," Colton added.

"Is it against the law to spy on drug dealers?" asked Seth.

To Trooper Steve, anything teenage boys do is against the law.

"Then you should call Trooper Laurie. She's more reasonable, and she said she would help, didn't she?" Seth said.

Colton considered Seth's reasoning. Laurie knows they are investigating the murder, and she offered to help. He turned to Seth and said, "You're right. We need to talk to Trooper Laurie. If anyone will help, she will. We're not equipped to handle drug dealers on our own."

The drive back to Pigeon was uneventful. Colton noticed every black SUV, and if he missed one, Seth pointed it out. They were on edge and eager to get home, but the question remained: how safe would home be with drug dealers angry at them for destroying their drug deal? *Only time will tell*, Colton thought.

The Jeep pulled into the Blackwell driveway around eight o'clock and parked next to Seth's Charger. Colton checked to make sure no strange black or white SUVs followed them.

"Well, when will we call Trooper Laurie?" Seth asked.

"I don't know. Do you think we should call now, or should we wait until after school tomorrow?"

"Colton, you're the detective, and I'm just an assistant. It's your decision, sir," Seth said.

"If I call her now, we won't finish until late tonight, and I don't know about you, but I'm tired. Almost getting killed, does that… it wears a person out."

"What about calling her in the morning?" Seth asked.

"If she comes to school, we will get in trouble again for using school time for our personal investigation. I'll call her in the morning, and we can meet her in the garage after football practice. Is that OK with you?"

"Hey, whatever you want. I'll talk to you at school. Don't forget to lock your doors. I'm not sure we can trust those killers to stay in Detroit."

Before Seth left for home, they went into the garage to make copies of the recordings they made of Mrs. Torengia's house and the drug dealers on Eight Mile. Colton also checked his Jeep to see if there was any white power left. He found traces of drugs on the back seat and put them into an envelope.

"You did a fantastic job cleaning the Jeep, Seth. The rain washed the dope off the outside, but how am I going to explain the hole in the mirror?" he asked, pointing to the hole that passed through his side mirror.

"Tell your dad it was from a deer's horns. With all the deer on The Point, he'll believe you."

"Dad will never believe a deer poked its horn through my mirror without hitting the Jeep." Getting serious, Colton put his hand on Seth's shoulder and said, "Seth, thank you for helping me. You make a great assistant detective, and if we ever start a business, I would be proud to have you as my partner."

The two did a high five and Seth walked to his car. "Remember to call Laurie in the morning. I'll sleep better when I know those hoods are in jail." With that, he shut his car door and left.

Colton closed up the garage and walked to the back door of the house. He could knew his brothers and sisters were already in bed because the house was silent. Hearing his mom and dad's voices in the living room, Colton walked in and sat on the couch.

His mom asked if he wanted something to eat, and he told her they had stopped for burgers in Imlay City.

"Well, what happened in Detroit?" his dad asked. "You look down. I take it you found no evidence to support your story?"

"Oh, I wouldn't say that. We know the killers' names, and we recorded them talking about how they killed Bobby Washington. They insinuated they dumped his body in the lake."

"Wow!" his mom said. "What will you do now?"

"I'm calling Trooper Laurie in the morning. We can't handle drug dealers by ourselves. It would be too dangerous, and we're trying to avoid anymore danger."

Colton didn't tell his parents about the shooting. Instead, he excused himself and went to bed. His parents knew something else had happened, but thcy didn't press the issue.

Chapter 28

A Date With Laurie

Five muscular black men walked up to Colton and placed a handgun in his open hand. "White boy, if you want to be a member, you must kill someone close to you. Each of us had to prove our loyalty. That's what it's about. Gang loyalty. Having brothers and sisters who care about you. Who'll have your back when you're in too deep? Brothers will protect you from the system."

"But I already have that. My family does all of those things for me."

"That's why you have to kill one of them."

"No, I don't want to be a member of your stupid gang. I never wanted to be a member."

"Too late, white boy, you are a member already. You took our drugs, so now you're ours. So which one will you waste? The little boy, little sis, or your other brother?"

"Kill me. I would rather die than hurt my family."

Colton woke with chills. His window was open, but it wasn't the cool breeze making him shiver. He felt chills because he sensed danger. This isn't over. This isn't over, he said to himself.

The clock showed five o'clock on Monday morning, and Colton couldn't go back to sleep. He researched on the internet and found that gangs are not a problem in Huron County as far as Colton knew. And he knew little about gangs. He searched the Internet for gang graffiti and recognized symbols he saw on the buildings near where the drug deal went bad. Colton couldn't decipher which gangs were in Detroit, but he was sure he wanted nothing to do with them. He recognized a few of the gang names he found: Micky Cobra's, Crips, Black Family Mafia, Latin Kings, Vice Lords, and Devil's Disciples.

At breakfast, Colton discussed his planned talk with the police. He said they had evidence to give Trooper Laurie and needed the police to help solve the case.

"We can't do it by ourselves. Somehow, we have to convince the police to look into our evidence and help us catch the killers," Colton explained.

It pleased Colton's parents to hear he and Seth were not continuing the investigation on their own.

"Thank God, Colton. This investigation mess has been making me sick. So much has happened this past week, and I keep thinking you will get hurt. Thank God," Colton's mom said as she picked up the breakfast dishes. "Now, about Friday, can you watch Terry during the homecoming game? You realize we will be in Bay City, and Jason and Steph want to go with my sister, Alice, and her kids, but Terry doesn't want to go with them."

"Colton, you promised you would take me to the game with you. Please, can I go with you to the game?"

"Sure, but after the game you need to go to bed when I tell you," said Colton.

"What time will you and Dad be back?"

"Around nine o'clock. So when we get home, you can go with your friends to the homecoming dance."

Colton turned to Terry, who awaited his answer. "Yes, Terry, it's a date for the homecoming game."

Terry yelled, "Yippee" and jumped into Colton's arms. "You're the greatest brother ever."

"Kiss up," said Jason.

Colton gave Jason his what's the problem glare and then said it was time to get to school. Everyone laughed because Colton was a half hour early. Colton smiled and said, "Got things to do at school this morning. Bye."

Before starting the Jeep, Colton dialed Trooper Laurie's number.

"Yes, it's Colton, Trooper Laurie. Can you meet Seth and me after school today at my place? We discovered evidence we need to give you. We found out who the killers are, and we discovered who the dead man was. It is drug related, and they shot at us yesterday afternoon in Detroit. The shooters included the two men I saw committing murder on The Point."

Laurie scolded Colton for going to Detroit looking for killers. "God knows there are plenty of them down there, but you need to be more careful," she said. "I imagine you will be at football practice, so is six o'clock all right?"

"That will be great. If you want to do some checking before the meeting, I'll give you the information we gathered," Colton said.

"OK. What evidence did you find?"

"The dead man's name is Bobby Washington, and he is from Sebewaing. One killer, Joey, is a relative of Mrs. Alberto Torengia of St. Clair Shores. He is in his thirties, dark complexion and drives a Lincoln MKX with the license number RUE-735K. The other killer, Donny, is a friend of his. He has been in the home of Mr. and Mrs. Alexander Stone, the parents of Mrs. Castle, the Lake Huron Community High School English teacher. We think Donny has been trying to kill her parents, but we have no idea why."

Trooper Laurie clarified a few details and said she would investigate as soon as she could. "I will tell my sergeant, but he might want Trooper Steve on the case. Is that acceptable to you?"

"No, but if he has to be on the case, just tell him to play nice," Colton said.

The Bad Calls Begin

Colton ended his call with Trooper Laurie and called Seth to let him know what she said. They talked during lunch and study period. Seth said he felt better knowing the police would help them. He wouldn't admit it, but Colton knew the close call on Eight Mile scared the crap out of him. Unfortunately, Colton still had a nagging feeling that something else was about to happen. His cell phone rang, but since he didn't recognize the number, he let it go to voicemail and headed to school.

Lacie stood next to Colton's locker, waiting for him to arrive. She became concerned because he never called to let her know how the trip to Detroit went. When things go well, Colton is eager to share the news. She feared this was not one of those moments.

"So what happened?" she asked.

"We saw the killers, and they are badasses. I want you to know I called the state police, and Trooper Laurie agreed to help us. I gave her the information, and from now on, it's her investigation. Lacie, we're dealing with nasty drug dealers, and they may even be part of a Detroit gang. They aren't the people we should mess with."

"That sounds like a smart decision. You can tell me the details in art class. I went with Kathy to Bay City and helped her pick out a formal for homecoming. She got a beautiful off-white, strapless flowing gown. I told her it reminds me of a dress a princess would wear. It's so pretty."

"How exciting," said Colton. "Do all the girls have to buy new dresses?"

"They do, and that's what makes homecoming so much fun. I even bought a new dress for the homecoming dance. Did you order my tux and my corsage?" she asked, knowing Colton didn't.

"Was I supposed to?" he asked.

"It would have been nice, but you can get away with wearing your nice black suit. You need to order the flowers now. Please order something in dark blue and soft white, and tell the florist you will pick it up Friday afternoon after school. You can keep them in a cooler with ice in the Jeep until the dance. I suggest taking your suit with you and changing in the locker room. The dance will start right after the game."

"I have to take my brother, Terry, to my aunt's home after the game."

"We will be late then?" She thought for a moment and then said, "No problem. I'll go with you when you take Terry back. We will have a grand entrance. Sometimes it's better to be late; it's more sophisticated."

"Damn! So many plans, and so much to do, and we even have to be sophisticated."

The first bell rang, and Colton gave Lacie a hug as they left for their first hour class. By the time art class came, Colton had received several phone messages from the same unknown number. He knew he should check the messages, but something told him it wasn't a message he wanted to hear, and besides, school rules said no cell phones.

Colton and Lacie sat together during art class, working on their watercolors. Colton told Lacie everything that had happened in Detroit, including the bullet that almost hit his head.

Dropping her brush on her artwork, Lacie said, "God, Colton, now I know why you want the police to help." Hearing his story upset her, but she didn't want to make a scene. "Did you tell your parents?"

"Some, but I didn't tell them everything that happened. I'm sure they know more happened than what I told them, but they don't know the details. If possible, I hope they never know. I don't want them to get upset."

"You're just afraid to tell them. Remember, it's best to be honest."

"We'll see."

Colton felt his phone ringing again. It was on vibrate. He pulled it from his pocket and noticed the same unknown number.

"I have been getting calls from someone I don't know."

"Why didn't you answer it? It could be important," Lacie said.

"I think it's from Detroit. You know... the bad guys," said Colton.

"OK, but how do you know if you don't answer it?"

"By the area code, and by my gut feeling. I've felt all day that something bad will happen."

"Since when do you have intuition? Check the voicemail and get it over with. It might be a stupid advertisement."

"Lacie, I can't. This is art class. Mr. Swansear is nice, but he won't be nice if he sees me using my phone again. He got upset last week when I left the room to take a call."

"Fine, coward! Wait until lunch. But check those messages; I suggest doing it sooner," Lacie said as she dabbed on her watercolor, trying to fix the blob she made when she dropped her paintbrush.

I Think They Are Angry

Colton sat with Seth during lunch, and together they listened to the voicemail messages. The first message received was, "Kid, we want our money back, now! If you don't get it to us, you're dead."

"That sounded like Joey, the drug dealing killer. I wonder what money he wants," said Seth.

"Here's the second message."

"I know you're getting these messages, chickenshit. Call me now."

"How many messages are there?" asked Seth.

"Five more," said Colton.

They listened to each message, which grew more angry and nasty. In the last message, Joey used every four letter word that Colton and Seth had ever heard, and a few new ones. If he were to be believed, Joey would make them suffer by removing vital parts of their body; and then, he would kill them if his money isn't returned.

"Well, we know he wants his money, but I don't know why he thinks we have it," said Colton.

"Could it be that the other group stole the money and blamed us?" asked Seth.

As they were talking, Colton's phone rang. He checked the incoming number and said, "Yes, it's him again."

"Well, tell the bastard we don't have his rotten money, and get him off our backs," said Seth.

"Hello, Joey. We don't have your money," Colton said.

"Bastard liar, you took it yesterday, and we saw you. I want that money back now, or you will be dead. I'm giving you effing turds twenty-four hours to bring it back to us. If you don't, I will kill you, then Donny will kill you, and then the Black Family Mafia will kill you. Get the idea, kid, and you will be dead!"

Joey hung up before Colton could tell him again that he didn't know where the money was. He looked at Seth and said, "I think he's mad at us."

"You think so? What makes you say that?" Seth said.

"I sure hope Trooper Laurie knows what we should do. I would rather not talk to Joey again. He sends chills down my spine. Just knowing he killed Bobby makes my stomach turn," said Colton.

"At least we have twenty-four hours. Joey must be talking about the money from the drug deal we messed up. I bet those gang members took the money when we drove over it, and now they want Joey to think we did it. They might have told Joey they saw us scoop it up as we drove by," suggested Seth.

"Sounds logical, Seth, but we still have to deal with Joey, and that isn't a good prospect," said Colton.

After hearing the first bell for the fifth hour, Colton and Seth found their seats in the multipurpose study room. Lacie and Jerry sat at the table to talk about the investigation. Miss Walker came by and told them they should do homework and not talk. When she walked away, the four continued their conversation.

"Man, Lacie told us you're being hunted down by drug dealers. That's a real bummer, Colton," said Jerry. "You figure out who they are?"

"Yes. Their names are Joey and Donny from St. Clair Shores. We don't know their last names, but they work with a group known as the Black Family Mafia. I read about them on the internet, and I only know that they have big handguns and know how to use them," said Colton.

"What does it feel like to have someone shoot at you, man?"

"Not good. Not good at all. When I saw those guys point their guns at me and pull the trigger, I thought I was dead. Trust me, Jerry, it's not a good feeling," Colton said.

Miss Walker came over to the table, and everyone tried to look busy. It didn't work, and she again told them to do homework and avoid detective work during school hours.

"Colton, the principal does not want you and your friends to continue playing detective. He told us to keep you on track with your schoolwork. Please help, and at least look busy. This is my first year teaching, and I can't afford any trouble," she said.

"I'm sorry, Miss Walker. Since we found the killers yesterday, the investigation is being completed by the police, and now we have to give them the evidence. We'll stop talking and do our homework," said Colton.

Everyone else agreed with him. Jerry and Lacie moved back to their table, and Seth took out his books and worked. Colton had no homework to do, so he asked if he could listen to his audiobook. Listening to another murder was just what he needed to relax.

Chapter 29

Football And Trooper Laurie

Monday begins the craziness of homecoming week. The students will decorate the halls in a special theme, and are expected to dress following a special theme for the day. Tuesday will be *Yesterday*; Wednesday: *At The Movies*; Thursday: *Casual Thursday*; and Friday: *Spirit Day*. Colton wasn't sure what to wear for each of these days, but he planned to wear his pirate outfit for Yesterday, and on Spirit Day a spirit t-shirt. Voting for homecoming queen takes place during Friday's lunch hour. The student will learn who the king and queen are during Friday's assembly.

Each class is building a float for the parade, but Colton isn't help-ing his class this year. Lacie spent several hours working on the class float over the weekend, and she told him it was a paper dragon eating the Bay City Cougars. She laughed when she told Colton because she thought it looked like a large lizard instead of a dragon.

When Colton reached Mrs. Castle's English class, he wanted to talk to her, but felt she should broach the subject. He grew tired of get-ting into trouble for putting his investigative nose into other people's business. To his surprise, she assigned individual reading time for the hour, and asked Colton to come to her desk to talk.

In a soft voice, Mrs. Castle said, "I've been talking to Trooper Laurie, and she has evidence to support that my brother and I had nothing to do with poisoning our parents. Colton, she said you and Seth could have been killed in Detroit trying to get the evidence to help me. I don't know how I can thank you."

"We did not only it for you, Mrs. Castle. I need to prove that I saw a murder, and we want to find out what happened to Rosa Washington's uncle."

"I understand and appreciate your efforts in helping me get through this hard experience. I know elder abuse is a real problem, but when you are accused of it, it hurts. My parents never thought we were involved, but the system requires an investigation, no matter who gets hurt."

"Seth and I will meet with Trooper Laurie after football practice today, and I hope we can finish our investigation. I am tired of being shot at... beat up... and I am just worn out. I want to enjoy homecoming without worrying that someone will kill us."

"Well, good luck, Colton. I was glad to hear the college scouts recommended scholarships for you, Aden, and the other players," Mrs. Castle said.

Colton returned to his desk as the entire class kept their eyes on him, wondering what the secret conversation was about. There were a few whispers and questions, but Colton brushed them off. It would be difficult to explain it to everyone.

Hoping for some stress relief, Colton looked forward to gym class. Coach Talbert asked him about the murder mystery, hoping that he could finish the foolishness. When Colton told him it was now in the police's hands, Coach was ecstatic and told him he needed to get his mind on the game. "Remember, we're facing Bay City, and they will be out for blood. They haven't lost a game yet this year, and after facing us, they will take on the Hampton Colts."

The coach gave Colton and several other players a list of weight routines to do for the rest of the week. He walked to the door and said, "Keep up the good work, guys, and I'll see you at practice," he said.

Football practice flew by. At the top of his game, Aden spent most of his time working with the receivers on passes. Both Colton and the other receivers were spot on, and the assistant coach beamed with pride when he congratulated them on a great practice.

"Tomorrow, I want to do handoffs because need to hone our skills to beat the Bay City Cougars," he said. "Now, hit the showers and get home. Remember, get lots of sleep and eat well. I want you in good condition for Friday."

Trooper To The Rescue

When Colton pulled into the driveway of his home, he could see that Seth and Trooper Laurie were already there. He walked to the garage and, to his relief, he didn't see Trooper Steve.

"Hello, Colton. Seth told me about the trip to Eight Mile. It sounds like it was dangerous. Do you see why I worried about you two?" she said.

"Yes, we called to tell you the investigation is all yours. Just catch them and make Joey stop calling me," Colton said.

"What do you mean, calling you?"

"Just that. Somehow he got my number, and he says he will kill us if we don't give him back the money."

"Money?"

"We do not have their money, but he thinks we took the drug deal money when we drove over their box of drugs. We think the money was in the duffel bag we ran over. He expects the money in twenty-four hours… well… less than that now… about 19 hours," Colton said, looking at his watch.

Seth added, "If we knew how much they wanted, perhaps my dad could help. I mean, if it came down to having me dead or alive, I would hope he would pay them."

"No one will give Joey Torengia or Donny Anderwood any money. We have their full names now, and with the evidence you gave me, I can go to the district attorney and seek a warrant for their arrest."

Trooper, Laurie said.

"Great. Is it OK that we used a camera on their personal property?" Seth asked.

"No, we can't use that video. But the camera at the drug deal and the audio recording are OK. They were in a public place, so you didn't intrude on their privacy, unless a judge says otherwise."

"Can you use the threats they made on my life against them?" Colton asked.

"Yes. I can download them from your voicemail. Do you have a computer?"

Colton pulled out his laptop and checked to make sure he could get a Wi-Fi signal. "Here you go. I accessed my voicemail and downloaded it to this file. Seth, let me see that USB memory stick, and I'll add it to the evidence you already recorded on it."

"Since Joey and Donny already know it's you who turned them in, I would be very careful about going anywhere. I'm not sure what they will do about the money they think you stole, so if you can, get someone else to do your route tonight," Trooper Laurie said.

"I can't, and I have to do the route again on Thursday and Friday morning. Can you catch them before then?"

"I don't think so, Colton. There won't be a warrant for their arrest until later tomorrow, and then it will take time to catch them," she said. "I guess you will just have to be careful. I'll let the sheriff know what's happening. County Deputy Ned Wooddell has been assisting me on this case. The sheriff has a drug unit that's interested in closing down the flow of drugs into this area, and they think Joey and Donny are the kingpins of the organization."

"I hope they can do that soon. I hate having two Detroit killers and an entire gang out to get the two of us," said Colton.

"That goes for me, too," added Seth.

Trooper Laurie gathered the evidence, including the sample of powder Colton collected from the Jeep, and started for her patrol car.

"I'll call you when I have information about the arrest of these guys. In the meantime, be careful."

As she drove off, Seth said, "Do you want me to come with you tonight? Like you said the other day, two sets of eyes are better than one."

"No, but thanks. Joey gave us twenty-four hours, and that won't be until tomorrow. I don't think he'll try anything tonight. But I might want help Thursday and Friday when he discovers we don't have the money."

"I'm going home then. I've got some explaining to do. Dad got the bill for the spy equipment, and he's a little upset. Not about the money, but because I didn't ask him for help." Seth closed his car door and turned around. He opened the window and said. "Good luck tonight and be careful."

Someone Is Following Me

Before Colton could get in the house to see about dinner, Terry was at the back door with his football. Colton ran up to him, picked him up, and ran to the backyard. Terry screamed with delight, and the two played catch for half an hour.

"Dinner's ready," Mrs. Blackwell yelled out the back door.

"Let's eat, little guy," Colton said. "You're getting good at throwing that ball, Terry. Next year I'm sure you will be the starting quarterback of the pewee team, and who knows, you could end up being the Loons' quarterback when you're in high school."

Terry loved Colton and the way he praised him. "Will you carry me back to the house? That was fun, Colton."

"No, you're getting too big, and my arms hurt. But I'll race you."

Colton let Terry win, and he acted like he was out of breath when they got into the kitchen. Steph and Jason were eating while their mom prepared two more plates of meatloaf, mashed potatoes, and garden fresh green beans. "Don't forget to wash your hands; they're filthy," she said.

After dinner, Colton called Lacie to discuss the homecoming and to tell her what Trooper Laurie said. It pleased Lacie that Colton was letting the police handle the rest of the investigation.

"Perhaps you can get back to normal now. The last two weeks have been an actual nightmare, Colton," she said.

"Yes, they have. I'll be glad when those murderers are behind bars, but Laurie says it will take several days, so we still have to be careful."

"You do that, and we can talk in art class tomorrow. I love you, Colton."

"I love you too, Lacie. Bye."

Colton slept well and was ready to start Tuesday morning's route at two o'clock. He worried about being on the road alone. With two killers on the loose, anything could happen. He had given Seth, Lacie, and Trooper Laurie his *I'll be OK mantra*, but he felt afraid.

To his pleasant surprise, no killers jumped out of the woods. He noticed more police cars around than normal. There were several county patrol cars, the Pigeon police and an officer from the Village of Caseville kept passing him as he did the route. It's not unusual to see police officers at night, but seeing so many was odd. Knowing the police were there made Colton feel secure.

He completed his last delivery at five o'clock on Tuesday morning, and he was fast asleep by five fifteen. He didn't have a dream, at least he didn't remember dreaming. When the alarm woke him at six-thirty, he felt rested and eager to get to school. After taking his shower, he remembered that this was the day he had to dress in a Yesterday outfit. He planned to wear his pirate pants and the eye-patch, but decided that he would wear the jeans and t-shirt he wore yesterday. That would be close enough.

Colton couldn't believe the strange costumes the students had worn. Lacie wore a Victorian lace dress. She looked like she could have been English royalty. Seth was a dandy from the 1800s, complete with an old brown suit, cowboy shoes, and a black derby hat.

"So, Seth, what are you?" asked Colton.

"I'm a Pinkerton detective. Isn't that neat?" he said. "What are you supposed to be?"

Lacie said, "Yes, Colton, and what are you supposed to be?"

"I was told to dress in clothing that represents yesterday, so I'm wearing the clothes I wore yesterday. Neat, huh?"

Lacie laughed and said, "Colton, that's so lame. You didn't want to dress up, so you came up with a dumb excuse."

Seth and Lacie walked away, looking like they were taking part in an old-time western movie. Colton felt left out until he saw Jerry. He was wearing red tights with a red and white shirt, pointy shoes and a hat that looked like it had two horns.

"Hey Jerry, what are you, a fairy?" Colton asked.

"No, man. Like can't you tell I'm a medieval jester?" he said. "And you're.. like... wearing yesterday's clothes? That's so lame."

"Thanks, Jerry. Do you have dumbbells for juggling? You jesters do that, don't you?"

Jerry walked away, laughing and muttering something about stupid jokes.

During fifth hour, Colton checked his messages and saw another call from Joey, the killer. He listened to it and called Trooper Laurie. "Hi, Colton here. I got another message. Joey said If I don't get him the money, I will be dead, my friend Seth will be dead, and my family will be dead. He wants to meet me Friday night at the game to make an exchange. The money for our lives."

Colton could hear Trooper Laurie confer with another person, then she said, "Call him back and see if you can make the exchange on your newspaper route Friday morning on Haist Road, south of

Bay Port. We can set a trap there and get this over with."

"I'll try, but wouldn't it be better to meet him Thursday morning?" Colton asked.

"No, we still don't have a warrant. I'm having trouble getting one, because we don't have a body, and we only have Seth and your eyewitness accounts. The recordings help, but they aren't a smoking gun. If you can, stall them until I can get more evidence."

Colton slid over to Seth's table and sat down next to him. Miss Walker wasn't paying attention, so the two could talk.

Colton told him about Trooper Laurie's suggestion and asked if he could be there when he called Joey.

"I can give moral support, but that's about all I have," said Seth.

Colton asked for permission to go to the restroom, and then a few minutes later Seth requested permission to get a book from his locker. They met up in the restroom. Colton dialed Joey's number and said, "I got your message. Let's meet Friday morning on Haist Road, south of Bay Port. I'll have the money for you then."

"No, it's got to be at the game," said Joey. "I'll meet you where there are lots of people, so there can't be any funny business."

Seth shook Colton's arm and whispered, "Find out how much money they want. Perhaps my dad could loan me enough so we could just give it to them and get them off our backs."

"It has to be Friday morning, but I need to know how much money I have to have for you."

"All of it. Everything you stole from us."

"Refresh my memory, Joey."

"Damn, you're stupid, kid. You stole five hundred thousand dollars. That's half a million bucks. And if you don't have it by Friday night, a lot of your friends and family will die," Joey said as he hung up.

"Well, how much do we need?" asked Seth.

"Half a million dollars."

"Oh, crap. My dad will not like that. Nope, he won't like that at all. I'd never be able to pay that back with my allowance… not even if he raised it a lot."

Chapter 30

Rosa's Uncle Floats To Shore

By the end of football practice, Colton felt exhausted. He wasn't sure why he was so tired, but he blamed it on stress. Since he didn't have to do a delivery this evening, he will get as much rest as possible.

When he got home, he told his mom not to wake him for dinner.

"Are you ill?" she asked. "If you don't feel good, tell me where it hurts, and I'll get medicine for you."

"Mom, I'm tired, and I think the stress of the investigation and football practice did a number on me. Hopefully, a lot of sleep will help."

"I know the feeling, Colton. Drink some warm milk before you go to bed. If you can't fall asleep, put on some soft music. Don't listen to any of those nasty detective stories; they'll just make you more tense," she said. "When you get hungry, there will be leftovers in the fridge."

"Thanks, Mom," Colton said as he went to his room. It was six o'clock in the evening, and he looked forward to a good twelve hour rest. Something he hadn't enjoyed for many years.

As he lay in bed, the events of the last two weeks kept playing like a silent movie, over and over. He wondered what had happened to Bobby Washington, Rosa's uncle? Why would Donny want to hurt Mrs. Castle's parents? What will he do when he has to give the Detroit gang their money, and all he has is an empty bag? What will he wear to school in the morning? Tomorrow's theme is *At The Movies*. Something from the movies, he thought. But before deciding on tomorrow's outfit, he was in dreamland.

Colton didn't wake until his alarm clock rang at six o'clock Wednesday morning, and the entire world looked fresh. He took a shower when his sister finished and settled on being a pirate today. Not because his tights wouldn't hurt his bruises, but because they looked like a pirate's. Today is movie day, and I can be from the Pirates of the Caribbean. Good enough, he thought.

"Are you hungry?" his mom asked, knowing he had was.

"A little. Could I have a dozen eggs and a pound of bacon?" he asked.

"No, but you can start on this stack of pancakes. More will come, and there's sausage on the stove. Leave some for your brothers and sister," she said.

On his way to school, Colton called Seth. "Hey, can you help with the route tonight, and can we use your Charger?" Colton asked.

"Sure, but why?" asked Seth.

"Well, I want to be safe, and if Joey and Donny look for us, they will look for my yellow Jeep, not your red Charger."

"Smart thought, Colton. Yes. What time do you want me to pick you up?"

"I'll drive over to your place, and we can put the Jeep in your garage. That way they won't see it parked at home," Colton said.

"OK, I'll see you fifth hour," Seth said.

At school, everyone welcomed the pirate back. The halls filled with characters from so many movies it looked like a Hollywood movie set. Lacie dressed as Snow White, and Colton wondered where her seven dwarfs were. Then he noticed two students who looked like dwarfs. They weren't, but they could have passed for one, short and rotund. He later learned that the two students were from The Wizard of Oz.

They dressed as Munchkins.

Since the students had dressed for the movies, most of the teachers had special projects and games that kept with the spirit of fun. It would have been difficult to do normal schoolwork. Mrs. Castle showed a video on theatrical costume making, and in chemistry they played a trivia game. The questions dealt with chemistry, but there were some nice prizes awarded.

With all the fun, Wednesday flew by, and Colton was in good spirits until his phone rang during fifth hour study period. He checked the number, and it was County Deputy Ned Wooddell. Colton didn't ask if he could use his phone; he went to the hallway and answered Ned's call. Miss Walker saw him and gave him a look of disapproval. Colton turned and walked to the office. There he told Miss Downer he had an emergency personal call and asked if he could use the conference room.

"Ned, I'm sorry about the delay, but I had to get approval to take the call. What's up?" he asked.

"Trooper Laurie asked me to tell you that Bobby Washington washed ashore at Oak Beach this morning. It was hard to identify him, because he didn't have a face left, but there was dental work and two tattoos that helped his brother and Rosa identify him."

"Damn, I don't know why, but that makes me feel sad. I thought I'd celebrate when I was proven right," Colton said.

"I know the feeling. At least Rosa and her family know what happened to him. I'm calling because you must be careful tonight. The word is, there are more gang members involved than just Joey and Donny. Some Detroit Black Family Mafia members are roaming around Bad Axe. We told them to leave the county, but we can't throw them in jail unless they break the law."

"What should I do?"

"Do your route, but keep alert and watch for any strange vehicles.

Have your cell phone on at all times."

"Seth will help me tonight, and we're using his red Dodge Charger instead of my yellow Jeep. I figured it would throw them off our trail."

"Good idea. Just be careful," said Ned. "And tell Lacie she looked beautiful in her outfit today. I saw her before school."

"I will, and yes, she is beautiful. Thanks, Ned."

When Colton walked out of the room, Mr. Zeller stood at the door.

"Care to tell me what was so important about that call, and why I shouldn't write you up for using it during school?" he said.

"It was the sheriff's department. They found Rosa's uncle, Bobby Washington, on the beach, dead from a gunshot wound to the back of his head, just like I said I saw. You know, Mr. Zeller, adults should show students more trust than they do. We don't always lie. As far as writing me up for using my cell phone, do whatever you want." Colton turned and walked away before Mr. Zeller could respond. He looked back and saw that the principal was on his cell phone confirming his story.

Of Life And Death

When Colton got back to study period, he told Miss Walker about the call, and she said she understood, and was sorry. He then told Seth and Lacie. The news spread like wildfire, and soon everyone knew about Rosa's uncle. Lacie guessed that this was why Rosa wasn't at school this morning. They took her to Bad Axe to make the identification.

"That's awful. Can you imagine having to see a dead relative like that? It's bad enough when they are all painted up in a fancy casket. Imagine what he looked like... fresh out of the lake? God, how sick is that?" said Seth.

"Like, I've seen dead guys that got messed up," said Jerry. "I saw a major accident and had to help guys who were in a serious condition. I mean, like body parts were missing. Talk about sick. I puked a bunch, and I'll never forget it... ever."

"Yes, I know the feeling, Jerry," said Colton. The bell rang, and the group walked silently to their next class.

Coach heard about Rosa's uncle and told Colton that he needed to clear his mind and concentrate on the game. I know it's hard, but if you can put the effort into the game, it will help. "Get those endorphins running and you will be in another world," he said.

"I know you're talking about the runner's high, but it sounds like you're condoning the use of drugs. And it was drugs that got Rosa's uncle killed."

"Well, runner's high is a natural drug. I meant to say that sometimes a good football game can get your mind off your other problems. It won't solve them, but it helps you forget... for a while."

"Still sounds like drugs," Colton said as he walked out of the locker room to the practice field. Coach Talbert didn't know what to think, but he felt he should avoid talking to Colton this afternoon.

Being vindicated pleased Colton, but the reality of a dead man brought the entire event into perspective. *It isn't just a brief investigation to prove I was right;* he thought... *It's a death. The violent killing of one man by two other men. He thought about how important the police are, and how much they have to endure every day. Being a detective isn't easy. Seeing daily crime, abuse, and death must hurt the soul;* a tear ran down his cheek.

At home, he told his mom about Rosa's uncle. She cried, "I know he was into drugs and wasn't the best person, but he didn't deserve to die that way," she said. "Colton, I am proud of you. You're turning into a good man. I can see that in your heart you feel pain for Rosa's loss. You're so much like your dad." Tears ran down her cheeks and Colton hugged her.

"I know, Mom, and Dad tells me I'm just like you. Go figure." They both laughed.

"Well, I have to be careful tonight, but I think the police will have my back this time," he said.

"Call your brothers and sister, and tell them dinner is ready. I will be so glad when your dad finishes the classes at Delta College. He's gone so much. We had no money when he wasn't working, but we could be poor together. Now, he's either at work or school."

"I know, Mom, but have you noticed the big smile on his face? He loves the work and school," said Colton.

His mom went back to the stove and dished up dinner. Colton went to call his siblings to the table and felt warm inside. *Damn, I love this family*, he thought. *Even Jason, the brat.*

Thunder And Lightning Return

At two o'clock, Colton drove into Seth's driveway. He had called him half an hour earlier to wake him. As he approached the garage, the door opened. Seth stood inside the garage and waved Colton into an empty spot next to his dad's Lexus. Colton took the newspaper delivery bags out of the Jeep and tossed them into the back seat of Seth's car.

"Did you bring something to drink?" asked Seth.

"No, I forgot. I was in a hurry and didn't make coffee."

Seth opened a small refrigerator in the garage and took out several cans of Coke. "Here, these will help us stay awake."

When they arrived in Pigeon at the storage shed, Joe's van sat next to the storage unit. Joe opened the door and walked up to their car.

"Colton, is that you in there?"

Colton looked out Seth's window and said, "Joe. Like my new car and personal driver? This job pays so well, I could get this baby with my first check."

Joe looked over the car, lit a cigarette and coughed. "Have you been smoking weed, or are you drunk?"

"It's my friend's. Joe, this is Seth."

"Glad to meet you, kid. Hey, the truck is here," he said, pointing to the company van driving into the parking lot. "Time to load our papers."

As they were loading papers, they could hear thunder in the distance. Seth laughed and said, "Damn, Colton, it looks like we will see thunder and lightning again tonight."

"Yes, we will, but not the dumb kind, just the wet kind."

Joe yelled to the boys, "Better hurry; it's raining. I think we're in for a nasty night."

Driving on the rural roads of Bay Port, the deliveries were slow. Colton had to tell Seth the exact location of each stop. "Seth, can I drive, please? At this rate, we will deliver papers through our second hour. I promise I won't wreck your shiny new red car."

Seth relented and said, "Fine, but you have to go outside in the rain. This weather is nastier than Hampton's Thunder and Lightning." While he spoke, a flash of lightning struck a tree a few hundred feet ahead of them. They both jumped, and Colton raced around and jumped into the driver's seat. "OK, I promise I won't hurt your car, and be sure to put the papers in plastic bags. The customers will be pissed if their papers are wet."

"Yeah, like they will be dry! It's raining, Colton. Everything's getting wet, including me!"

With Colton driving, the deliveries took less time. By three o'clock they were delivering newspapers on The Point, where he saw at least five police vehicles. There were city, county and state patrol cars everywhere. When they drove down the main street, a county patrol car flashed its lights and drove out of a driveway. The car drove toward the red Charger and stopped beside it.

Opening the window, Colton could see it was Ned Wooddell.

"Nasty night, isn't it?" Ned said. "Have you noticed a few police cars tonight, Colton?"

"Yes, what's up with that?"

"We are here to protect and serve. Protect you guys and serve an arrest warrant on Joey and Donny."

"Clever use of words, Ned," said Seth.

"We appreciate your watching out for us. Has anyone seen them yet? The only people I've seen are the police officers."

"Not yet, but when we do, we'll get them. Enjoy the rain and have fun doing your deliveries," Deputy Ned said as he rolled up his window.

Colton drove to the next stop. Seth felt that Colton deliberately made all the stops on his side of the road. "Why am I the only one who's getting his arm wet, Colton? Can't you deliver some of these on your side of the road?" he asked.

"I can, but I'm having too much fun watching you get wet."

Colton gave Seth a break and delivered on his side. As they got to the end of The Point, Colton turned down the wooded road, where they had the altercation with Thunder and Lightning last week.

"Have you noticed that the rain is stopping?" he asked.

Seth looked up and said, "Yes, but I still see lightning, and I hope there isn't anyone down this road waiting for us again." As Colton drove, he noticed a state police car behind him. The car had stopped, waiting for him to deliver his paper and turn around. When Colton got to the end of the road, he drove into the driveway, dropped a paper into the tube, and started back.

From the woods, a white Cadillac Escalade drove up to the road, and three men ran into the center of the road facing the Dodge Charger. They were pointing handguns at the car's front window.

The largest black man yelled, "Hey, boy, we want our money now!"

Colton opened his window and yelled, "We don't have it."

The second black man fired over Colton's head, and yelled. "Next one goes through your forehead. Get out of the car and walk over here. Both of you!"

Colton could see the state police car coming from the end of the road without its lights. It stopped, and an officer jumped out and yelled, "Stop, this is the police and you're under arrest."

The men turned and fired at the officers. Colton could see that one bullet hit the officer in the leg and he fell to the ground.

"Colton, that's Trooper Steve. The bullet hit him in the leg," yelled Seth. Colton put the Charger in drive and drove toward the men standing in the road. They jumped back, and Colton stopped the car next to the downed officer. He jumped out and pulled Trooper Steve into the back seat. The gang members shot three times, and they could hear bullets hitting the back of the Charger. Colton drove to the end of the road and sped down Main Street. Three police cars rushed to the scene. A county patrol car stopped, and Colton pulled up next to it. Deputy Ned saw that a dazed Trooper Steve was in the back seat.

"Deputy Ned, call an ambulance. Trooper Steve got shot in the leg, said Colton."

Steve looked at Ned and yelled. "I'll be OK. Throw me your first aid kit and get down there. The other officers will need your help. Those gang members we stopped in Bad Axe today are there. They'll kill anyone in their way, Ned. Don't let them."

Ned threw the kit to Colton and raced down the street, turning onto the wooded lane. He heard a series of gunshots and men yelling.

"Are you going to be OK, Trooper Steve?" Colton asked. Sitting in the front seat, and looking back at the trooper, he could see Steve's bloody leg. Steve tore his pant leg up to his thigh.

"Yeah, kid. It'll be fine. Just a bloody flesh wound. You know, you guys saved my life back there. I guess I owe you one."

"No, if it weren't for you, Steve, we would be dead. Those gang members wanted money we don't have. And I could tell that if they didn't get it.... Well, we'd be dead. Thank you for being there, sir," Colton said.

Seth added, "That goes for me too. Do you want us to take you to the hospital?"

"No, I'll stop there after we get those bastards."

The gunshots had stopped, and several police cars drove out of the woods. They stopped behind Seth's Charger and walked up to the car. Five police officers stood there, looking in at Steve.

"You OK, Steve?" asked the village police officer.

"I'm fine, George. Guys, what went down back there?" Steve opened the back door of the Charger and stood up. He was favoring his bloody leg, now bandaged up and no longer bleeding. He looked back into the Charger and said, "Sorry, Seth, I made a mess of your back seat."

"Hey, what's a little blood? At least there aren't bullet holes in my windshield and forehead," Seth said.

"Sir, when we pulled up, they shot at us. But when they realized we had five guns shooting at them and there was no exit, they dropped their guns and asked for their lawyers. We will take them back to Bad Axe. Deputy Lee Coldfield has your patrol car at the end of the line. Do you want him to drive you to the hospital?"

"Sounds good, but someone has to stay with Colton and Seth," Steve said, as he turned to the two. "You want to finish your route, don't you?"

"Yes, sir. It will take another hour," said Colton.

Ned stepped out of the group of officers and said. "I'll follow them. If I see Joey and Donny, I'll radio for backup. But I don't think they will be around tonight. The last report had them still hiding in Detroit."

Chapter 31

Yes! They Shot At Us

By the time Colton and Seth finished the route, there was less than an hour to get ready for school.

"What are you wearing today, Seth?"

"It's Casual Thursday. I don't understand what that's supposed to mean. Everything I always wear casual clothing. Blue jeans and a t-shirt. I could wear my pajamas because I'm tired enough to sleep all day," Seth said.

"I always get into trouble when I sleep in school," said Colton.

"You've been getting into trouble every day at school. You might as well sleep through today and save yourself for the big game. I have an idea. Why don't we skip school and go to Bad Axe to make faces at the gang members when they're talking to the judge? That would be fun," Seth said.

Colton wasn't sure if Seth was joking, but he knew better than to skip school. "No, I want to be at school. Will you tell your parents about the fun we had last night?"

"Hell, yes! If they hear my name on the radio, and I didn't warn them, I'll wish the gang had shot me."

"Same here. I'm going home now to break the news. See you tomorrow, Seth."

Seth opened the garage door, and Colton jumped in his Jeep.

"Bye, Colton. Good luck with your parents," Seth said.

When Colton walked into the kitchen, his dad and mom were

218

listening to the Bad Axe radio station. The broadcaster said, "Three Detroit gang members were arrested on The Point early Thursday morning. There were gunshots fired, and a state police officer is reported to have been shot. More details will follow as they become available."

"Son," said Colton's dad, "this sounds like something to do with you. Care to tell us about it?"

"Trooper Steve got shot, but he's OK. It was a flesh wound. He saved us from the Detroit gang that thought we had stolen their money. Oh, I forgot to tell you, they believe we stole five hundred thousand dollars that belong to them," Colton said. "But we have none of their money. At least they are in jail now, and the police don't think the other two guys will bother us. There is a warrant out for their arrest, and they went into hiding."

"Well, that makes me feel better," said Colton's mom. "I'm glad you and Seth didn't get hurt, and you can never leave this house again.. *ever*!"

"But Mom, I need to go to school," Colton insisted.

"I know. Take a shower, and I'll make you an egg and English muffin sandwich. Your dad picked up some of Walsh's Canadian bacon, and it's good," Colton's mom said, as she reached out and gave him an enormous hug. His dad looked on and smiled.

"Thanks Mom. You can make two for me. I'll be down in a few minutes." He passed Steph on the stairs and told her she looked beautiful. Jason was in the bathroom and told Colton he wouldn't hurry because he was here first.

Colton gathered his clothes and ran down to his parents' bathroom. It was super clean. Not like upstairs. He shaved and splashed on his dad's cologne.

Walking into the kitchen, he said, "Dad, I hope you don't mind, but I used your cologne."

"No problem, but watch out for the girls; they might attack you today."

"It's Avon, Colton. Powerful stuff," his mom said as she handed him his breakfast sandwich.

Terry asked if he could use cologne, and Colton said, "It won't help, kid, because you must wait until you're my age before it affects the girls."

Terry made a face and said, "Girls? Yuck."

Your Statement Please

The Jeep raced down the road and slid through the intersection heading to Lake Huron High School. Colton was late again. He ran into the building and was the only one in the hallway. Damn, he thought, Mr. Dinger will get upset again. When he reached the door, it was locked. He knocked, and a student dressed in gym shorts and a tank top opened the door. The students were wearing every type of garb… pajamas, shorts, and sweatpants were the most popular.

"Welcome to my nightmare," said Mr. Dinger.

"Sir, I'm sorry I was late; there was trouble on my route last night."

"You mean something like three Detroit gang members shooting a State Trooper?" said Mr. Dinger.

"Yes, Sir. Something like that."

"Have a seat; you're not late at all today."

The class applauded Colton as he found his desk. He didn't know why they did, but later he learned that Mr. Dinger had told the class what he heard on the radio. He said Trooper Steve credited Colton and Seth with saving his life. They were heroes.

The entire school had heard about the events on The Point. Seth was in heaven. He told Colton that he loved having students treat him like a hero. It was almost worth getting shot at.

"Is this what it's like when you have great moments in sports?"

he asked Colton as they ate lunch.

"Not as intense. It's crazy enough with homecoming, but I can't believe all the excitement about what happened last night. You know, it was Trooper Steve who risked his life for us. If he hadn't got those gang members to turn around and shoot at him, they would have shot us. And now, we're getting all the praise," Colton said.

"Yeah, ain't life great," added Seth.

An announcement came over the intercom requesting that Colton and Seth come to the office.

Colton looked at Seth and said, "Crap, now what do they want?"

"Perhaps we're in trouble for causing too much excitement on school property, or something like that."

The two walked to the office and saw Deputy Ned Wooddell standing with Mr. Zeller.

"Colton," said Deputy Ned, "you and Seth are to drive to Bad Axe to see the district attorney. They want your statement regarding last night, and Seth, they want to check your car for bullet holes."

"Any idea how long it will take?" asked Colton.

"You should be back before football practice, if that's what you're wondering."

"That's great. I don't want to miss practice. Friday is the big game, you know."

Colton turned to Seth and said, "I'll drive with you, if that's OK with Ned?"

"That's fine. I already gave them my statement, so I'm heading to Bay Port on other business," he said.

"Mr. Zeller, we will be back as soon as possible," Colton said.

Mr. Zeller said, "You know I didn't believe you saw a murder, Colton, but your persistence has resulted in the capture of a Detroit gang of drug dealers, and your actions saved the life of a state police officer. I am impressed with the two of you."

Seth shook Mr. Zeller's hand and said, "Thank you sir, it was all in a day's work."

Mr. Zeller smiled. Colton and Seth walked out of the office and to their lockers. Once they put their things away, they headed to Seth's car.

"You know, Seth, the police want to find the bullets that went into your trunk. I hope there's nothing in there that you don't want them to find."

"Oh, my God. I have a half million dollars in there. I wanted to split it with you when we got done with this caper," he said with a huge grin.

Colton laughed and put his arm around Seth's shoulder. "Never joke like that around the police, Seth. Steve will have you put in handcuffs and leg irons before you can finish laughing."

The two jumped into the Charger and headed for Bad Axe.

When they entered the police station, the middle-aged, gray-haired county sheriff walked up to them and shook their hands. "Boys, I want to commend you for the fine work you did on behalf of our county. We have a drug problem here, and thanks to you, it is now reduced by a factor of three."

"What about the two killers, Joey and Donny?" asked Colton.

"We will catch them. There is an APB out, and the entire state is looking for them."

The sheriff led Colton and Seth to the district attorney's office. "Here you go, boys. Seth, we'll be checking your car for evidence, and I told the boys in the garage they only have an hour. So, your car will be ready for you when you're done here."

"Thanks, Sheriff," said Seth.

The district attorney opened his door and welcomed Colton and Seth. "Boys, I'm glad to see you. Trooper Steve has informed us about your actions on behalf of our community. I need to get a few statements from you before I see the judge. The men who were shooting at you are drug dealers and gang members from the Detroit area. The entire state of Michigan thanks you for providing evidence resulting in their arrest."

Colton grew weary of all the attention. All he did was attempt to prove that he saw a murder, and now he must listen to long-winded old men talk on for hours. "Thank you, sir," was all he could say.

The sheriff's men found three bullets in the trunk of Seth's car. They may be damaged but they can be used as evidence. Finally, the district attorney finished his questions and walked with Colton and Seth to the door. He added, "We will let you know when we go to trial. You may have to testify at the trial."

"Great, we'll be looking forward to that," said Colton as he walked down the hallway. "Well, Seth, it looks like the investigation ends here. Now we can enjoy homecoming and the dance without killers trying to eliminate us."

"Yeah, Colton. But after all the excitement we've been through, homecoming will be a dull experience."

"Seth, you need a hobby."

Seth laughed and asked, "Do you need me to help with the route again tonight?"

"No, there have been no calls from Joey and Donny, and the police said they would give me protection until they arrest them. I'll use the Jeep, and I don't expect any problems."

"Great, I have a ton of homework. I'm so far behind that Dad might have to hire a tutor or bribe my teachers. Which reminds me, can I bribe you to vote for my new girlfriend, Linda? The entire high school gets to vote for homecoming queen on Friday, and if she wins, I'll be her homecoming king. Wouldn't that be outstanding?"

"I'll think about it, Seth. But I know Lacie will want me to vote for her friend, Kathy," Colton said.

"Will she be king if Kathy wins? I think not. But I will be if Linda wins. I think it's obvious what you should do, Colton."

By the time they arrived back at school, the buses had left and the football team was already on the field. Colton rushed to the locker room, and Seth started for home. He said he had to explain to his dad why there were three large holes in the back of his new Dodge Charger. *Does auto insurance cover gunshots?* he wondered.

Chapter 32

Thursday Night - Good Night

Football practice was easy and fun. Colton had to run extra laps because he was late. Coach Talbert accepts no excuses, so Colton didn't bother to tell him where he was. The other players only knew the police visited Seth and him at school.

After running, he worked with the assistant coach on his footwork.

"You're good at running around the defense, Colton, but you have to learn how to avoid injuries. If you aren't prepared for the tackle, which comes often, you can hurt yourself, so you must learn how to fall gracefully," the coach said.

"Fall gracefully?"

"Well, follow these tips. Stay as low as possible, run as fast as possible, keep that arm out to push the tackler away, and when you know you're being tackled, just fall down around the ball. You must hold on to the ball! It's when you're running and standing up straight you will get hurt, and if you tuck your head down, you can hurt your neck when you get tackled," the coach advised.

Colton ran a series of plays with two men trying to tackle him. The coach kept saying, "Come on, Colton, let them tackle you! I want to see how you fall."

Colton got tackled twice, and Coach Talbert turned to the assistant coach and said, "See, it's like trying to catch a fly; get in his way, and he'll just jump over you."

In the locker room, a few of his teammates wanted to know about the events on The Point, but Colton avoided going into detail. He tired of the attention and just wanted to have his life get back to normal. *Like it was three weeks ago,* he thought.

At home, Colton helped his mom take canned vegetables she had processed down to the basement. He also picked squash, dug up potatoes, and cleaned out parts of the garden that were no longer productive. He enjoyed doing this work because the garden helped to save money, and he loved fresh vegetables.

At suppertime, he told Terry what to wear to the football game, and when to be ready to leave. Terry got excited when Colton told him he could be in the locker room before the game and he could sit on the team benches during the game.

"Wow, Colton. I'll be just like a football player, won't I?" he said.

"Yes, but you better not get in anyone's way, or they'll step on you. Remember, there are some big players on our team, and you're just a little kid."

"I'm not so little," Terry insisted.

"You are too. I'm a lot bigger than you are," said Jason. "Colton, why didn't you ask me to the game?"

"Well, Jason, why didn't you say you wanted to go? Mom said you wanted to go with Aunt Alice and the cousins."

"I do, but sometime I would like to go with you, too."

"Sure, pal. We can do things together sometime soon. Just the two of us," Colton said.

"Cool. The kids at school say you are something. I don't know what something is, but whatever it is, you got it."

"All I've got, Jason, is two great brothers." Colton looked at his sister and added, "And one hot little sister."

Colton went to bed by eight o'clock. He set the alarm clock for two in the morning and looked forward to doing the newspaper route. *Tonight I'll be able to listen to my audio book, without having to worry about getting shot at,* he thought.

Friday Is Spirit Day

When Colton started the Jeep, he checked to make sure every-thing he needed was there. Bags? Check: Coke? Check: Coat to keep warm? Check. Enough gas? Check. Audiobook? Check. He pulled out of the driveway and headed for the storage unit. As he drove, he started listening to his next novel. He had listened to two Baldacci books, but his dad told him to try some James Patterson. Tonight, Colton would listen to a book by James Patterson entitled Step on a Crack. According to the description, it's the first novel in the Michael Bennett series featuring Detective Michael Bennett and his ten kids. Colton listened to this book because he liked the book's name, and he also hoped that he might learn more about being a detective.

After listening to the first ten minutes of the audiobook, he was hooked because it was about the murder of the president's wife.

As he listened and ran the route, Colton kept seeing cars turning their lights on and off as he drove. He saw two patrol cars on The Point. He knew the police would be out, but he thought they would just follow him. Instead, they stayed out of his sight, just observing.

He was lucky because no gang members or drug dealers were hiding in the woods. There were no problems with the route, and Colton finished before five o'clock on Friday morning. When he pulled up to the garage, he stopped and continued listening to his book. He was hooked and didn't want to stop. Time, however, also didn't stop. It was now five-thirty, and he had to head into the house. Instead of taking a nap, he listened to his book for another hour.

Friday is Spirit Day, and Colton put on his spirit t-shirt and a pair of jeans. He considered dressing up in an old football jersey, but thought it would be too much. Besides, he would dress for football tonight.

As he got ready for school, Colton collected his black suit, black shoes, socks, a pastel blue dress shirt, and a clean pair of boxer briefs. He wanted to be ready for the homecoming dance and figured that he would just put his clothes in the Jeep now. That way he wouldn't forget. He also found a small styrofoam cooler and put it in the back of the Jeep. Flowers for my date, he thought. I can't forget to pick the corsage up after school.

After a quick breakfast, he jumped into the Jeep and took off. Turning around at the end of the driveway, he drove back to the garage.

He ran into the house, and his mom asked, "What did you forget?"

"A tie. Lacie would kill me if I wore my suit without a tie. Can I borrow a good one of Dad's?" he asked.

"I'll get one." She came out of the bedroom with a beautiful crimson red tie. "This will go with your black suit and a blue shirt. Don't mess it up; it's your dad's favorite."

The Spirits Are High

The buzz at the school was unmistakable. Almost everyone dressed in the school colors, or they wore a glowing yellow spirit t-shirt. The principal ordered hundreds of them, sold some, and gave many away as rewards. Now, when there is a game, the students glow with spirit.

Colton met Lacie at his locker and gave her a big hug. "You're beautiful today, all decked out in your spirit T-shirt," he said. "I want you to know, everything is ready for tonight. I packed the Jeep, ordered the corsage, and now I'm good with the world," he said.

"Well, aren't we in a cheerful mood? I take it they caught Joey and Donny?" she asked.

"No, but they will. At least Joey stopped calling me. I guess he got the message I don't have their money."

"A half a million dollars. Can you imagine having that much money? I would buy a car. A classy used car," Lacie said.

"Cheap... Cheap... Cheap," Colton chirped. "With that money, you could get a Lexus, or better yet, a new Jeep."

"We can discuss money later. Now I have to get to class. Don't forget to vote today before seventh hour. Seventh hour is the pep rally, and remember you must vote for Kathy. The entire school body gets to vote for homecoming queen today; so it's your duty to vote for Kathy. Understood?" she asked.

"Is this a free and secret ballot?"

"No, you must vote for Kathy. She's my friend, and I want her to win," Lacie insisted.

The first hour bell rang, and they went their separate ways. Colton wasn't sure who he would vote for. Seth asked him to vote for his new girlfriend, Linda Canberry. As head cheerleader, she would have a lot of support. But Kathy was a nice girl, and she was Lacie's friend. Decisions, decisions, decisions. I hate them; he thought.

All during art class, Lacie could only talk about how important it is that Kathy win.

Colton reminded Lacie that if Kathy becomes homecoming queen, then Aden would be king. That would be fine because Aden is a good friend. But if Linda gets elected queen, then his best friend, Seth, will be the king. And that would be even better. Decisions, decisions, decisions. I hate them, he thought.

"Colton, you want Aden to be king because I want Kathy to be queen. Understood?" Lacie asked.

During the lunch hour, Colton went to the office and cast his ballot for homecoming queen. He told Lacie that he voted for Kathy, and then he told Seth that he voted for Linda. He hoped the two would not compare notes, but they did, and after talking to each other they approached him.

"Well, smartass, who did you vote for?" they asked in unison.

"I wrote in Lacie's name. It was the only person I wanted to win, even if she isn't a senior," he said.

"Awe, that's so sweet, Colton," Lacie said. "I don't believe you, though. But it's a gracious gesture."

By the seventh hour, the entire school body was ready for the big game. The pep rally only made them more energized. If the students could control fate, their football team would have no problem beating the Bay City Cougars. After the last cheer, they dismissed the students for the weekend, and a mad rush of bodies made its way to the buses. Colton and Lacie took the back door out of the gym. In the back hallway, Colton told Lacie that he would see her after the game. They kissed, and she went out to find her bus, and he walked to the Jeep. *In four hours, I will be on the football field fighting the Bay City Cougars*, he thought. *I'm glad they don't have a Thunder and Lightning on their team.*

Chapter 33

Kick OFF

At six o'clock, Colton placed Lacie's corsage in the small Styrofoam cooler he had in the back of the Jeep. He added ice and set it next to his suit, tie, shirt, and shoes.

"Terry, I'm ready to go," he yelled. Terry came running out of the house in his T-shirt and jeans.

"I'm ready, Colton."

"No, you're not. Get in the house and find a sweatshirt and overcoat. It will be under 40 degrees tonight, and I don't want you freezing your butt off," he said.

"OK, but don't leave without me," Terry said.

In a few minutes, the two brothers were ready to go. Terry was so excited that he couldn't stop bouncing around the front seat. Colton reminded him he should settle down and use his seat belt, which he did, but he was still excited.

"Colton, I've never been to a homecoming. Why do they call it that?"

"Because old school friends come home and visit the school, so they call it, homecoming."

"OK. I think I know what you mean," Terry said.

When they got to the high school parking lot, Colton drove by the lineup of floats. They went through the one hometown and now they would drive around the football field during halftime. Lacie was right; the junior class float looked like a lizard eating a huge cat. The lizard had wings, like the dragon it was supposed to represent. The senior float was awesome. A Bay City Cougar lay hogtied on the ground, with a huge cowboy wearing a Loons' jersey standing over it. The motto read: Victory Is Ours. Behind the floats, five convertibles for the homecoming queen candidates sat ready for halftime. The convertible impressed Terry.

"I want one of those when I get to your age," he said.

"So do I, and I am my age. We better get to the locker room; it's getting late."

Seth drove up and yelled to Colton through his open window, "Ready to win tonight?"

"You bet I am, but if I don't get into the locker room, Coach will be mad. Talk to you after the game."

The locker room was buzzing with guys in every state of dress. Colton told Terry to sit on a bench and stay there. He then put on his football uniform. A few guys tried to tease Terry, telling him he's too small to be on the team, but Colton reminded them they were once the same size, "So shut up and leave my brother alone." They did.

Coach gave a rousing pep talk to the team. He reminded them that Bay City has a great coach and that they are out for victory. "We can't assume that they are weaker than us. My sources say they are a stronger team, so don't sluff off. Get your minds off the girls, the floats, the homecoming queen, and stay focused on the game. Win this one for yourselves, and the alumni who came tonight."

The team did a group high-five and ran for the door. Colton told Coach that Terry was there, and he would stay out of the way. Coach said it would be fine. Bay C was already on the field, doing warm-up exercises. Colton sensed they were ready for the battle. As the Lake Huron Loons ran onto the field, everyone in the bleachers stood and cheered. It was a great feeling and pushed the Loons' spirits higher.

The announcer called the names of The Bay City, and a few fans, cheerleaders, students, and family members screamed after each player's name got called. Then, it was time to introduce the Loons' players. Before calling the first name, the announcer had to ask that the fans lower their screams so they could hear the names. The screams were unbearable, and no one could hear a word the announcer said.

After introducing the team members and coaching staff, Aden and the captain of the Bay City Cougars met with the official in the center of the field. They tossed a coin and announced that the Loons would kick off, with the Cougars receiving. The game was on.

The kick was good, and the Bay City team ran it back to their forty-five yard line. They inched closer to a first and ten, but none of their passes got completed. On their fourth and one, they tried to run up the middle, but hit a giant roadblock, known as the Loons' defensive line: a wall of farm-boys unwilling to move.

The Loons' first play was a pass to Colton, deep down-field. It was good, and Colton was off. He skirted the defense, but on the Loons' ten yard line, a quick Bay City player snagged him from behind. The fans were on their feet, chanting: Colton, Colton, Colton. Aden asked that they stop yelling so he could call the next play.

The Cougars watched for another pass; so, Aden faked a pass and ran the ten yards for a touchdown. Suddenly the bleachers erupted, and Aden was *the man*. The extra point was good, and the Loons were leading seven to zero.

The first half of the game became stagnant after the lone touchdown, and Cougars couldn't move against the Loons, and the Loons' offense was being blocked at every turn. Coach tried every trick he knew, but as long as they could hold the Bay City Cougars from getting a touchdown, they were closer to victory. The team ran to the lockers, and Coach gave a pep-talk, had them use the restroom, and sent them back to the field for the halftime events.

Terry was behaving. He knew how to keep himself out of the way, and Coach gave him some pointers about the game. He told Colton that Terry was an ace player in the making, which made Colton very proud.

When they reached the field, the floats had just finished making the trip around the track. The senior's float won first place, second place went to the freshmen, third place to the sophomores, and the juniors won last place. Colton felt guilty for not helping. Then he thought, *with my artistic talent, I wouldn't have helped much.*

As the line of convertibles rolled down the track, the crowd roared with excitement. Lacie walked up to Colton to stand with him. They hugged and then listened to the announcer as he said, "Ladies and gentlemen, I present the royal court." When the girls reached the podium, the band played, and they introduced each girl and her date for the homecoming dance, who would become her homecoming king. Both Seth and Aden looked so proud to be standing next to their girlfriends. Of course, the others were proud too.

Lacie beamed with excitement, and Colton took her hand. Together, they listened for the winner's name.

The booming voice rang through the night. "Ladies and gentlemen, I present to you Queen Kathy Dorsher, and her King, Aden Carville." The crowd roared, and Lacie jumped up and kissed Colton. "She won! She won! Oh my God, she won!"

"Of course she did, Lacie. I nominated her, didn't I?" Lacie hit him in the arm and said, "Yes, but did you vote for her?"

As the band played, the queen and her court returned to the convertibles and left the field. Coach Talbert yelled for his team to warm up, and Colton gave Lacie a hug and ran to the far end of the football field to be with his teammates.

Second Half Troubles

Coach was right. The Bay City Cougars were a stronger team than the Hampton Colts. They were using their skills instead of relying on thugs. In the third quarter, they broke out and ran a beautiful pass down the side. Their star halfback, Lawrence Slodem, ran forty yards for a touchdown. Then, at the start of the fourth quarter, the Bay City quarterback worked his team down to their ten yard line and handed off to his fullback for a perfect run down the middle. The Loon line was tired and expected a pass.

Coach Talbert could have been livid, but he told his boys, "I want you to just buckle down and do your job. We can still win this."

Bay City had the ball again, but Colton got called to the sideline. Coach Talbert put another player in for him.

"What's the problem, Coach? Did I do something wrong?" Colton asked.

"No, but someone handed me this message. I read it, and we have a big problem."

Colton took the note and read: "We have Terry. Give us the money or watch him die."

Colton looked around for his brother and couldn't see him. He ran down the sidelines and at the far end of the field, two large men stood with Terry at their side. The men were Joey and Donny, dressed in long overcoats and oversized hats. When they saw Colton, they made a gun with their fingers and pointed it at the side of Terry's head.

"Oh God, not this, not Terry," Colton cried. He ran back to Coach Talbert. "What do we do, Coach? Crap, what am I going to do?"

Coach Talbert took Colton by the shoulder and pulled him around so they were facing. Looking him in the eyes, he said, "Colton, I've talked to the police. They don't want you to try anything; they'll be here in about fifteen minutes."

"Crap, the game will be over in less than a minute. And, those guys want money I don't have," Colton said.

Coach took his notepad and wrote. "I will get you the money after the last play of the game. Meet me in the parking lot by my Jeep. Don't hurt Terry!"

Coach sent the note back to the two thugs with his team manager. He said, "Say nothing, just give them the note, and run back here as fast as you can."

It was the fourth quarter; the ball was in the hands of the Loons on their forty-five yard line. They were down by five points and needed a touchdown to win the game. Terry was being held by the killers on the Loons' ten yard line. With only a few seconds left in the game, the coach called another time-out.

"Guys, we will win this game and save Colton's brother, and here is how we'll do it." He gave the team the details of their last play… the most important play of Colton's life.

Running back to the huddle, Aden told Colton that he would not make any mistakes. "You have my word, Colton."

At the line, Colton positioned himself as a wide receiver, far to the right, with two Bay City players guarding him. On the snap, Colton ran around the guards, forcing one of them to stumble and fall. He leaped over the other and ran toward the end zone. Aden threw a long pass, and Colton turned as the ball glided into his hands. He was off, running for his and Terry's lives, toward the end zone.

As he ran, the entire Loon team followed him down the field. Aden ran along the sideline with three guards. When he reached the killers, he snatched Terry into his arms, as the two guards ran into Joey and Donny, knocking them to the ground. Aden ran with Terry and passed him off to Colton, who had just made the touchdown. The crowd was on its feet, but screamed when there were three gunshots. The team ran away from Joey and Donny, who were brandishing their handguns.

Colton carried Terry to the Jeep and threw him into the passenger seat. He told him, "Lay down under the dash, and don't move." Terry had tears in his eyes, and Colton could tell he was scared to death, but at least he was alive.

Colton started the Jeep and sped to the parking lot exit. There was no traffic, so he didn't stop at the main road. He turned left, heading toward Bad Axe and the county sheriff's office. He hoped the killers wouldn't follow him, but they did. Brandishing their guns, they ran off the football field and jumped into their Lincoln MKX. Just minutes behind Colton, they skidded around the corner and hit the gas, trying to catch up to the Jeep.

Colton had the gas pedal pushed down to the floorboard. He pulled his cell phone out of the glove box and dialed Trooper Laurie. "I'm on my way to Bad Axe, and the killers are right behind me." There were two shots, and Colton could hear the bullets hitting his Jeep's tailgate. "Oh crap, they want to kill me now; they're shooting at the Jeep."

"We have cars covering you. Don't stop or slow down; we'll clear the roads for you, as best we can. Just watch out for the corners, in case someone is on the roadway," she said as Colton flew through Elkton where two patrol cars blocked off the intersection. The Lincoln was three car lengths from him and closing in. Another two shots hit the back window and flew past Colton's ear and out the front window. He tried to weave across the road and kept the accelerator pushed down to the floor.

The Lincoln came up to his side, but Colton forced them off the road. Running on the gravel shoulder slowed the Lincoln down, and Joey and Donny fell behind.

"Colton, are you still there?" asked Trooper Laurie.

"Yes, about seven miles from the M-53 intersection."

"Listen, Colton. Here's the plan. Don't stop at the intersection. Cross M-53 even if the light is red. Just keep going east. When you cross M-53, your tires will blow out. We're putting down traffic spikes, and they will puncture your tires and also the tires on Joey's Lincoln. When you run over them, just remember to let the Jeep roll to a stop. Hold the wheel steady and don't hit the brakes. Is that understood?"

"Got it. Oh, crap... they're behind me again!" Two more gunshots flew into the back of the Jeep, and Colton could hear the bullets ricochet. "I hope we are still alive when we get there."

A mile from the intersection, Joey tried to pass again. Colton ran him off into the gravel, forcing Joey to back off again. Then, they shot another round into the back window, just missing Colton's head. Terry screamed as he held his hands over his ears and curled up on the Jeep floor.

"Doing OK, Terry? Isn't this a lot of fun?" Colton said.

"No! I want my mom and dad."

Colton could see the police cars at the intersection. He ran over the spikes and could hear his tires explode. The Jeep shimmied and weaved, but he held the steering wheel and allowed the Jeep to roll to a stop. Behind him, he saw a cloud of dust as the Lincoln rolled over in the parking lot of a furniture store on the corner. A horde of police officers descended on the SUV and pulled Joey and Donny out of the wreck.

Deputy Ned Wooddell pulled up to Colton's Jeep and ran to Colton's door yelling, "Are either of you injured?"

"No, we're fine. All those bullets, and we didn't get hit once... thank God."

"Yes, thank God, Colton, we were afraid you had gotten injured."

Colton got out of the Jeep and helped Terry stand. Still shaky, but he was finding his legs.

"Colton, I gotta pee," he said.

"Here, kid," said Ned as he opened his patrol car doors, so Terry could go on the side of the road. "I'm surprised you could hold it with all those gunshots, Terry."

Terry smiled and said, "Well, I sort of didn't." The front of his jeans was slightly damp.

"That's OK, Terry," said Colton. "I almost wet myself when that last bullet nearly took my ear off."

Colton walked around his Jeep and cringed at all the damage. Multiple holes in the back tailgate, and several holes in the glass.

He looked inside and saw that his clothes were still there, but there were two gunshot holes in the Styrofoam cooler. He looked in, and it appeared the corsage box was fine.

Chapter 34

Homecoming Dance

Trooper Laurie walked up and asked Colton and Terry to jump in her patrol car, so she could take them back to the Sheriff's office. Colton could see Seth's car, with Lacie in the front seat, pull up to the intersection. He yelled for them to meet him at the sheriff's office. Seth nodded and headed south on M-53.

It took half an hour for the Sheriff to take statements, fingerprint, and book Joey and Donny.

Out of curiosity, Colton yelled out, "Donny, why did you try to kill Mr. and Mrs. Stone?"

It surprised him when Donny yelled back, "Because they bought my grandfather's house, and they promised I would get it when he died. I'll be damned if anyone else ever lives in my house!" The deputy then took him to a holding cell.

While Colton waited for word on his Jeep, the doors burst open and his mom and dad ran into the police station.

"Colton, Terry, are you OK? We got a call you were here. We were on our way home from Delta and came straight here. What happened?"

Long story, Mom, but we're fine.

"Mommy, we got shot at, and Colton blew out all his tires. It was fun," Terry said, running into her arms. She picked him up, looked at Colton and said, "I thought you said this was all over! You told me there wouldn't be any more problems. Damn, Colton, you could have gotten yourself and Terry killed."

Colton said nothing because he knew she was right and he had no defense.

Two deputies walked into the office, holding Colton's clothing, cooler, and duffel bag from the Jeep. "Are these the items you wanted retrieved from the Jeep?"

"Yes, but what's with the duffel bag?" Colton asked.

"The craziest thing, this was stuck under the Jeep... wedged really tight," the deputy said.

"What's in it?" asked Seth.

The deputy opened the case and whistled. "Holy crap, I've never seen so much money." He dumped the contents onto the table. There was a mountain of cash.

"That's my money, damn it," yelled Joey from his holding cell. "I want my effing money."

The sheriff laughed. "It looks like it's the county's money now, gentlemen. And you know, we could always use a few new patrol cars," he laughed. "We'll just call this drug money and confiscate it. Too bad you guys wrecked that nice new Lincoln, 'cause I could have used that too."

As Colton and his parents came out of the Sheriff's headquarters, Seth and Lacie were standing outside. Lacie ran into Colton's arms and hugged him.

"Are you OK?" she asked.

"We're fine. My Jeep needs some new tires, windows, and Bondo over the gunshot holes, but it'll be fine."

Terry said, "Colton, I had fun at the game. Let's do it again!"

"Colton, are there more killers looking for you tonight?" asked his mother. "If there are, I don't want to know."

"None, Mom. I will go dancing with this lovely girl, and I'll be home when Seth has time to drive me there."

Colton's dad gave him a hug and said, "Son, don't do this again, OK?"

"Promise Dad, I'm out of the detective business. Of course, Seth and I solved the mystery; so I guess we are excellent investigators."

"You were lucky you didn't get killed," Adam said.

Colton threw his clothes and the cooler into the trunk of Seth's Charger and jumped in the back seat with Lacie.

"Where's your date, Seth?" Colton asked.

"At the dance, waiting for me. They had to take pictures, and she didn't want to drive to Bad Axe and miss being in them. I hope she's still there."

"She will be, Seth," said Lacie. "You're worth the wait."

When they got back to Lake Huron High School, Colton went into the locker room to change out of his football uniform. He took a hot shower, shaved and threw on some cologne. When he put his dress pants on, he noticed several holes in the back of the pants, showing his white shorts. The suit jacket had a gunshot in the side and through one sleeve. He slid the tie on and saw a large bullet hole where you would expect a tie tack to be. Holding the corsage box, he went into the hallway where Lacie was.

One look at Colton and she chuckled, "I'm just glad there isn't blood coming out of those holes."

"Damn, me too! But Dad will be pissed. This is his favorite tie."

"He'll get over it, Colton," Lacie said, holding the tie between her fingers. She looked into his eyes. "You look nice all dressed up."

"Thanks, Lacie. You look beautiful in that dress, too. Oh, here is the corsage. The cooler had a bullet hole in it, but I think the flowers are OK."

She took the cardboard box and opened it. There was a shattered corsage. One green stem with a few pale blue sprigs still attached. She laughed.

"Oh God, Lacie, I'm sorry it's ruined." Colton said.

"No, they're fine." She took the flowers and had Colton pin them to her dress. "I love these flowers, Colton. And I love you too. Let's go in and dance."

To Be Continued

Deadly Dance

The Spirit Walker Series

Book 3

The big bands are playing your favorite tunes,
but a killer is on the loose. Can Tianna and Charlie help
stop a killer from Detroit's 1930s?

If you liked this book, you will love Duane's other novels.

In Search Of Elysium

A touching sci-fi adventure for all ages!

Kevin Carpenter is learning disabled. In a touching adventure he leads his friends on a search for God, taking them deep into space, in search of a planet called Elysium.

Death on the Point

No. 1 - The Blackwell Series

Colton Blackwell, a football star and teenage detective, stars in this fast moving mystery series. A humorous and romantic novel filled with action and adventure

Blood Bath

No. 2 - The Blackwell Series

Colton Blackwell is faced with another murder. The humor, romance, and adventure continues.

Deadly Sixteen - Killer Within

No. 1 - The Spirit Walker Series

This reincarnation story takes you through the history of Detroit, Michigan, investigating a 300 year murder mystery.

Doyle Mysteries

No. 1 - The Scent Of Murder

New series. Check Website For Details.

Doyle, a retired police detective and master chef, and his Bloodhound (Copper) face a life filled with luxury and murder. A cozy mystery for all ages.

www.duanewurst.com ~ duane0w@gmail.com

Share your opinion and do a review on Amazon.com

Duane Wurst

COMING SOON

Deadly Guilt and Shame

A Halocaust story you will never forget.

The Spirit Walker Series

Book 4

www.duanewurst.com
duanewurst.com@gmail.com